ROGUE

B
RE

Rogue threw Zero onto the ramp and pulled himself on board as the Nort armoured vehicles rounded the street corner, pushing waves of water, bodies and debris before them. "Get us out of here!" A cannon on the lead tank spat smoke and flame, and Ferris flinched as a shell shrieked over the shuttle and demolished a nearby building. "Whoa! That ain't friendly!" He slammed the throttle forward to full burn. "Hang on to something!"

The atmocraft's engine bells threw a sheet of fusion fire out behind them and the ship leapt to supersonic velocity, cracking the sound barrier with a thunderous boom of compacted air.

More Rogue Trooper from Black Flame

#1: CRUCIBLE
Gordon Rennie

More 2000 AD action from Black Flame

Judge Dredd

#1: DREDD vs DEATH
Gordon Rennie

#2: BAD MOON RISING
David Bishop

#3: BLACK ATLANTIC
Simon Jowett & Peter J Evans

#4: ECLIPSE
James Swallow

#5: KINGDOM OF THE BLIND
David Bishop

#6: THE FINAL CUT
Matthew Smith

Durham Red

#1: THE UNQUIET GRAVE
Peter J Evans

Strontium Dog

#1: BAD TIMING
Rebecca Levene

#2: PROPHET MARGIN
Simon Spurrier

The ABC Warriors

#1: THE MEDUSA WAR
Pat Mills & Alan Mitchell

Nikolai Dante

#1: THE STRANGELOVE GAMBIT
David Bishop

Rogue Trooper created by **Gerry Finley-Day**
and **Dave Gibbons**.

ROGUE TROOPER

BLOOD RELATIVE

JAMES SWALLOW

BLACK FLAME

For The Enfield Suicide Squad,
The Friday Nighters
and The Friends of the 58th.
Semper Fidelis.

A Black Flame Publication
www.blackflame.com

First published in 2005 by BL Publishing, Games Workshop Ltd.,
Willow Road, Nottingham NG7 2WS, UK.

Distributed in the US by Simon & Schuster, 1230 Avenue of the
Americas, New York, NY 10020, USA.

10 9 8 7 6 5 4 3 2 1

Cover illustration by Dylan Teague.

ISBN 13: 978 1 84416 167 6
ISBN 10: 1 84416 167 6

A CIP record for this book is available from the British Library.

Printed in the UK by Bookmarque, Surrey, UK.

THE LEGEND OF THE ROGUE TROOPER

Nu Earth is a hellish, nightmare planet ravaged by war. The planet's atmosphere is devoid of life, poisoned by repeated chemical attacks and deadly to inhale. But the planet is close to a vital wormhole in space, a fact which has dragged its two rival factions - the Norts and the Southers - into a never-ending war. Now Nu Earth is a toxic, hell-blasted rock, where millions of soldiers in bio-suits wage bloody battles and die in their millions. Nu Earth is too important to lose. Not an inch of ground can be lost!

Here is where the legend of Rogue Trooper was born. Created by Souther forces, Rogue Trooper is the sole surviving example of the Genetic Infantrymen: a regiment of soldiers grown in vats and bio-engineered to be the perfect killing machine. Complete with protective blue skin and the ability to breathe the venomous atmosphere, the Genetic Infantrymen became renowned figures on both sides of the conflict. Moreover, the mind and soul of the GI could be downloaded onto a silicon chip in case of a mortal wound on the battlefield. Once downloaded, the dog-chip could then be slotted into special equipment and preserved until the soldier could grace a newly grown body.

Betrayed by a general in their own high command, almost the entire regiment of GIs were wiped out in the Quartz Zone Massacre.

The sole survivor managed to save just three chips from his former comrades and slot them into his gun, helmet and backpack. Now he is a loner, with just the disembodied personalities of his comrades for company, roaming the chemical wasteland in search of revenge: the Rogue Trooper.

ONE
THE SCHEME'S THE THING

Sequence Begins: Reference PBI2743#987. Digi-Orchestra setting: "Southern Freedom March Suite". SynthVox selection: Female. Subliminals at interval grade alpha. Training vid commences.

"Courage. Faith. Honour. These are the values that you, as a soldier of the Confederacy of the Southern Cross Republics, embody. Even now, as you watch this vid, thousands of your fellow troopers are fighting for those very same values on battlefields across the galactic frontier. Like you, they have bravely volunteered for a duty that no ordinary person could be capable of. Like them, you have proven that you have the stamina, the fitness and the keen mind that the Souther Army expects in all its men and women. Take a moment and look around you."

SynthVox pause, approximately four seconds.

"What do you see? Your fellow soldiers, brothers and sisters-in-arms preparing for their first day of military service to the people of the Confederacy. Together you are the very tip of the spear, honed to a fine, deadly point. Think of your family and friends; if they could see you now, they would be filled with pride at your accomplishments."

Open planetary data file. Image: Reference NUE97104/A#X45.

"Because of your level of excellence, your unit has been selected for operations at our most important conflict site: the planet Nu Earth."

Galactic map graphic. Scroll and zoom in to star system 97104, planet A.

"Our war with the vicious rogue nations of Nordland is at a critical juncture here, and you alone may be the one to help turn the tide. Nu Earth is of crucial strategic value because of its proximity to the Valhalla Gate, a Type Epsilon Wormhole Crossroads which links it to other important star systems; ask your line officer for more information if you would like to learn about black hole hyperspace travel. To allow this world to fall into Nort hands would leave our peace-loving home colonies open to their savage and pitiless attacks."

Sublimininal optic trigger #34 (Anger/Hatred/Determination analogue).

"Your tour on Nu Earth will not be an easy one, and you will be tested. During your rotation, you will face extremes of warfare never dreamed of in other battle zones – ruthless Nort weapons such as the cursed Hell-streaks, Decapitator drone mines and the sinister psychogenic Dream-Weavers – but your trusted leaders at Milli-Com are deploying the finest counter-forces to these evil devices, including advanced Robo-Gunners, the latest fighters and even genetically engineered super-soldiers. Alongside these allies, you will prevail. Have faith in your commanders. The Southern Nation has confidence in your superlative skills; your four weeks of training and orientation have moulded you into the best fighting force the South has to offer."

Sublimininal optic trigger #197 (Pride/Arrogance analogue).

"The transport ship you are currently aboard will begin its landing pattern in a few moments. Remember! The bombardments by the cowardly Norts have poisoned the atmosphere of planet Nu Earth through their destructive use of chem-weapons, bio-toxins and nuclear munitions! Under no circumstances are you to remove your chemsuit while outside a sealed environment! Stay alert, watch your teammates and keep your suit patches to hand!"

Digi-Orchestra volume to maximum. SynthVox tones to setting 4.

"Follow your training and you will be unbeaten! Discipline, teamwork, belief in the unit – these are the keys to victory. Know your directives! Obey orders. Trust your commander. Destroy all enemies. Show no mercy. If in doubt, consult your war book. And remember – The Scheme's The Thing!"

Sequence ends.

Ivar rolled the kaff-stik around his mouth as he patted his pockets in search of a lighter tab. The bitter flavour of the artificial caffeine substitute had not been improved by spending a few days inside the pocket of his combat fatigues and the thin white tube was bent a little in the middle, but for Ivar it was a taste of heaven and it flattened the twitches that came from his near-addiction to the mild stimulant. He counted himself lucky that his posting to Nu Sealand freed him of the need to wear a full-hood chem-suit.

The Nort base hid itself in the midst of a rusting stilt-town out in the shallows of the Orange Sea, off the Dix-I coastline; once Nu Sealand had been the site of a geothermal power plant, built in the heyday of the colonisation years. Back then, when the Orange Sea had been called the Crystal Sea and the waters had actually been blue, the facility was hammered into the ocean floor with plans to tap into Nu Earth's magma core for cheap, clean energy. Had it worked, the plant would have lit up half the continent, but construction was never completed, as the wars took more and more money from the coffers of the Nordland Territories and gave less and less to civilian contracts like the rig. By the time the ocean had been turned to a dirty umber by rust-fungus bio-bombs, Nu Sealand had accreted a shantytown on its half-finished decks, packed with refugees fleeing the warfare.

Ivar found the tab and touched it to the kaff-stick; he was rewarded with a warm gust of vaporised caffeine molecules and sucked them into his lungs. He'd been in school then, during the early throes of the war, and the vidiganda shows had captivated him. Ivar joined the Nort army as soon as he was old enough, gleeful that he would be sent to Nu Earth to torch the arrogant Southers just as the proud men on the screen had done. Reality gave him a different view on things, though. He soiled his chem-suit on the first day he fought the enemy, and there, cowering in a foxhole on the outskirts of the Toron-2 citiplex, Ivar realised what a terrible mistake he had made.

His dumb luck saved him; a senior officer with the same surname was killed half a world away, and because of a related foul-up in assignments at High Command, Ivar found himself sent back from the frontline and placed here, out in the ruddy waters where nothing really happened. At some point in the past decade, the Norts had flamed the rig to kill all the civvies clinging to its grimy framework and then quietly set up shop on board. It was a choice spot, just over the horizon from Souther-held Dix-I, a perfect listening post and staging point for Filth Columnist missions. When the push from Greater Nordland had come just a few weeks ago, Dix-I fell to the Nort war machine – thanks in part to the operations of the Nu Sealand crew.

Technically, the rig was a naval outpost, but the sensitive nature of what was done there mandated an army presence too – hence Ivar and the rest of the cadre garrisoned in the mid-levels. Ivar didn't really know the exact ins and outs of what happened in the core decks of the stilt-rig and he didn't really care. It was something to do with computers and communications, that he was sure of. Even the slowest soldier couldn't fail to notice the clusters of antennae and sat-dishes concealed among the rusty metalwork, painted with fake mutie-gull guano to blend in. They had a word for what was done on Nu Sealand: Sig-Int.

Signals Intelligence, that was the term. In the core, a weasely gaggle of techs studied and evaluated millions of pieces of radio traffic from all across the hemisphere, sifting and collating it for analysis by a different gaggle of techs at some other secret base. To Ivar, the idea of reading Souther emails every day was the most boring thing he could imagine, so he was thankful that he had been given the job of standing guard while someone else ploughed through the endless pile of communications. Out here, far from the dirt, mud and blood of the real fighting, Ivar's only mission was to walk a route that never changed, circling the western face of the vast rig, watching for contrails or the signs of ships on the horizon.

Like all the polluted waters of Nu Earth, the foetid stench of the Orange Sea's marine microclimate was enough to keep the virulent chem-clouds at bay; so while the air around Nu Sealand was breathable, it was a cocktail of the most repellent scents imaginable. Ivar's commander had once described it as being similar to "a boiling pot of excrement, vomit and caustic soda". Still, you got used to it after a while, and it meant that the Norts on the platform could go about barefaced, at least when there weren't any acid storms in the vicinity.

Ivar took a long drag on the kaff-stick. He couldn't stand the idea of being sealed into a chem-suit, maybe for days on end, incapable of having even the briefest of smokes. Sure, this place smelled like puke and if he fell over the side, the toxins in the water would turn him into meaty slurry in a matter of minutes, but at least he could light up.

He cast a lazy eye over the poisoned ocean, but Ivar didn't expect to see anything of interest. Since the Norts had taken Dix-I, the only thing coming over the horizon were broadcasts from the Nordland forces simulant sweetheart DeeTrick, her synth singing bawdy tunes about her exploits in Nu Atlanta. Ivar sighed. He hoped that the fall of Dix-I wouldn't mean the end of Nu Sealand's usefulness to High Command, because that would mean reassignment, and maybe some actual exposure to warfare.

Little of the kaff-stick remained and Ivar began the return leg of his patrol to the post where Lindquist would be waiting; newly promoted to sergeant and one pay grade above Korporal Ivar, Lindquist would probably be polishing his rank pins again. Ivar rounded a stanchion and saw the sergeant leaning over the guardrail, staring down at the russet froth around the stilt legs. It wasn't until he got closer that Ivar started to become concerned. It seemed like Lindquist wasn't breathing.

"Hoi!" he said around the cigarette, reaching for the other man's shoulder, "Are you–"

Ivar took a handful of Lindquist's jacket and pulled him up from his crooked stance. He almost swallowed the kaff-stick in surprise. "Stak!" Protruding from the sergeant's pale neck were three small knives made from a dull, matte plastic. The blades of the little weapons had swelled up after they penetrated his skin, thickening enough to choke the soldier to death. Every detail of the silent murder imprinted itself on the Nort's eyes.

Korporal Ivar felt the onset of loosening bowels as he imagined where the knives might have come from – had they been thrown? Not from the sea, no, too far. Not from above... That meant the killer was on the same deck! Ivar went cold as he realised that he'd walked right past a pool of shadows cast by the stanchion, large enough to conceal a man. He clutched his rifle, brought it up and fumbled at the safety catch.

The length of chain was connected at one end to a pulley mechanism that had served some forgotten purpose during the rig's construction; the other end was wrapped around a balled fist belonging to a figure that stood, not in the shadows, but directly behind Korporal Ivar. With brutal economy of movement, the grimy line of metal links looped over Ivar's head and coiled around his neck. The chain bit into his throat and tightened inexorably. Ivar had the brief impression that the figure behind him was bare-chested, but the lack of air in his lungs seemed to be playing tricks on his eyesight, warping his sense of colour. The Nort soldier let the gun drop and clawed at his neck, tearing his skin as he tried to lever the makeshift garrotte from its deadly embrace. However, his trachea collapsed under the pressure and the lifeless body slumped to the ground.

As he exhaled a final puff of air, the smouldering kaff-stick dropped from Ivar's mouth and was sent tumbling over the rail. His assassin, with the speed and deadly grace of a coiled cobra, snapped at the falling cigarette and caught it before it could fall down below; the chance was slight, but a burning cigarette butt could ignite a pool of flammable tox-sludge. The killer ground the butt into the palm of his hand, ignoring the faint sizzle as it snuffed out – the hot tip left no marks on the vat-grown plastiform flesh. He threw the dead korporal a blank look. "These things will kill you." The voice was low but intense.

Satisfied, Ivar's murderer moved silently to Lindquist's corpse and recovered the three D-Daggers in his neck, collapsing them back to their original throwing mode. He made sure that there were no other observers in sight and then pitched the two men into the sea. If anything remained of them once the chem-sludge had done its work, there might be a few meaty morsels for the slug-sharks.

Powerful fingers dug into lips of rusted metal, revealing where epoxy seals had been placed to hold a wide ventilator grid closed. Silently, the killer marshalled the musculature of his arms and chest, and with a sharp squeak, the grid came away. He slipped into the vent shaft and pulled the grille back with him. Inside the conduit, the air was hot and thin streams of burning steam coiled upward; the heat would have blinded a normal man, but he would be unaffected for quite a while. The biological machine of his body was far more efficient than the crude design made by human evolution – he was a finely tooled organic instrument that had never been subject to the random whims of nature.

Gently, the killer made his way downward, searching for the branch shafts that led to his target.

Data fell through the computers like sand through a sieve; trillions of bits of information, terabytes of code, voices, images, all of it ceaseless and unstoppable. The work of making sense of the "catch", as the technicians liked to call it, belonged to Nu Sealand's most important team member. Vok-IV was one of hundreds of similar units scattered in bases across Nu Earth, a dedicated artificial intelligence that could trace its lineage back to the primitive smart machines of the twentieth century, devices with names like "Echelon" and "Zagadka".

Vok-IV's sole purpose was to listen and parse communications traffic into discreet packets of intel for Nort High Command's cryptography and logistics battalions. Every three hours, it would squirt a compressed stream of lexicode to a secure transmitter and pass along another million lines of battle plans from the Southern lines. Both sides rotated their code keys on a daily basis – some of the more sensitive units did it on a hourly basis – so a lot of what Vok-IV handled was unreadable, given classification through point of origin or destination rather than content. However, there were some Souther ciphers that the Norts had torn wide open and their text streamed across the screens of the monitor techs, giving them something to do in between the checking of the AI's coolant systems.

Tek-Specialist Erno was on desk duty shift, and he cocked his head to watch the clear data stream race past him. The other technicians passed the time by placing bets on the content of certain messages or reading the enemy soldiers' letters home; such activity would have been grounds for serious charges if the unit's political officer knew of it, of course. Erno stifled a yawn. A solboat convoy in the Western Sea was calling for rescue from a wolf pack of Nort Mantas; Private First Class Taylor of the 151st Rangers was getting a "Dear Joan" letter from her lover; a neutron missile had hit a railhead in Nu Dakota; an outbreak of black rictus was being reported in Toxville. Another uneventful afternoon in this small corner of the galaxy's longest running war.

Of course, Vok-IV didn't just listen to the enemy. The wide-band scanners tuned in to frequencies used by the scattered independents and Freeport zones across the planet, looking out for information from battlefield looters and profiteers. And unbeknownst to all but a select group of staff (of which Erno was one), Nu Sealand also eaves-dropped on its own side. A special section of Vok-IV's operational memory was devoted exclusively to checking the parity and content of Nort communications, looking for any signs of duplicity, treachery or malfeasance. After all, there were traitors and opportunists on both sides of the Nu Earth war.

Erno frowned at this thought, remembering the lengthy series of loyalty tests and biometric checks he'd had to undergo before being stationed here. High Command ensured that everyone with direct access to Vok-IV was a staunch Nordland party member; anyone who came up short by their stringent standards swiftly found themselves posted to front-line operations like Nu Paree's endless street fights or the lethal Morrok Combat Zone.

Such a "reassignment" had happened quite recently – one of the scanalysists from F-Sector had made a few imperti-nent comments about Grand Marshal Von Gort, only to be escorted on to the next jumpshuttle out, bound for what the base commander called "a more challenging appointment". The errant technician's shuttle had never made it to what-ever meat grinder it was destined for, though. A day later Erno had noticed comm traffic from a search and rescue unit as it passed through the datastream, reporting that the transport ship had been shot down by a Souther orbital lancer. If Erno ever entertained the idea of even *thinking* something disloyal, he would remind himself of the stills of that crashed flyer, reduced to a ball of indistinct wreckage somewhere on the Dix-I plains.

He glanced around the room. Erno was alone. He could see the shape of a guard through the frosted glass of the core chamber's hatch, but he was behind five centimetres of plastisteel; Erno could shout obscenities at the trooper and never be heard. Erno gave his chair an experimental spin. As he turned in place, his eyes ranged over the banks of consoles, the ducting from the power core and then the central frame of the Vok unit itself. Big, like the magazine from some giant's pistol, Vok-IV was a block of machined aluminium riddled with tubes carrying pinkish coolants. At this angle, Erno could see the heart of the machine, the oval module of the datacore. He watched a blinking green light turn red on its surface; the unit had just fired off another databurst. In three hours time, the greedy little code-monkeys at crypto would be ready for another helping. The core was such a small thing really, no bigger than a handball, and yet it was the very reason for Nu Sealand's continued existence; had the listening post not been here, the Norts would have reduced the rusting rig to slag years ago. Erno's commander was fond of telling his men that the Vok-IV was much more important than any of them. In the balance of things, the officer often said, the lives of all the technicians combined were worth less than the least expensive component inside the datacore. How this knowledge was supposed to motivate them, Erno wasn't sure. They were glorified watchmen, really, observers looking over the machine's shoulder on the million-to-one chance that the unit might suffer a breakdown. It was dull work, but at least it was safe.

Erno spun on his chair again, quicker this time. He saw monitors, ducts, Vok-IV, more monitors, the wall. Another spin. Monitors, ducts, a blue man, Vok-IV, more monitors.

The Nort fell off the chair in surprise when his brain caught up with the images from his eyes. "Buh," he managed, attempting to force himself back up from the floor. The intruder crossed the room in quick, lightning-fast steps, snatching at Erno's tunic. The technician drew in a breath to scream – not that it would have mattered – but then found it impossible as the swift figure pressed a serrated combat knife to his lips.

"Quiet," he was told.

Erno looked into inhuman eyes, greenish-yellow without a trace of pupil, eyes that regarded him with clinical, detached precision. The face they were set in was a strong, sculpted mask, hard and much abused like that of a prize-fighter, but also curiously smooth. The technician suddenly thought of the classical sculptures looted from old Earth in the museums on Norta Sekunda.

Erno had spent his entire tour on this planet reading Souther comm signals, so he knew exactly who and what had walked into the computer chamber. There was a legend in the room with him, a blue-skinned ghost conjured up by the worst of battlefield science. A freak. A monster.

A Rogue.

"Key," it said.

Erno blinked. He had never really believed the stories that the Genetic Infantrymen actually existed, instead considering them to be some weird piece of Souther misinformation and propaganda set out to encourage tall tales among the war zones. And for long moments he found it hard to connect the creature holding him by his throat to that abstract idea.

"Your key," repeated the GI.

Dutifully, Erno produced the beam-key from its loop on his belt and handed it over, thumb and forefinger extending. It wasn't like the enemy soldier would be able to use it, anyhow. Erno had to be in direct physical contact for it to work, so the bio-lock could read his DNA pattern.

The Rogue Trooper gave Tek-Soldat Erno the smallest of smiles. "Thanks," he added, and then with a single stroke of his knife, he cut the technician's thumb and forefinger clean off.

As pain and shock shot throughout his body, Erno fell back into his chair, screaming. Rogue crossed to the Vok-IV and squeezed the severed digits and the key into the right slots on the module, absently wiping blood off his broad chest. The computer core flowered open and offered him the datacore like a gift. Rogue reached into the rain of vaporous sub-zero liquids that kept the AI just above freezing and tore the unit out, ignoring the rime of frost that snapped and crackled over his fingers.

Erno skittered backwards on his chair's castors, kicking and flailing, and a trail of blood marking a dot-dash path after him. He could now see where the vent shaft had been opened from the inside, the marks in the metal where bare hands hard as iron had pulled and tore it. With the most total physical exertion of his life, Erno forced away the blazing pain from his injury and used his off-hand to slam a circular button on the desk. Instantly, a siren began to wail.

The GI ignored him, unhurried in his task, and placed the datacore in one of two blocky pannier packs strapped to the thighs of his fatigue trousers. Erno's vision began to tunnel from shock and the sound in the chamber was becoming woolly and indistinct. He saw the hatch slide open and a guard barrel in, a heavy flechette pistol in his grip; standard firearms were not permitted inside the computer chamber, for fear that an accidental discharge could strike a vital component. The frangible micro-arrows the guard's weapon fired could make a red ruin of flesh but would bounce harmlessly off any solid surface.

The pistol made a coughing sound and suddenly there were dozens of plastic darts embedded in the GI's chest. The trooper, who appeared annoyed with this untimely intrusion, bushed them away with one hand, tossing his bloodstained knife with the other. The blade buried itself in the guard's forehead and he fell away, out of Erno's line of sight. The technician blinked slowly. Peculiar that the Souther soldier had no weapon of his own. Where was his rifle, his headgear or his backpack? The question followed Erno into unconsciousness and faded with him.

Rogue recovered his combat blade from the guard's corpse with a sucking noise and took up the handgun as an afterthought, then he sprinted away toward the main elevator. The dense Nort datacore thumped against his leg as he ran.

TWO
DISPATCHES

Nu Sealand's command centre was on the platform's largest tower, built inside the shell of a vast gas ventilation chimney. Hidden by thick armourplas baffles, an outside observer would never know of the chaos that was unfolding inside; shrieking alarms blared from all sides of the room as the officer of the watch found three sets of critical alerts screaming for his attention.

An emergency signal from the computer core was jockeying for attention with anguished shouts from loading bay two where someone had detonated a plasma sphere and a chorus of sporadic gunfire from mid-deck.

"Voices down here!" a guardsman on the deck was shouting. "Dozens of them, coming from all over the place!"

The watch officer swore – that particular section of the rig was a perfect conduit for echoes, so for all he knew that dolt was firing at himself – but the grenade? On cue, a pair of dull thumps resonated through the floor plating. "It's an attack!" he snapped, gesturing to his second in command. "Open the blinds!"

"Kapten. Is that wise?"

"Do it!" he snapped, the veins in his neck throbbing with anger and frustration.

The junior officer did as he was ordered and with the flick of a switch the steel shields that covered the windows of the control deck folded away, giving the watch officer an uninterrupted view of the whole rig. But it also made the command crew visible to the triad optics of a GI-issue assault rifle that had been set up on a bipod on a shorter neighbouring tower.

Automatic mechanisms inside the gun had already shifted its internal balance to that of sniper mode, altering its lens, scope and barrel configuration. Although no finger was on the rifle's trigger and no eye was at its scope, the weapon was live to fire. Its breech held a magazine packed full of high-energy laser round capacitor cartridges, the ultra-dense kind that were usually used for cracking the engine blocks of Nort trucks. With a ripping noise, the rifle tore through the rounds, moderating its own recoil to scatter bolts of coherent light across the deck. Hot streaks of colour punched through the armoured glasseen windows and struck flesh, boiling blood to pink steam wherever they hit their mark.

For a long moment, nothing moved on the command level. Then the elevator's doors opened and the rifle's owner burst out, flechette gun and knife at the ready. Rogue paused and nodded at the perfect fire pattern with satisfaction. He ignored the moans of the dying and kicked out the remains of one of the shattered windows. The GI leapt from the tower and fell ten feet to the nearby platform where the smoking rifle lay. He had set the gun in place a few hours earlier, before the dawn had illuminated the upper decks with weak yellow light.

"About time." The rifle's voice was terse. "Dump that sissy gun and let's get out of here. I need ammo."

Rogue tossed the pistol away and retrieved his weapon, replacing the empty cartridge with a new magazine of shells; his actions were so automatic that it was as natural a reflex to him as breathing. "Nice grouping, Gunnar."

"Eh?" The word was the synthetic equivalent of a shrug. "Easy meat."

Rogue slung the rifle over his shoulder and then grasped a trailing cable. With a swift shift of his weight, he came off the platform and began to slide down the long wire.

The metallic cable fizzed as it passed through his bare fingers, the heat of the friction raising thin threads of smoke from his skin. Rogue registered the pain as a minor irritation and dismissed it. Below his feet, the mid-deck loomed.

"I'm telling you, there's someone in here!" bellowed Kawso. "Grenades don't just throw themselves!"

Furni shook his head, studying the infra-scan. "But there's no body heat traces! If there was an intruder here before, they're gone now... "

"That's what those Sud bastards want us to think!" Sergeant Kawso spat and stepped over the remains of another Nort soldier. There were five or six dead men in the loading bay – it was tough to make an exact count because of all the scattered body parts – and broad holes in the decking where plasma spheres had rolled out of the dark corners to detonate under their feet. The lethal grenades cast out deadly globes of superheated gas when they exploded, metallic vapour as hot as the surface of a sun, incinerating men and hardware with equal power.

"Wait," Furni said, pointing at something. "What is that?"

Kawso took a cautious step closer and saw a rectangular box sitting on the deck. It had a pair of optic sensors on the upper face and straps dangling down from one side.

"Don't touch it! It could be a booby trap!" Furni warned.

The Nort sergeant gave him a silencing grimace and gingerly picked up the object, holding it waist high. He turned it over in his hands: one side had a chip slot. "Huh," he made a low chuckle. "It's just a skevving backpack."

An opening on one face of the pack glinted in the dimness and a synthetic voice replied, "No, I'm not."

A three-pronged steel claw snapped out of the opening and grabbed a large handful of Kawso's crotch in a vice-like grip. Furni was startled as the Nort let out a high scream. "Aaaaaaa! Get it off me!"

He hesitated at the peculiar sight of Kawso dancing about with a pack attached to his genitals, afraid to shoot at the thing for fear he would miss and hit the sergeant. Furni heard swift footsteps behind him and turned, expecting reinforcements; they were, but just not for him.

"Lights out," said Rogue and his fist came at the Nort trooper like a missile, the punch propelling a GI helmet in his hand like a huge mutant knuckle-duster. The hardhat smashed Furni aside trailing blood, teeth and fragments of jawbone.

"Hey!" the helmet complained. "What am I now, a boxing glove?"

Rogue ignored the comment and flipped the armoured gear onto his head, moving to grab Kawso. The claw released its killer grip and the sergeant tumbled backwards. Rogue tugged the off-balance Nort by the shoulder strap of his autogun and before he could react, the GI pitched him into one of the blast holes.

Sergeant Kawso hit the scummy ocean cursing and screaming as the orange murk gushed in through his open mouth. He drowned in a dilution of foetid poison and his own liquefied organs. Rogue snatched up the backpack and secured it over his shoulders. "Helm, you got the frequency for the charge locked in?"

A voice issued from a chip bearing a morose skull image and the digit "1" on the brow of his helmet. "Affirmative, Rogue. Give me the word and it's done."

"Tell me you got it." Another chip, this one slotted in the backpack, spoke aloud. The flat face of the microcircuit had the number three visible on it.

"He's got it, Bagman," said Gunnar from the number two slot on the rifle. "And he woke up half the damn Nort Army doing it."

Rogue ignored the chatter, his heightened hearing concentrating on the screams of sirens and the noise of approaching boots on the metal decks. "Blow it, Helm. We're outta here." Without waiting for confirmation, the

GI stepped lightly over the edge of the same hole he'd thrown Kawso down. As he struck the water, the drag from his gear flipped Rogue over, just in time for him to see shimmering balls of yellow flame erupt from the centre of the Nu Sealand rig. The C9 detonator charges had been placed in just the right locations, along weak lines of rusted pipe and vital conduits that fed hot gases from the geothermal sink below the ocean floor.

He hovered under the waterline for a moment, as the first chunks of metal and plastic began to fall away past him into the depths below. The acidic embrace of the Orange Sea was already burning into his bare skin and stinging the protective nictitating membranes over his eyes. Rogue turned from his target and struck out in a hard, measured pace, swimming down and away.

Nu Sealand became a torch, vomiting flames and black smoke up into the air, adding a little more toxic matter and poison to the planet's ruined atmosphere.

They said Pitt City was a Freeport, but in truth there was absolutely nothing free about it. If you didn't have money in Pitt City, you might as well be dead. As Ferris saw it, it was all about degrees of how rich you were. Nobody here was too rich, because if they had that many nu-credits, the first thing they would do would be to buy a ride off the chem-infested rock. There were a few folks who were just rich enough – like Gog here, the alien dealer-fixer-pimp-whatever sitting across from Ferris in all his insectile glory – and they stayed in Pitt City because they were too greedy to leave. Gog and his kind cut up the Freeport like a pie, paying bribes to the Souther Divisional Command that technically had jurisdiction over the settlement, running their own pieces of the city as little empires. Guys like Ferris, who were forever looking for a big score and were never rich enough, were always scrabbling for enough bluebacks to pay for fuel and grub as well as getting into scrapes that inevitably ended up emptying their pockets.

And then there were the folks at the bottom, the ones who worked as "rentals" for soldiers on liberty, or who hovered on the edges of malnutrition, living on what they could beg or steal. Money was exactly the reason why Ferris was in Gog's nightclub, and money was why Ferris had accepted the alien's commission to fly a cargo of "tractor parts" to Kyro. He'd caught some Nort flak on the return leg and lost a drive baffle. He now needed the cash more than ever, and not just because he owed hundreds in dock fees from here to the Rockies-2.

The alien looked like the unpleasant result of cross-breeding a cockroach and a mantis, all five feet and six legs of him squatting on a broad cushion like some Old Earth Arabian prince. There weren't a lot of XT species on Nu Earth, as most of them had been smart enough to get going when the colony had turned into a war zone, but the insect had earned itself a nice piece of the action and showed no intentions of leaving.

"F-f-f-Ferris," Gog chattered. "Nice work-k-k. I saw the hole in your thruster. Kik-kik. Other pilot wouldn't have been able to land that. Other pilot would have landed in the Pitt-t-t."

"Hey," his reply was languid and full of studied cool. "Some guys got the skills, some guys don't." Ferris wasn't about to admit to the bug that he'd almost lost it on the touchdown, barely keeping his strato-shuttle from nose-diving into the vast crater that gave Pitt City its name.

Gog's head bobbed. "Kik. Kyro connection was very satisfied with the merchandise."

"Right." Ferris nodded. His jaw hardened as he thought about the boxes as they'd been hauled off the shuttle, the white armourplas containers with their stasis units. He thought about the noises the boxes had made. People noises. *Scared* people noises. Ferris forced the memory away; what Gog had made him carry was none of his damn business. He had to have the nu-creds, or else he'd lose his ship, his lifeline and probably a few internal organs if the syndicate's muscle boys caught up with him. Ferris couldn't help but feel sick inside as he asked, "So, my payment, then?"

"Aaaaah," the insect wheezed. "Kik. Small problem."

Dread, cold and sudden, flooded Ferris's chest. "Problem?" he repeated. "What kinda problem?" He let his hand drop to where the vibro-dagger he habitually carried was holstered.

Gog made an airy gesture with two of his claws. "K-k-cash flow. I don't think I can pay you."

Ferris's eyes narrowed. Cash flow? The damned bug was sitting next to a gold hookah and planting his scaly ass on a Nibian silk pillow, both of which were worth more than the pilot made in a year. "If not now, then when?" he demanded.

"No," said Gog. "Not now. Not ever." It made a clicking sound that was the alien's equivalent of a laugh. "Perils of being a freelancer, F-f-Ferris. Kik."

The pilot surged to his feet, the vibro-dag humming into his hand. "You son of a roach, where's my damn money?"

"Gaaah!" Gog's legs came up defensively. "Thought you might take it badly, kik. Made a call in k-k-case."

Ferris hesitated, and in that moment he heard the rising-falling hoots of an approaching military police siren. "What did you do?"

"Remember those fuel rods you boosted from the T-t-Twentieth Mobilised last month? Kik-kik? T-told the MPs where to find you. Be here any second."

"Ah, sneck." Just like that, the money, the paid-off debts, all the problems Gog's fee would have solved slammed back into Ferris like a hammer blow. The humming knife in his hand was hot and ready, and for a second the pilot thought about ramming it into Gog's big compound eye, but he could hear the squeal of tyres as the Milli-Fuzz cruiser skidded to a halt outside the building and the gruff shouts of army cops as they kicked in the door. Ferris had been on the wrong end of Souther military justice before and he'd pissed blood for a week afterwards; he really didn't have much of a choice. He would be executed for stealing combat supplies, there was no question.

"Bastard!" Ferris kicked over the hookah and broke it, sending Gog into a hissing, clacking fit of insect swearing, and then he ran for the exit and staircase that would take him to the roof. From there, he could climb up to the underside of the port's dome and make a run for it. Hopefully. Ferris was now officially broke, and in Pitt City that was a death sentence.

The black sand crunched under Rogue's boots as he walked lightly across the flat expanse of beach. The cold air over his bare arms helped the anti-tox aerosol to soothe the inflammation of his tough, rubbery skin; although Rogue and his kind were built to weather the worst extremes of Nu Earth's murderous environment, swimming for hours in water like battery acid was hard even on him. The breeze moaned through the curls of obsidian sandstone that bordered the seashore. The soft black rock looked like frozen waves where the winds had cut and shaped it. The GI held his rifle shoulder high, tracing the horizon through its optical sights. At the edge of the visual acuity, a quick, stubby shape was crossing the stagnant waters.

"Nort foil." Gunnar's voice was close to Rogue's ear. "Going for the rig, maybe?"

"Reckon so." Rogue watched the vessel until it went out of sight. He slipped the rifle to a stand-easy stance and ran a hand through the queue of wire-hard white hair that bisected the top of his head.

"Chalk up another victory for the mysterious Rogue Trooper and his biochip buddies," Gunnar mimicked the slick tones of a vid announcer. "Just hope it was worth the effort."

The GI walked back toward the mouth of a small cavern, flicking out the legs of Gunnar's bipod. "We'll know soon enough." He placed the rifle on the sand, facing across the beach. "You know the drill. Watch and wait."

"Yeah, yeah," the chip retorted irritably. "I hear you."

"I mean it, Gunnar. You get trigger-happy and I'll swap you with Helm. See how you like the view from up there."

"Whatever."

Rogue threw the gun a last look and then ducked into the cave. Bagman was propped against a wall, his manipulator claw exploring the datacore's innards, trails of fibre-optic cable running into his service ports. Helm rested on a rock, watching over a cluster of G-rations on a heater pad. Helm was in full flow, recounting his exploits on the rig. "So I pushed up the gain on my output, right, and started broadcasting the sounds of the Nort guys looking for me! Footsteps, voices, the works! I swear they were running around in circles down there, chasing echoes!"

"Helm..." Bagman's artificial voice was curt.

"And when they started firing, I beamed that out too! They must've thought we had a whole platoon on board!"

"Helm!"

"Then Rogue and Gunnar turn up and snag me, but the Norts were real close, so quick as you like I pull punchbag duty and break those Norty noses like a–"

"Helm, for synth's sake, will you quit it?" Bagman snarled. "I'm trying to bust a class nine encryption here. I don't wanna hear your damn hero stories!"

"Well, excuse me, ya miserable kook!"

"Don't call me a kook, you tin-plate piece of–"

"Hey!" Rogue silenced them both with a sharp growl. "Can't you two ladies stop bickering for ten mikes? Keep it down, the pair of you." The GI sat heavily and took a bite from the ration pack.

"Sorry, Rogue," said Helm. "I was just talking, is all."

"Well, talk to me. Don't bother Bagman." He swallowed the last of the tasteless freezemeat and washed it down with a sip from his canteen.

"You really think we're gonna find something in that box of chips?" Helm asked. "I mean, we went a long way on the word of some half-dead Nort technogeek."

"That we did." Rogue remembered the injured technician they'd discovered inside the crashed atmocraft, desperate for air, desperate enough to spill his guts about the listening post. "It's not like we had a choice. We lost his trail after the Norts took Dix-I and this is the best chance to pick it up again." He nodded at the datacore. "If there's even a scrap of intel in that thing about the Traitor General, it's more than we got now."

Talking about the Traitor brought a sudden silence into the cave. The faceless nemesis that Rogue had dedicated his life to hunting had slipped out of his grasp, and with him the Genetic Infantryman's purpose for living. Out there somewhere in the Nu Earth wilderness, the unnamed man still drew breath, and every moment he was alive was an insult to the legions of Rogue's brother GIs who had died because of his duplicity. Rogue looked away from the dingy depths of the sandstone cave, where the shadows called up black memories of drop-pods blossoming into smoke, of bloodshed on fields of glass and the screams of betrayed soldiers. His eyes ranged over Helm, Bagman and Gunnar. Three minds rescued from the massacre, entombed on biochips: three dead comrades and him. They were all that remained of the GI legions and if they had a purpose beyond revenge, Rogue could not see it.

"That tech would have given up his own mother for a fresh ox-bottle," he said quietly. "We're gonna find that rat bastard traitor soon. I know it."

"Ah," Bagman made a satisfied noise. "Here we are... " A string of indicators on the surface of the datacore blinked from blue to green. "And the crowd goes wild."

"You cracked it?" Helm was surprised.

"Never doubt my skills."

Rogue smiled thinly. "Good work, Bagman. Run the search; you know the drill, look for the keywords, GI,

Rogue, Buzzard." Buzzard-Three was the closest they had ever got to naming the Traitor General, a code designation given by the Norts when the double-agent had served aboard an orbital Souther command satellite – perhaps as some kind of twisted private joke, the traitor sometimes used the title. It had almost been his undoing at Glasshouse-G, a Nort stockade where Rogue had tightened the noose on the spy. However, the traitor had played the game of espionage long enough to have had an escape route prepared and the GI had been left chasing a shadow.

"I got something!" Bagman's voice couldn't hide a tone of excitement. "Listen to this; an advisory from Nort High Command to one General Rössa, Internal Affairs Apparat. Regarding NexGen Project at Domain Delta lab complex, proceed to facility and initiate directive 'S'."

"What does that have to do with us?" said Helm.

"There's a reference attached to the message with two code words. 'Prog #228' and 'Buzzard'."

Rogue cursed to himself. Programme #228 had been the Souther Army's classification for the research and development that had created the Genetic Infantrymen, a top-secret operation that the Norts had never been able to duplicate. The enemy's crude attempts at making their own Genetik Soldats had been a spectacular failure where Rogue and his brethren could easily breathe poisoned air and survive the harsh toxins of the battlefield. Their Nort "cousins" soon succumbed to the relentless taints and died on their feet after just a few weeks of service.

"You thinking what I'm thinking?" said Helm.

"Reckon so. This Domain Delta has gotta be a gene-lab, maybe where the Norts are still trying to cook up their own brand of GI troopers." Rogue considered this for a moment. "We know the Traitor General sold us out to the Norts when we dropped on the Quartz Zone... But what if that's not all he gave them?"

"You reckon he passed on data from Programme #228?"

"Some of it, at least. Why else would his code be tagged to this message?"

"Then we gotta find this Delta place," said Helm. "Bag, you got a location?"

"Negative," Bagman replied. "This is just an addendum to orders already sent. Wherever this Domain Delta place is, it's too sensitive for standard channels."

"Damn!" growled Rogue. "Then we're back at square one."

"Maybe not." Bagman sent a new set of pulses down the cables to the datacore. "I'm gonna widen the search, see if I can find anything else that..." His words trailed off into silence. When he spoke again, it was in a hushed whisper. "Synth me..."

Helm's voice was low. "What you got?"

"Forget that Delta stuff for a second. You ain't gonna believe this." He paused, and then from the opening on the pack, the manipulator produced a digi-pad. "Here, see for yourself."

Rogue took the panel and activated the screen. The tell-tale Nort symbology of a lightning bolt striking downwards from a darkened sky filled the display. "It's a vidiganda broadcast."

"Time-stamp says it's going to air tomorrow. Keep watching."

The Nort simulant DeeTrick appeared on the screen and winked. "Hello my brave boychiks! Oh, do I have a surprise for you! I'm here in the cityplex of San Diablo, which you might recall we took from those silly Suds like candy from a baby, yah? Well, our handsome lads in covert operations have asked me to announce the capture of a very, very special person." The svelte android woman was walking through the streets of the captured city toward the stadium that lay at its centre. Her tone turned serious and grim; Rogue's ultra-sensitive hearing picked out the subliminal audio cues as she spoke. "Many of you have heard the legend of a Sud super-duper-soldier that stalks the combat zones, preying on our fighters and performing unspeakable acts of barbarism." DeeTrick paused and wiped a theatrically large tear from her eye. "Those poor boys... But now they're going to have their debts paid in full! The proud army of the Nordland Territories has seized one of Nu Earth's most horrific and deadly Souther war criminals!" The simulant threw open the stadium doors and there in the middle of the vast arena was a lone figure strapped to an X-shaped crucifix. "Sons of Nordland, I bring before you the monstrous Genetik Infantryman: the Rogue Trooper!"

The camera's view panned in to reveal a blue-skinned male, heavily beaten, hanging loosely in his restraints. DeeTrick clasped his chin and held up his face; weak yellow eyes blinked back at them from the screen.

"What the hell is this?" Rogue hissed.

"The war criminal's trial will take place here in twenty-four hours, after which he will be found guilty and executed by firing squad," the android said happily. "Don't forget to tune in, folks! We'll be live across Nu Earth to say bye-bye to blue-boy!"

The screen went blank. "If that's a trap, then it's the most overdone one I've ever come across."

"It's gotta be," insisted Helm. "That tech in the wreck, he had to be a plant."

"I don't think so," Bagman broke in. "I've been monitoring the comm channels since we left Dix-I, and there's some hush-hush stuff going on in San Diablo. This vid and the radio traffic I'm seeing in the datacore... It looks legit."

Rogue called out. "Gunnar, you hearing this?"

"Yeah," came the reply. "Maybe we oughta let the Norts ice that guy. The pressure would be off if they thought we were dead."

"I'm gonna pretend I didn't hear that," Bagman snapped. "Rogue, whoever the Norts have got there, he ain't you but he *is* a GI. I got the bio-scans right here."

"But Rogue's the last of us still breathing, right? We know everyone else got scragged in the Zone. So who's that joker?"

After a long moment, Rogue gave the only answer he could. "There's one way to find out."

Helm made an electronic snort. "You want to go get him? What are we gonna do, just waltz into the middle of a fortified Nort city and ask politely?"

"Wasn't thinking about being polite, Helm."

"San Diablo's clear across the continent," rumbled Gunnar. "If the bot-babe is right, we'd never make it there before they killed him."

Rogue buried the remains of his meal and then picked up his helmet. "Bagman, check the digi-map. Where's the nearest airstrip?"

"Searching... There's a Nort base about fifty klicks southwest, but it's a tough nut to crack. How about Pitt City? It's closer and the defences are lame."

"Freeport, huh? Sounds like a plan. We'll slip in and find an atmocraft."

"And how are you going to convince someone to fly us?" snapped Helm.

Rogue picked up Bagman and walked out on to the sands. "I'll let Gunnar do the talking."

THREE
ESCAPE KEY

Ferris's breathing echoed about his chem-hood with every exhalation. He'd been running all day, dodging patrols and skirting the more heavily populated parts of Pitt City. It wasn't easy; the settlement was an aggregation of linked bubbledomes that sat in a fat ring around the mouth of the Pitt, the huge crater that a stray meteor-bomb had gouged in the Nu Earth landscape. There were only ever two directions you could go in Pitt City – for or against the clock – and that made it simpler to find someone on the run. The Milli-Fuzz were running a standard sweep for Ferris, two packs of MPs going around the ring in different directions. Eventually, he'd run out of places to hide.

The army cops were cracking down; anyone who broke the rules was being prosecuted to the full extent of the Confederate Military Code of Justice, which usually meant a .50 calibre "pardon" to the back of the head. That worthless bug Gog had turned Ferris into a dead man running. Once the MPs got him, he was cold meat. The pilot paused in the lee of a hab-capsule, struggling to even out his breathing. He was out of condition; he wasn't cut out for the fugitive life. Ferris wondered why Gog hadn't just had him killed. It was just like the loathsome little insect to amuse itself by letting him scurry and run while the cops closed in on him. Hell, Gog probably had a betting pool going for how long Ferris would survive.

He gave a hollow, dry cough, steaming up the murky faceplate of his civilian chem-suit. His air filter needed replacing and all this exertion wasn't helping the jury-rigged oxy-scrubber in his backpack. Ferris had to get to safety and un-hood, or it wouldn't matter about the MPs. They'd find him collapsed in a corner somewhere, choked to death on his own carbon dioxide. He crossed the mud-slick street and walked as quickly as he dared towards the shuttle pads, peeling back a ragged edge of chain-link fence instead of taking the suicidal route through the main entrance. His luck held; there was a Mili-Fuzz trooper on the gate, spinning his baton with idle menace, but the Souther never saw Ferris as he ducked and wove between fuel bowsers and bombed-out blockhouses. Not for the first time today, Ferris found himself wishing he had a gun; but he'd lost his pistol in a card game and had barely managed to keep hold of the dagger in his belt – a lot of good that would do him against a dozen MPs, if it came down to it.

There were lots of shuttles, hoppers and assorted atmocraft parked on the Pitt City airstrip. It was always busy with cargo, military craft dropping in and civvie ships coming from other Freeports and Disputed Zones. The fuzz would never think of looking for Ferris here, because no one being hunted by MPs would be stupid enough to sneak onto an airfield crawling with Southers. Nobody except Ferris, of course.

He had never felt this nervous before in his life, and his eyes were darting everywhere, desperately trying to look in all directions at once. The pilot almost screamed in fright when he saw something shapeless move at the edge of the rockcrete.

"Damn!" Ferris recovered quickly, watching a bent figure wreathed in a camu-cape shambling toward the vent ducts from the launch pits. Just one of the city's massive number of derelicts, some poor chem-sodden wretch trying to stave off the cold night air by clustering around steam that billowed from the ducts. Vagrants were ten a cred and their life expectancy was short. Ferris was sobered by the realisation that this could be his fate, too, unless he got his ass out of the settlement.

His strato-shuttle was still where he had left it and for the first time that night, Ferris felt a vague twinge of hope. The aircraft's holds were empty and he was lacking in supplies, but he had plenty of fuel – plenty of stolen Souther fuel, as Gog had pointed out – and despite the busted drive baffle, it wouldn't be a problem getting airborne. As he approached, he began to entertain the idea that he could get away clean. All Ferris needed now was somewhere to escape *to*.

He was at the hatch when they emerged from the shadows; four stocky Mili-Fuzz enforcers with the standard armoured shoulder pads and hoods with face-guards. One had a pistol, but the other three held batons in ready stances. Ferris sagged against the hull, his knees turning to water. Of course they would have been waiting for him. Why would he ever have thought otherwise?

"Hey," he began lamely. "I can explain..."

"Really?" said the MP with the gun. "You can explain why a no-good thief like you has Souther military property on board his tub?" His face wore a crooked smile. "We'd like to hear that, wouldn't we, lads?"

There was a chorus of nods. "Yeah," said the closest man, the anticipation of imminent ultra-violence in his eyes, "This punk can tell us all about it while we're giving him a beating."

Ferris held up a hand. "Wait, you don't–"

"Oh," said another MP, "did you see that? He's resisting arrest."

The gunman nodded. "Take him."

A studded truncheon came down on Ferris as he tried to wheel away; the impact struck his shoulder and threw him to the ground. With every bone in his arm singing in pain, he scrambled under the shuttle's landing gear.

"Get him out of there!" someone shouted.

A hand closed around his ankle and pulled; Ferris slid across the oil-stained ferrocrete and into the clutches of the MPs. Turning, something caught his eye – the hobo from the vents, standing close by. An arm emerged from the dark depths of the camu-cloak and rolled something small and cylindrical towards the Mili-Fuzz.

The trooper with the pistol was shouting at the vagrant. "Get lost, rummy, else you want us to put you down too!" The object halted at his feet. "What the–"

The sunflare grenade exploded with a fizzing shriek and everything was flooded with brilliant white. Ferris recoiled from the dazzling light, twin shards of pure agony lancing into his skull. He felt flat on the runway, flash-blinded, eyes alive with horrible pain.

The MPs were yelling and cursing as well, and one of them kicked Ferris as he stumbled around, flailing with his baton. "What was that?" said a voice.

"Someone's here!" That was the one with the pistol. "Aaagh! Damn it. I can't see!"

"Quiet!" called the guy with the baton. "You hear something?"

Ferris stayed very silent and very still, the grey-white haze filling his vision.

"Hey, Fuzz. Over here." Ferris didn't recognise this new voice. He heard a noise like bone crunching and the heavy sound of a man collapsing.

"Watch it!" shouted the gunman.

"Rogue, on your nine." Another voice, quite close; then a crack.

"Ugh! My knee! He broke my knee!" The sound of a choke, another falling body.

"Lights out, creep." A third newcomer, gruff and nasty. "I'd spit on him if I had a mouth."

"Two left."

"I hear him!" shouted the MP with the gun. Two rapid snap-shots sizzled over Ferris's head. "You like that, huh?" Then the trooper made a surprised yelp and fell silent.

The last MP said nothing, but Ferris heard his footsteps as he ran, boots skipping off the ferrocrete.

"Where's that dink goin'?" said the gruff voice.

"He's gonna run straight into that–"

Ferris heard an echoing clang as something struck a metallic object.

"–fuel truck."

There was a long silence. When the pain in his eyes had lessened from a murderous burning to a dull ache, Ferris dared to gather himself up. His vision was a blurry collection of grey shapes and black shadows.

"You a pilot?" The voice startled him and Ferris jerked. "What's your name?"

"Uh, yeah. When I can see, I am. I'm Ferris, just Ferris."

"This your ship, Ferris?"

"I think so. Registration number 1138 on the hull..."

A strong arm clamped around his elbow. "This way." Ferris let himself be guided, feeling the decking of the strato-shuttle beneath his feet as he was led on board. He blinked. He could make out the shape of a man, dark against the light from the port floods. Just one guy? He could have sworn he heard more than one voice...

The airlock slammed shut and the decontam process began, detergent spray spitting over the pair of them. Ferris removed his helmet and rubbed at his raw eyes. "Who are you? What did you do out there?"

"I need a ride to San Diablo and you look like you need to get out of town quick. Figured one good turn deserves another."

"Uh-huh." Now on familiar ground, Ferris fumbled his way by touch to a medi-kit on the wall and recovered an analgesic spray. He jetted puffs of vapour into his weeping eyes and blinked furiously. The pilot looked up at his erstwhile saviour. "Ah, crap. Your little lightshow's screwed up my vision. I've gone colour-blind!"

Rogue sighed. "No, you haven't. I'm always like this."

"But your skin is–" Ferris's brain caught up with his mouth and he gaped. "Blue. Your skin is blue." He swallowed hard. "You're that GI... The Rogue Soldier, or something..."

"Eh?" said Gunnar. "Why do we have to go through this every time we meet someone? Next he's gonna say 'Holy Skev! Your gun can talk!'."

Ferris shook his head as he made his way through the shuttle's interior, as if that would dispel the phantom of the Genetic Infantryman. He'd heard of the deserter – hell, everyone on Nu Earth had heard the tale of the lone gene-freak stalking the war zones – but it was almost too surreal for it... for *him* to come out of the darkness and pull Ferris's backside out of the fire. "I gotta sit down for a second."

"We don't have time for this," said a new voice, calling over Rogue's shoulder from his backpack. "We need to get airborne now, before those Mili-Fuzz creeps wake up."

Ferris glanced out the cockpit window and saw the sprawled forms of the MPs on the landing pad. A couple of them sported broken limbs. He blinked again.

"How about it?" asked Rogue. "Can you see straight? Can you get this thing in the air?"

"No," Ferris replied, running through the pre-flight check with quick, deft movements, "but that never stopped me before." In the heart of the shuttle, the thruster array went live and ignited. The pilot switched off the radio chatter streaming from Pitt City traffic control and grasped the throttle and joystick. "You better strap in, GI."

Rogue leapt into a seat and tugged a restraint harness tight over his chest, then a lead cushion of G-force pressed into him, as the strato-shuttle thundered into the night sky.

• • •

Ferris used the cover of a chem-storm to mask their flight over the no-man's-land near the Ash Wastes and dropped the transport down to treetop level – or what would have been treetop level if there had been any trees down below. His eyesight gradually returned, leaving him with just a mild headache and the gut-sick sensation of an adrenaline comedown. He glanced at the trooper.

"So. San Diablo, huh? What's the big rush to get there?"

The GI didn't look up from the digi-pad that held his attention. "Someone I know needs my help."

"Oh yeah? What's his name?" Ferris could just about see the image of another GI on the screen.

"Not sure yet."

"You know that city's swarming with Norts, right? I mean, I'm a civilian. I could probably make it in okay on my own, but you... They'll waste you the second they see blue."

"I can handle it."

"Right," Ferris replied. "Well, if it's all the same to you, I'm not going to stick around when we land. You saved my ass, I give you a lift, we're even."

Rogue's rifle made a derisive snort. "Huh. Civvies. Got no stomach for a fight, have ya?"

"You're a gun. What the hell do you know about anything?"

The GI broke in before Gunnar could frame an angry reply. "He used to be a soldier, like me." He indicated the biochips in his helmet and backpack. "They all were, once."

Ferris looked away, his expression souring. "Yeah, well, it ain't my war. You know, if I had my head straight, I should land at the nearest Souther base and turn you in. I'm guessing the reward for a deserter is pretty high."

Rogue gave a dry chuckle. "You're not going to do that. Those MPs weren't busting you up for fun, you must have a Milli-Fuzz warrant on you. You'd be about as welcome as me if you touched down on Souther turf right now." The soldier leaned forward. "And if it's nu-credits you're after, how about a little business proposition?"

Part of Ferris's mind, the rational, sensible part of it, rang an alarm bell the moment the words left the infantry-man's mouth; hooking up with this battlefield horror story would be worse than flying for Gog. And yet... The well-honed sense of greed that guided most of Ferris's deals was smiling widely, sensing the taste of money in the air. "Keep talking," he said automatically.

"Rogue, why do we need this guy–" began Helm.

"Quiet," said the GI, removing a cluster of circuits from his pack. "You know what this is, Ferris?"

The pilot's bloodshot eyes widened. "Datacore, right? Looks like Nort issue."

"Good call. I stole it from a listening post in the Orange Sea. The contents are less than a day old. Now, I'm willing to bet you know some dealers who'd pay very well for a look at what's on here."

He nodded. "If it's genuine."

"Oh, it is," said Bagman. "Count on it."

Rogue pocketed the device. "I'm gonna need to leave San Diablo in a hurry. You keep the meter running for me and you get the core. Do we have a deal?"

Ferris didn't hesitate. "Deal."

"And don't even think about a double-cross," growled Gunnar. "Compared to the guys we've rubbed out, you're a wet fart in a chem-shower. Got me?"

"Uh-huh," said Ferris. "Nice to be, uh, working with you."

San Diablo, like so many cities on Nu Earth, was built on a foundation of broken promises and half-truths. The Southers had proclaimed it would be a model community, constructed using advanced techniques from the rocky buttes of the NuVada plateau, powered by the fierce energy of the Diablo Springs. The searing hot sulphurous waters that surged and plumed like clockwork would turn massive turbines to light the metropolis, and the population would be able to move from place to place via a state-of-the art sub-train network. It looked good on paper, but like so many things, the war changed it for the worse. Half-built, the vast construction site of a city became the focal point of a Nort armoured thrust from Oman-3, and so began its metamorphosis from township of the future to a nightmare of sniper corridors and six-foot deep drifts of broken glass from the unoccupied skyscrapers.

The Norts had been holding San Diablo for over four years now and they were well settled in; two divisions of Blackmare tanks kept the land approaches clear and Grendel air patrols swept the skies. On their initial capture of the city, the Nort occupation force was dogged by Souther sappers, who used the incomplete sub-train tunnels to pop up amid ammo dumps and barracks for hit-and-run attacks. Brigadier Trager, the officer in charge of the Nort units, was a clever soldier with an eye for the dramatic; he set geomag charges at points along the tunnels where the thermal vents from the springs were closest and blew them open. When the daily surges came, boiling fluid flooded the San Diablo transit network and every Souther who didn't emerge into the guns of waiting Nort soldiers was scalded to death. Trager's victory over the so-called "tubeway army" earned him command of the sector and cemented Nordland's hold on the landscape.

The torrid, fuming waters still gushed under San Diablo's streets, blocking any attempts to enter the city by underground means. The heat and pressure would cook a soldier venturing down there. An *ordinary* soldier.

Rogue waded waist-high through the yellowish liquid, the stinging fumes from the sulphur and chem-agents coiling around him. The engineered internal regulatory organs in his torso worked at full capacity, bleeding the heat off the GI in streams of thick, oily sweat. "Time?"

Bagman checked an internal clock. "Plenty. The geyser upsurge won't be until the top of the hour."

"We're close," added Helm, over the constant hiss of bubbles. "About fifty metres up, south-south-west."

"Got it." Rogue peered through the mists and saw the lip of a sub-train platform close by. "End of the line, guys." The GI made his way along the reeking tunnel and into the underground station. Dirty yellow slurry coated everything, thick and glutinous on every surface.

"Is this the right place?" asked Bagman. "All those turns and branches, we could be back at the airport for all I know."

"I loaded the network map from the battle computer," Helm replied. "We walked right in under their tanks. Beautiful!"

"Aside from those four wrong turns." Gunnar said brusquely.

Rogue hauled himself up and out of the water. "We're here now. That's all that matters."

"Good," Gunnar continued. "Much more of that heat and my chips would have been fried."

"Think of it as a much-needed bath," Bagman's tone was mocking.

"Minds on the mission, fellas." Rogue growled. He reached up and wiped a layer of thick silt off the station sign. "Stadium Loop. This is the one." Unlimbering his rifle, the GI picked his way through the remains of a broken escalator and made for the surface. The fumes thinned out, to be replaced with the cocktail of lethal chemistry that was Nu Earth's sorry excuse for an atmosphere.

"You gonna clue us in on the plan, then?" Bagman said quietly. "Or is this going to be another make-it-up-as-you-go sortie?"

Gunnar broke in. "I still reckon you should have left one of us with that flyboy. I don't trust him."

"Synth out," Rogue retorted. "Ferris's not going anywhere. He's on a Nort airstrip surrounded by enemy soldiers. He may be a civilian but he's Souther-born. He's not gonna turn us over. We're his meal ticket."

"That all depends on how hungry he is."

"Quiet!" The entrance lobby of the station was clogged with debris and fallen masonry, but the GI's fleet-footed passage was almost silent. He shifted into a position where he could see the street, and beyond it, the flat disc of the stadium. The Norts outside were thinly spread – it would be a few hours before the main event took place – and most of the figures milling around were patrolmen and auxiliaries. Hung from the sides of buildings were huge flopscreens, some of them damaged with broken patches of errant pixels visible here and there. That braying robot female DeeTrick was pouting and posing across the panels, dolling out canned slogans and pithy bits of Nort propaganda in both Nordsprache and English.

Rogue looked away. "Bagman, dispense binox." He held the imaging unit to his eyes and studied the stadium entrance. A pair of light AFVs were parked in positions where their fields of fire overlapped and watchful line troopers scanned the walkways for interlopers. Micro-drones hummed over their heads, casting clusters of camera lenses across the area. Rogue watched an officer approach the scan grid at the main doors and saw him undergo an optical retina check and a passive DNA scan. The grid blinked green and he entered, the defence web confident of his identity. The GI frowned; he only had himself to blame for such increased security. Recently, he'd decided to show the Norts a little payback for their invasion of Dix-I sector by sneaking into a rally at Nu Nuremburg; that little operation had seen him assassinate Mooler and Marvin, two top-level Nort officers. As such, the enemy had quadrupled security on every other public event.

"Won't be able to get by with a disguise this time," whispered Helm, guessing Rogue's thoughts.

On the screens, the vidiganda broadcast Bagman had picked from the datacore was playing a loop from the announcement earlier in the day. DeeTrick's flawless metallic face was grinning out at them, to the wolf-whistles and catcalls of the Norts on the street. "Don't forget to tune in, folks!" she said. "We'll be live across Nu Earth to say bye-bye to blue-boy!" Then the image flickered and changed; now there was a "live broadcast" logo in the bottom corner and the simulant was shaking hands with a stocky, hard-eyed man in a commander's dress uniform.

"I'm here with Brigadier Trager," said DeeTrick silkily. "San Diablo's most senior – and certainly one of the most handsome – officers!"

"Oh please," said Bagman quietly. "That guy's got a face like a bucket of smashed crabs."

Trager began to talk about how difficult it had been to capture the "Rogue Trooper" and of the awesome responsibility that his command placed upon him. The GI watched his face, three storeys high on the side of the building, examining the Nort with a predator's eye. Trager had the stuffed-shirt pomposity that was virtually a trademark of the old school Nordland officer corps; it had to be something that was drilled into them, Rogue assumed, along with battle tactics and that typical arrogance that always made them underestimate Souther ingenuity. "And to think," he sneered to the simulant interviewer, "the pathetic creature actually tried to suggest that we'd captured the wrong person!" He gave a rough chug of laughter. "As if there's more than one of these blue freaks walking around!"

DeeTrick winked at the camera. "Our brave boys in the Kashan Legion made sure that wasn't so, right?"

"Bitch," Gunnar growled, voicing the thoughts of his three squad-mates.

Rogue replaced the binox and removed his helmet. "Okay, here's how it's going to go down." He dipped his hands in some muddy run-off and smeared it across his chest and face. "We can't bust our way in and we can't sneak our way in. So that leaves us one option."

"This is going to be good," Bagman was sarcastic. "We're going to walk in through the front door? And how will we do that exactly?"

"Easy," said Rogue. "We're going to let the Norts capture us."

"And, of course, although some officers might find the idea of a static posting to be unchallenging, I have found my command here to be most satisfactory."

DeeTrick nodded; where Trager's dull monotone and self-aggrandising manner might have put off a human interviewer, the android was positively enraptured by the brigadier's answers. The simulant had no choice in the matter – it was the way the Nordland Overt Media Apparat had programmed her to be. She hung on his every word, occasionally casting the odd saucy smile to her hovercam and flashing come-hither eyes that were modelled on star-lets from more than four centuries of history. "So, if I might ask," she interjected, "who will have the honour of terminating the Rogue Trooper?"

"I've personally selected a group of eight–" Trager's words were suddenly drowned out by the shrill cry of an alert siren. The brigadier shot to his feet and crossed the room to a console. "Report!" he demanded.

"Patrol Three-Alfa is at the lower lock," came the instant reply. "They captured the Genetik Infantryman!"

"*Captured* him? What the hell do you mean? We already..." Trager glanced at DeeTrick, suddenly aware that the unfolding events were being caught on vid. "I'm on my way!"

The simulant followed him as he raced for the door. "Oh, brigadier," her voice had a singsong cadence. "Our inter-view isn't over yet!"

Line troopers and junior officers alike saw the thunderous look on Trager's face as he swept down the stadium corri-dors, and they parted like a bow wave. Two steps behind him, DeeTrick blew kisses to the soldiers as she passed, the elliptical hovercam trailing behind her like a toy balloon.

Trager punched his command code into the hatchlock and shoved the sliding door open to enter the holding area. There were four men waiting inside and they snapped to parade ground attention as he strode in. The brigadier's angry gaze ranged the room and came across the sight of a blue-skinned man slumped on the floor. He swore a gutter oath, forgetting the camera's eye upon him.

"What is this?" he roared, grabbing the GI's chin, then casting him away. He stabbed a finger at the nearest soldier, a twitchy korporal. "Explain!"

"Sir, we spotted the creature in an alley off the boulevard. It was making for the warehouse district." He hesitated. "It, uh, appeared to be injured..."

Trager rounded on the duty officer in the holding area and the man blanched. "It escaped?" he bellowed, stabbing a finger at the slumped GI. "This unholy abortion of a thing escaped from its cell and you knew nothing about it?"

"But brigadier," the officer faltered, "the confinement cell is a sealed ferrocrete cube with a solid plastisteel door!" He jerked his thumb at the thick circular hatch behind him. "The vent shafts are no bigger than a credicard, there's no way out!" He togged a screen, and the display showed a lone, blue-skinned figure slumped in a featureless grey cell. "This is a live feed from the monitor in there!"

Trager's temper fractured and he cuffed the officer about the head. "Dolt! The camera has obviously been tampered with!" The commander glanced at the korporal. "Fortunate for you that this observant trooper was able to apprehend the freak before it could go to ground."

"Sir, I–" the officer spoke again, "let me just–" He worked the console, beginning the unlocking sequence that would open the cell.

"You are a disgrace!" Trager snapped, and in one swift motion, he drew his pistol and shot the officer between the eyes. "I will not have incompetents in my command!"

"Yes sir!" snapped the korporal. He gestured to one of the other troopers, who clutched a peculiar-looking rifle and backpack. "It was carrying some unfamiliar equipment, brigadier..."

As the cell door yawned open, something in Trager's mind rang a wrong note. He'd seen the weapon before, on briefing files about the GI – but the one they captured in the desert had been carrying looted Nort gear, not GI-issue hardware. "Wait, where did he get–"

"Oh my," simpered DeeTrick, pointing into the cell. "That can't be right."

Trager looked at the GI on the floor, and then at the *other* GI in the cell. "Two?" he managed.

"Surprise," said the prone infantryman.

FOUR
ZERO SUM

Everything happened at once. The GI on the floor – the second one, Trager realised with surprise – flashed across the room in a streak of blue, slamming into the trooper holding the backpack. At the same moment, the peculiar rifle cradled in a lazy grip by the other soldier clattered and charged into life. On full autofire, las-rounds roared through the confines of the holding area and tore the third member of Patrol Three-Alfa to pieces. The man grasping the gun had two choices and he made the wrong one; instead of dropping the weapon instantly, he tried to hold it down, like a rider dealing with a troublesome mount. The rifle rose on its own recoil, past the falling corpse of the third trooper and marched energy bolts up the seamless silver torso of DeeTrick.

The feminine simulant did not scream; she wasn't programmed to. Instead, she twittered and babbled as the shots tore though the logic centres in her midriff. The robot crashed to the floor, her velvet voice now a shower of gibberish.

All of this in seconds. The GI they had brought before Trager, broken and sickly, had exhibited none of this power. The new arrival was a whirlwind. The Nort with the backpack in his hand was already dead, neck broken in an instant when Trager's mind had been elsewhere. Abruptly, the brigadier became aware of the pistol in his hand, its barrel still hot from where he had exercised his displeasure on the duty officer. He brought it to bear on the GI, but the soldier with the rifle was in front of his intended target. Trager shot him; he had to regain control of the situation quickly and the hapless fool was in his way.

Throughout the unfolding melee, DeeTrick's hovercam was continuing to broadcast the live vid to screens all over the city. There might be quick-witted Norts on the way to assist him, but Trager had no way of knowing – just as he had no way of seeing the other GI in the cell stirring, getting to his feet, coming at him. Trager had enjoyed himself with the prisoner before DeeTrick had been allowed to compose her vidiganda footage. By a quirk of fate, the Nort officer's unit had been replaced by the 7th Kashan Legion on the eve of the ambush that both sides would later call the Quartz Zone Massacre, and on some level, Trager had always resented the fact that he had never been able to kill some of the Souther genetic freaks. Trager was a strict Church of Sekunda zealot – the approved religion of the Nordland party – and his personal faith looked upon gene-manipulation as unholy and inhuman. The lucky turn of events that had landed him with the prisoner had given him the chance to work through some of his issues on that matter, taking a sap glove to the creature's dull, blue-grey skin. Payback now came to Trager tenfold.

Rogue saw the injured GI slam an iron-hard fist into the small of the brigadier's back and a couple of vital vertebrae came apart with a sharp crack. The other infantryman followed up with two more punishing strikes, not for any reasons of efficiency, but for the sheer violence of it.

"Rogue, the hovercam!" snapped Bagman, and in answer the GI dragged the machine out of the air, servos whining, and battered it against the wall. Surrounded by dead and dying Norts, Rogue took his first good look at his fellow soldier. "You know me?" he asked.

The other GI looked in bad shape and it wasn't just the after-effects of the beatings. His skin lacked the dark, near-midnight hue of Rogue's – it was pale and in places the cultured plastiflesh was broken. Welts and unpleasant lesions of black blood matter marred his arms and torso.

"Who...?" His voice was hoarse. "Who you with?"

"Battalion M-C Five," Rogue replied automatically.

"Rogue... You're the Rogue... I found you!"

Gunnar made a low noise. "Synth me! I know him! That you, Zero?"

"Zero?" Rogue repeated, helping the GI to walk. Like all the nicknames the GIs used, his was one that the Milli-Com genetic engineers had coined, half joking, for each of their vat-grown killers-in-training. Rogue had never served directly with Zero, but he knew of him. He'd been in top percentile on the roster boards after they were decanted and noted as an exceptional sniper.

To any observer, the faces of the two GIs would have looked virtually identical – and that fact was what had made Rogue's daring plan work – but to the troopers themselves, subtle differences made them as individual as any pure-bred human.

"Zero, man. How did you make it out of the zone alive?" said Gunnar.

"Time for that later," snapped Rogue, recovering Helm from a compartment in the backpack. He snatched up a weapon from one of the dead Norts and tossed it to Zero. "Can you make it, brother?"

Zero managed a shaky smile. "I'm tactical, Rogue. Solid blue."

"We got incoming," said Helm. "I'm picking up human heat signatures through the walls."

"Let's go." Rogue grabbed his gear and beckoned Zero toward the hatch. "We're on the clock."

Zero gave a weary nod. "How... we gonna get out of this place?"

"Helm, how long we got?" said Rogue.

"Five mikes, give or take."

Rogue gave Zero a nod. "Can you swim?"

. . .

As any general worth his stars would tell you, the problem with developing a new military tactic was that the moment you used it, the enemy would be able to use it against you. Trager's brutal flooding of the San Diablo sub-train network had made him a war criminal in the eyes of Souther Command and his callous actions were now a part of the training briefs that upper echelon officer-cadets received in Milli-Com's battle schools. His actions were also documented in the war books of Souther line troopers; on the hundreds of cold and lonely nights that Rogue had spent on Nu Earth's wasted landscape, the GI had pored over salvaged digi-texts, learning all he needed to know about Trager's callous strategy and how to turn it against him.

Ferris had complained loudly when Rogue helped himself to one of the hyper-densified fuel canisters in the strato-shuttle's stores, but the infantryman simply tapped a finger on the upward-thrusting arrow on the casing, the symbol of the Souther Forces. Reminded of where he stole them from, the pilot opted for silence, and Rogue took the container with him into the tunnel network. The GI made short work of his improvised munition, wiring the last of the C9 detonator charges to the connector nozzle on the fuel tank before taking the jury-rigged bomb and positioning it in the optimum location. The overseer-teachers, the men the GIs called the "Genies", had taught their creations well, instilling in them the skills to innovate weapons from scraps of hardware and battlefield leftovers; Rogue could do everything from carving flint arrowheads to operating a piece of field artillery, if the need arose.

The Diablo Springs ran on geological clockwork, regular surge tides of hot, metallic waters bubbling up and then receding as Nu Earth's tectonic plates were massaged by the gravity tides of its moons and the distant energies of the Valhalla wormhole. Trager had known the tidal pattern and used it against the Souther sappers; now Rogue returned the favour, but with a new twist.

The water rose, lapping up at the walls of the dead sub-train tunnels, filling the tubeways with yellowed liquid. Soon, acrid moisture licked at the tip of a hydro sensor salvaged from a broken geoscanner module and a switch was tripped. The thin detonator rod spat sparks into the firing charge, chain-reacting. The block of C9 explosive flashed, puncturing the tank; suddenly the volatile shuttle fuel – a thick, tarry slurry in its inert state – was burning in one brilliant instant. Everything in its vicinity was instantly reduced to a ball of gas, stone and metal, vaporising and collapsing dozens of the ferrocrete pylons that were the foundations of the city stadium.

Tonnes of earth sank into the sulphurous floodwaters, displacing and choking the smaller tributary tunnels, and with nowhere else to go, the boiling surge from the toxic springs blew upward into San Diablo's streets, punching through the basements of buildings and ripping open the stadium plaza.

Gushes of murky liquid burst forth and engulfed Nort soldiers and vehicles alike, knocking them over and flattening them with caustic waves. Troopers used to the protection of their chem-suits from Nu Earth's toxins found the thin plastimesh to be no match for the boiling acids and they were cooked inside their war gear. Streams of the floodwater cut into the sealed corridors of the stadium interior, spurting out of fresh cracks in the ferrocrete like liquid knives. The water rose and chaos came with it.

Rogue forced his way through the rising tide in big, splashing steps, sparing only the occasional las-round for Nort troopers who were able enough to defend themselves. The majority of the enemy were far too occupied with more important things, like trying to breathe, to concern themselves with the two GIs in their midst.

Zero was having difficulty matching Rogue's pace, so the infantryman kept stopping to bring his fellow soldier along, guiding him through corridors choked with corpses floating in chest-high water. "Come on, brother. Just a little further."

Zero gave a laboured nod and Rogue frowned; he couldn't begin to imagine the hell that the other GI had been through at the hands of his Nort interrogators, and he felt a sting of guilt. In a way, he was responsible – the enemy believed that Zero was Rogue and undoubtedly they had tried to tear a confession from him for all the Norts that he had sent to their graves. He imagined Zero in that cramped cell, suffering intolerable agony as they beat and burned him, unable to answer the demands of his captors.

There was a distant, higher part of Rogue's tactical mind that still marvelled at the sight of another living, breathing Genetic Infantryman. It had been so long since the killings at the Quartz Zone – somewhere along the way he had become used to the idea that he was the last of his kind – the sole survivor of an artificially created species. If Zero was still alive, could there be more? What if there were other survivors out there, other Rogues?

He shook the thought away with a sharp turn of his head. No time to think about that now, he told himself. They still had to make it to the shuttle.

The entrance atrium had been turned into a seething pool of coarse, bubbling water, and the infantrymen half-swam, half-waded across the open area and into the flooded city streets. There were corpses as far they could see as well as great floating drifts of debris. Men were desperately scaling the exteriors of abandoned towers to escape the churn of the corrosive rivers. Shots cut into the torrents around the two troopers, slicing down from a rifleman in a high vantage point.

"Shooter, three o'clock high!" called Helm.

"Mark him," Rogue replied, and turned, bringing Gunnar to bear. Through the GI rifle's optics, Rogue saw the outlined heat-blob of a man on the thermographic scope. He squeezed the trigger and a red-orange laser light shot across the brickwork to flush the Nort out. The rifleman bolted from his cover, a blur through the sight scope, and abruptly came apart in a storm of crimson. Rogue's gaze flicked to his side to see that Zero had taken the kill shot himself, ripping into the Nort with the very same make of weapon that the enemy trooper had used on them. The rifleman's shredded corpse fell out of his sniper nest and landed in the water with a heavy splash.

Zero took a laboured breath. The effort of the escape was getting to him and they were a long way short. He caught Rogue looking at him and managed a quizzical jut of the chin. "Your show, Rogue. Where now?"

"Bagman, dispense macro-raft."

With a click, the backpack's servo arm extended, clasping a fat grey packet. "Uh, Rogue. This thing's Nort-issue junk. You sure it's gonna work?"

The GI grabbed the plastic pack and tore it open, revealing a striped pull-cord. "Unless you got a couple of surfboards in there, this is the only option." Rogue gave the cord a tug, and the packet hissed back at him, inflating.

"Where'd you get that?" Zero asked.

"Salvage from Harpo's Ferry. Thought it might come in useful." The macro-raft unfolded, memory-plastic bladders opening up to full size. The compact brick of flexible material transformed into a small boat, a shallow canoe big enough for two at a pinch. "Come on. We're gonna ride the flood right out of here."

"You thought of everything," Zero grunted.

Rogue hauled himself into the raft and extended a hand. "Tactics, improvisation, execution," he said, recalling the combat litany the Genies had drilled into them the moment they stepped from the breeder tubes. "That's how they made us."

"Right." With effort, Zero scrambled over the gunwale and Rogue grabbed his arm to pull him in. His fingers clamped around Zero's forearm and he felt atrophied, weak flesh there, not the hard muscle of a GI's normal physique. The other trooper almost fell into the boat, face-first. Rogue's eyes automatically caught sight of something anomalous on the back of Zero's neck, a slight distension like a malignant growth on the left side, just under the base of the skull. He hesitated; GIs knew their own physiology as well as any corpsman – there were no medics in the GI platoons, but every one of them had the knowledge to repair even the most serious of wounds and the surgical skill to operate on one another. It was a necessary talent, and along with all his fellow soldiers, Rogue had been trained to use a las-scalpel to open the cerebellum of a dying compatriot and recover the biochip that lay wired into the rubbery meat of a GI cortex. The lump on Zero's neck was in exactly that spot, something flat and bony just beneath the skin.

Helm's words in the cave returned to him. This was a trap; Zero was some sort of Trojan horse, part of a complex scheme to capture the Rogue Trooper. He didn't want to believe that.

Zero turned over and glanced around, meeting Rogue's gaze. "Let's go."

Rogue searched the other trooper's blank yellow eyes for a moment, looking for the merest hint of deception; he found nothing.

"Rogue?" said Helm. "Tide's at the maximum now. The flood's gonna start ebbing from this point onward."

The GI turned away and activated the single-use chemical squirt-jet motor in the raft's keel. "We're going." The inflatable surged forward at high speed, cutting a path into the drowning city. He dropped into a low prone position along the line of the boat and propped Gunnar on the bow. "Bagman, keep a watch on my six."

"Check," came the reply from the biochip. It was only one word, but after so long in each other's company, Rogue knew that Bagman had instantly understood the meaning of the order. If Zero suddenly turned on him, he'd be warned; but what he would do if that happened, he wasn't really sure.

■ ■ ■

Trager couldn't feel anything below his waist. He slapped at the inert flesh of his legs, but it was like touching raw, dead meat. He swore an oath that dated back to the first Great War and spat. The Brigadier fumbled at a communicator and shouted into it. "The Genetik Infantryman has broken out... There are two! Intercept and terminate them both!"

He listened for a confirmation of his order, but only static replied. Trager discarded the unit and tried to pull himself up. Nearby, the broken chassis of the android reporter was stuttering to itself, some fractured piece of programming repeating a string of words over and over. The simulant was stuttering and singing in a sultry, honeyed synth, dragging itself across the floor to where one of its perfectly-proportioned arms was lying, severed by las-fire in the breakout. "Fuh. Fuh. Falling apart again," she chimed, "Wh-what am I to do?"

Trager's nerve broke. "Be silent, you clockwork moron!" He attempted to push himself off the floor and as his hands touched the ferrocrete he felt a building vibration there, resonating into his bones. "Verkammt..." The Nort officer slid his bulk to the hatch and slammed the heel of his hand on the lock control.

The door juddered open, and in that moment he realised that he had killed himself; the rumbling in the floor was the rush of floodwater thudding against the corridor walls outside. Brigadier Trager screamed as a wall of acid swamped the chamber, submerging him, the robot and the dead troopers in stinking yellow water. Trager's lungs filled with burning, corrosive sulphates, drowning him in the milky fluids as DeeTrick's stammering final performance sang him into oblivion.

"Ferris."

The pilot jerked as the voice growled in his headset. He'd felt the rumble as the floods blew open the roadways just minutes earlier and with growing trepidation

Ferris had watched the waters lapping around the landing legs of the strato-shuttle. He was convinced that the GI had done something wrong and got himself killed, and for the fourth time in as many minutes he'd been thinking of cutting his losses and leaving. "Whoa, you made it?"

"We're coming to you. Get the ship warmed up and ready to lift." There was a crackling sound in the background.

"Copy that." The noise came again over the open channel, strident and very close. "You got trouble?"

"Nothing we can't handle. Be ready." The GI's voice cut off sharply.

"Okay," Ferris said to the empty cockpit. "Point of no return, then. Do I fly blue-boy and his talkative gear outta here, or do I cut and run?" His hand hovered over the thruster controls as he turned over the choice in his mind.

Thick anti-vehicle rounds spattered off the surface of the flooded street and rocked the macro-raft from side to side. Rogue coiled a length of pull-cord around one fist and used it to keep himself steady as he fired Gunnar with his other hand, sending arcs of las-fire into the air. His target jinked easily, the beams cutting through empty air. The Nort hopper had come out of nowhere, emerging from behind the top of a housing block like a huge and irate hornet. It ducked and wove along the canyon of the city street, null-grav engines humming with raw power. There were clusters of armour-piercing rockets in fat drums on the hopper's stubby winglets, but the flyer's crew hadn't opted to use them just yet – at such close quarters in the tight confines of the city proper, a miss might strike a derelict tower and send a whole decrepit neighbourhood tumbling down.

The Nort pilot, his hooded face visible though the armourglas cockpit canopy, was hunched forward, urging his ship on after the fleeing dart of the raft. Rogue couldn't see the gunnery crew sequestered behind the pilot's chair, but he knew the model of hopper and guessed where they would be sitting. Even now, they were probably looking right at him through the scopes of the flyer's twin chatter-guns, squeezing out bolts of depleted uranium ammo. The AV shells were overkill where the inflatable raft was con-cerned – one solid hit and the memory-plastic would be ripped to shreds – but subtlety had never been a hallmark of either side in the Nu Earth conflict.

The boat rose out of the water and slapped back down hard as it rode over a couple of floating corpses. For a sec-ond, the GI lost his grip on the steering cord and the raft listed dangerously to port, threatening to tip the passengers into the flood.

"Damn it, Rogue!" snapped Helm. "Steer or shoot, you can't do both!"

"Son of a tube!" Zero cursed, working the slide of his stolen enemy rifle. "I got a breech jam... Nort piece of scrap!"

The hopper pilot flared his ailerons and used the down-wash from his engines to batter the boat, trying to force a capsize. Rogue fired again and missed again.

Zero tossed the Nort rifle aside and held out a hand. "Gunnar! Give him to me!" When Rogue hesitated, he shouted over the whine of the jets. "I can swat this fly, brother! Come on!"

"Do it, Rogue!" Gunnar added. "No choice."

"Here!" Rogue flipped the GI rifle over in his grip and shoved it at Zero.

The other infantryman eagerly accepted it and the gun sank into his grip like it was one well-oiled component fit-ting into another.

"You want a Sammy?" Bagman called.

Zero shook his head. "I got this. Gunnar, give me thermo." The sniper raised the rifle to his cheek just as the hopper unleashed another punishing salvo of rounds.

Rogue rocked the raft from side to side, steering the thing with his body movements. Fragments of shot nicked his bare skin like dull needles.

The hopper loomed large in Gunnar's scope, moving wildly with the shock from the shots and the rise and fall of the floodwater. Zero took a breath, released half and held the rest. He fired.

Nort Komet-class hoppers used a forward-looking infrared scope mounted in the nose, but the lens that protected it was a notorious weak point. Zero's kill was impeccably placed, piercing the scope's housing and cutting up through the cockpit dashboard to strike the sternum of the pilot. The las-round blew most of his lungs out the back of his chem-suit and the Nort slumped forward on his flight yoke. The hopper veered away wildly and collided with a low bridge, erupting into a fireball.

"Nice shot," said Helm.

Rogue nodded in appreciation as the raft bumped and scraped off the broken roadway. "Floodwater's sinking back, we got nothing under the keel. Time to abandon ship, boys." The GI pulled the inflatable boat to a halt and leapt out. The waters were at his knees now and receding quickly. "Zero, let's go, double-time."

Zero wavered for a moment. "Rogue, I think I gotta..." He turned gently and Gunnar dropped from his fingers. There was a large triangle of shrapnel, probably part of the hopper's fuselage, buried in Zero's chest. Turquoise blood bubbled up around the edges of the wound, streaming down his torso. He fell forward and Rogue caught him.

"No, damn it!" Rogue cursed. "We got you out. You ain't gonna die on me now!"

"We got incoming," said Helm. "I'm picking up track noises from the west. AFVs maybe, or light tanks."

Rogue shook his head, discounting the unspoken thought in all their minds at once. "We're not leaving him behind." The GI gathered up his rifle and drew a walkie-talkie from his belt. "Ferris! Ferris, do you read me? I need a dust-off right now!" Dead static hissed back at him.

"I knew it!" Gunnar snarled. "That worthless pink-skin puke! He's left us twistin' in the wind!"

"Oh ye of little faith," said the radio. From behind the broken fingers of the city towers, the bullet shape of the strato-shuttle appeared, the sudden roar of the ship's vector jets like a tornado. Ferris brought the atmocraft to a hover above the GIs and dropped the boarding ramp. "Someone call for a taxi?"

Rogue bodily threw Zero on to the ramp and pulled himself on board as the Nort armoured vehicles rounded the street corner, pushing waves of water, bodies and debris before them. "Get us out of here!"

A cannon on the lead tank spat smoke and flame, and Ferris flinched as a shell shrieked over the shuttle and demolished a nearby building. "Whoa! That ain't friendly!" He slammed the throttle forward to full burn. "Hang on to something!"

The atmocraft's engine bells threw a sheet of fusion fire out behind them and the ship leapt to supersonic velocity, cracking the sound barrier with a thunderous boom of compacted air. San Diablo flashed past beneath the aircraft's underbelly and then they were in the desert plains, racing away.

Rogue stumbled to where Zero lay. "Steady, brother. You'll make it."

Zero managed a shake of the head. "Ah, no. I won't. I was dying before I got hit, Rogue. I know you saw it. I was... just holding on, see? I knew you were out there... I knew you'd come get me."

Bagman's manipulator unfolded, holding a compact medikit. "Rogue," he said in a low voice, "got the las-scalpel here and a chip support frame. We can still save his mind."

"Listen," Zero coughed up foamy azure blood. "Rogue, you gotta know... Domain Delta... You have to stop her..." The GI's eyes fluttered and closed.

"Her? Zero, who do you mean? What do you know about Delta?"

"Rogue, he's a goner," said Helm urgently. "You know the drill, the biochip has absorbed his personality matrix. Sixty seconds, that's all we got!"

"You have to get the chip," Bagman added. "If he knows something about that Nort lab, we can't let it die with him!"

Rogue thumbed the stud on the las-scalpel and a knife-beam glittered into existence. "Swore I was never gonna do this again."

With quick, careful cuts, Rogue began to slice away the pallid blue skin and the dull fleshy matter surrounding Zero's biochip implant.

FIVE
HEART OF GLASS

A soldier is an investment. To train them, feed them, clothe them, to educate them in the myriad ways of weapons and killing takes hundreds of thousands of nu-credits and infinitely more man hours. For the Genetic Infantrymen, that cost was geometrically higher. They were decanted as infants and trained without pause for twenty standard years; every hour of every day of their pre-war lives dedicated to the craft of controlled murder. The clone soldiers represented time and money that the Souther Armed Forces simply couldn't afford to spend recklessly on the battlefield. The expense and the sheer effort required by the GI programme had almost ended it on dozens of occasions; while Rogue and his compatriots had grown and learned, unknown to them figures in the Confederate government had tried again and again to end the super-soldier project – but there were men in positions of authority with too much invested, financial influences from the gargantuan mega-corporations like Clavel and Steiner-Bisley, power-players who refused to allow the GIs to die in the cradle. The fact that the project was also gen-erating millions in spin-off biotechnology patents and refining the discipline of human cloning was just coinci-dental. After all, war had always been the greatest spur for the advancement of new science.

Rogue cursed quietly under his breath as Zero's skin peeled away in his hands, revealing the necrotising flesh beneath the hardy, almost rubber-like surface. "There's major internal damage here. More than he would have got from just a beating..." The GI's fingers closed around a grey knot of bone-like material and pulled it free with a sound like tearing cloth. He considered it for a second, then put the object aside and kept working.

"You think its some sorta infection, a bio-agent?" Helm said urgently. "Like that paralysis toxin from the polar zone?"

"Negative," Rogue used the las-scalpel to dig deeper. "More like a blood disease, or organ failure."

"If Zero had a virus, then we all got it now," Bagman grated.

Rogue's fingers found the metallic edge of the biochip implant in among the soft organic matter. "Don't think so. I'd say it was genetic breakdown." He tuned the beam to a fine, pencil-thin setting and set to work cutting away the filaments that held the chip in place. It was warm, a tell-tale sign that the matrix within was active.

Those who opposed the GIs saw them as an expensive folly, a "wonder weapon" that would be obsolete before it even saw action. A normal human foot soldier could easily be replaced with just a few forced colonial conscriptions and some hypno-tape conditioning, but the death of a Genetic Infantryman represented a nu-cred cost somewhere close to that of a light strike bomber. All it would take was one lucky Nort sniper and an exorbitant Souther Army investment would be cold meat, so Milli-Com found a way to make their soldiers immortal, a method of life preservation that would sentence the GIs to an eternity of warfare no matter how many times they died. It didn't matter that it was callous, as long as it was cost effective.

When their bodies matured as the clones reached adolescence, the Genies "tagged" them. One by one, every GI was implanted with a "dog-chip". On the most basic level, the microcircuits served as electronic trooper identity cards, but the full function of the hardware was much more far-reaching. The chips were semi-organic, made from a matrix of complex artificial proteins suspended in an electromagnetic field that emulated the workings of living brain tissue. When death came, as it inevitably would, the biochips were ready. Silent and watchful, the small rectangles of silicon gradually altered their circuits to mimic the neural patterns of their physical hosts, waiting for the moment when they would come to life. By year twenty, as the GI troopers were prepared for final deployment, the chips were webbed into their cerebral cortex with nests of neurofibres.

The hatch to the shuttle's cockpit hissed open and Ferris emerged, his face pale and sweaty, fixed with an expression that was trying and failing to look cocksure and cool. "We're out of the Nort sensor range, I reckon," he began. "I put us on autopilot, programmed a loop-and-evade..." The pilot's voice trailed off as he caught a glimpse of Rogue ministering to Zero's fresh corpse. "What the hell are you doing to him?" Ferris started forward and grabbed at Rogue's arm.

"Back off, idiot. You're in his light!" Gunnar grated.

"You're cuttin' him open!" Ferris retorted. "You said you wanted to save this guy!"

"He *is* saving him, pinky. Now get away!"

Ferris's gut flipped over as he realised he was standing in an expanding puddle of sapphire-coloured blood. "Oh shit..."

The laser beam sizzled against dead flesh and sent a wisp of acrid cooked meat odour up and into the cargo bay compartment. "Ah, I've got it." Rogue held out his hand to Bagman's manipulator. "Clips?"

The backpack produced a pair of slender tongs and the GI used them to remove the biochip. The silicon plate came free with a sucking noise. Ferris covered his mouth. "Ugh."

Rogue quickly slipped the chip into a flat unit the size of a digi-pad. "Time?"

"Forty-three seconds," said Helm. "You're getting slow."

"I'm out of practice," Rogue replied, a grim set to his war-mask features.

A fatal wound to the host trooper flooded his bloodstream with an endorphin analogue that set the biochip implant into a rapid scan mode, and in those dying moments the protein circuits copied the GI's mental engrams like a data tape. As they perished, everything that made the soldiers who they were, their skills, their history, their random personality quirks, all of it would be sucked into the implant like a bottled ghost. If a GI fell in battle, his chip could be recovered and returned to Milli-Com for regeneration and in a matter of hours the same soldier could be back in the war, his biochip loaded into a fresh adult "blank". The Genies estimated that the biochips could withstand dozens, perhaps even hundreds of these "relocation trauma" experiences before the GI's consciousness would start to suffer any deleterious psychological effects.

There was just one drawback. The protein circuits could only exist for a maximum of sixty seconds outside of an organic host before they began to degrade, bleeding off memory and intellect with every passing moment; they required a constant power source to maintain an active matrix. Ever inventive, Milli-Com's tek-division supplied the troopers with chip support units and added energised slots to every major item of GI-issue hardware: to rifles, backpacks, helmets, pistols – and so dead men could survive and accompany their squad mates, staying out in the field for days or weeks before returning to be regened, synthetic souls inhabiting their war gear like possessive spirits.

The biochips would serve the will of the officers in command even when their bodies were destroyed; that was the plan. But the Quartz Zone changed all that. Some said it was a turncoat inside Souther Command, others talked about a conspiracy of corporate and military interests opposed to the GI programme, or even a combination of both. However it happened, the first mass capsule drop into enemy territory by Genetic Infantrymen was a descent into hell. The Norts were waiting and they wiped out the clone soldiers. When the massacre ended, the GI programme was scrapped, a costly failure that had wasted billions of nu-creds and almost three decades of research. Nothing remained; nothing but one man.

Ferris watched, forcing his gut to stay down, as Rogue quickly patted Zero's body, looking for any gear that might be of use to him. The dead GI had nothing but a pair of ripped fatigue trousers and Ferris noticed for the first time that the other man hadn't been wearing any boots.

"Hey, uh, Rogue," he nodded at the body. "I got some tarps, if you wanna wrap him up–"

"Where are we now?" The piercing yellow eyes cut into him like lasers.

"Crossing over a chem-swamp."

"Good enough." Rogue hit the hatch control and pushed Zero's corpse into the airlock.

"Don't you want to, I dunno, bury him or something?"

"What would be the point?" The GI pushed another button and the lock opened, venting Zero out into the air. The body tumbled away from the shuttle, falling toward the toxic marshes. Rogue nodded at the chip frame. "It's not like he's dead."

"Don't be so sure," said Bagman carefully. The backpack's diagnostic cables were connected to the unit holding Zero's biochip. "We got a situation here."

"Let's hear it."

Ferris heard the hesitation in the synthetic voice. "Rogue, I'm running a chip-check through the internal sensors on the frame and I'm coming up with some bad numbers. Zero's dog-chip has got some serious degradation, I'm talking major loss of deep memory and engram failure across the board."

"What the hell are you saying, Bag?" Gunnar demanded.

"I'm saying that we're looking at a matrix failure."

Rogue drew a sharp breath. Those last two words were a death sentence for a Genetic Infantryman; the spectre of physical trauma resulting in organic termination was almost an occupational hazard for the GI corps. The Genies had trained them not to fear death as the end to their existence it was for normal soldiers, but the corruption of their biochips held the very same terror that "real" termination did for a human. Matrix failure was quite simply the death of a GI mind, total and unrecoverable.

"Can you patch him into your synth?"

"I can try," Bagman said. "Wait one."

There was a sharp crackle of static from the pack's chip slot and then a thin, ghostly mimic of Zero's voice emerged. "Rogue? NNNnnnnnhear me?"

"We hear you, pal," Gunnar broke in. "Hang in there."

"Aaaagain!" The word was a cry of pain. "Dead again! Rogue, help meeee."

"Zero!" Rogue snapped. "I need you to focus! We don't have much time."

"I nnnnnnknow. Leaking like rrrrrain. Losing myself. Self. Self."

Ferris swallowed hard. "Can't you do something for him?"

Helm answered for all of them. "No."

Rogue knelt close to the synth pickup, as if that would make the strength of his words all the more urgent. "You were at the Quartz Zone with the rest of us, Zero. Gunnar, Bagman, Helm, everyone else, they were killed... How did you survive? Where have you been all this time?"

"Dead," came the flat, toneless reply. "Died in the glassssss."

"But he was alive..." Ferris gave an involuntary glance at the pool of blood.

"Rrrrrreborn, Rogue. Reborn where I fell. Ddddddomain Delta. She did it."

"Who, Zero? Who did it?" hissed Rogue.

"I'm losing him," said Bagman. "He's cracking up on me."

"Got away. Came looking for youuuuuuu." Violent crackles and barks of static punctuated every one of Zero's words. "Get her-*zzzzzt*. Ssssstop her. Delta. Ddddelta."

"Where?" Rogue demanded. "Where is it?"

"Kill it," Zero spat. "Savezzzzt−" The static hum rose to a peak and then suddenly ceased.

"No matrix function detected," said Bagman, after a long moment. "He's gone."

With infinite care, Rogue decoupled the support unit and removed Zero's dog-chip from the device. He turned it over in his blood-stained fingers, watching the play of light off the metallic surface. The chip was cold to the touch, bereft of life. The GI ran his thumb over the raised code number etched on the silicon and then thoughtfully placed it in one of his panniers.

Ferris watched Rogue handle the tiny sliver of memory-circuit. The GI treated the corpse of his comrade with all the respect of a piece of rotten meat, but he held the biochip like it was the most fragile thing in the world. The pilot understood; if there was any place that a GI's soul rested, then it had to be there.

Helm broke the silence. "Domain Delta again. There's gotta be something to that place, we just need to find it."

"Reckon we already have," said Rogue quietly. "You heard Zero."

"His mind was falling apart, Rogue," Gunnar snapped. "I didn't hear anything but garbage."

"He said he was holding on, waiting for me to come get him," Rogue was introspective, weighing the dead soldier's words. "He wanted to tell me about Domain Delta."

"He said 'reborn'," Ferris spoke without thinking. Rogue looked up at him and suddenly the pilot felt like he had intruded on a private moment. "Uh, sorry."

"No, you're right," Rogue replied. "He said he was 'reborn where I fell'. He was regened in the place where he died."

"You know where that is?" Ferris asked.

"Oh yeah," said Bagman coldly, "we know."

Rogue got to his feet and fished the Vok-IV datacore from his pocket. "Here, take it. You got us out like I asked. Here's your payment."

Ferris took the device and weighed it in his palm. He could almost feel the crisp nu-credits it represented. "So, uh, can I drop you off somewhere?"

"You could do that," said Rogue, considering, "or you could take us a little further."

The datacore vanished into the pilot's pocket. "Hey, no offence, but hanging out with deserters isn't exactly going to improve my standing with the Milli-Fuzz..."

"Can't say the Norts will be pleased to see you, either," drawled Bagman. "Reckon they'll have your ident code flagged from here to Timbuk-2, which pretty much makes you a wanted man north of the borders, and after that little disagreement with the law in Pitt City, you ain't exactly welcome in Southside turf."

The pilot's expression soured. "Son of a bitch..." he said to himself, the realisation of his predicament dawning. "Anywhere I land I'm a dead man walking."

Gunnar made an electronic grunt. "Catches on quick, doesn't he?"

Rogue inclined his head. "We're not done with this yet."

Ferris gave a slow nod; he wasn't a fool. His options had just shrunk to zero. "I'm guessing you all are going to need another ride, right?" He sighed, resigned to the situation. "How about a fresh trade, then? I get you where you wanna go, you help me keep breathin'."

Rogue considered this for a moment. "We can do that."

"What?" said Gunnar hotly. "We looking after waifs and strays now? I still don't trust this flyboy. We can just kiss mud and leave this airhead to watch his own pink behind!"

"Gunnar's got a point," began Bagman, "but a shuttle could get us there in hours instead of footslogging it all the way."

"There?" repeated Ferris. "Where's there, exactly?"

"The place where we fell," said Rogue. "The Quartz Zone."

The orb-drone caught up with her as she reached the upper tier of the central dome, the whine of the spherical robot's impellers matching the resolute clatter of her boots on the polished neoplastic floor. It held a sample case in one thin steel arm which dangled below its drifting fuselage. The drone looked like an errant balloon tethered to a silver brick. It spoke with a synthetic analogue of her voice; all the drones in the facility did, from the smallest auto-tek to the large autonomous robo-gunner patrol units. It was a subtle conceit, but one that Schrader felt underlined her position of authority here.

"Kolonel-Doktor," it chimed. "Here is the item you requested."

Schrader took the case without halting, flipping it open to double-check the contents before locking it shut once more. "Dismissed," she told the machine, and obediently it fled, vanishing down the curving corridor toward the lower levels.

She paused for just a moment outside the conference room, examining herself in the reflection of a polished steel panel displaying the Nordland sigil. Her ice-blond hair was impeccable as ever, framing a milky face so pale it was almost blue. From behind a set of wafer-thin data-glasses, Schrader's expressionless, doll-like eyes studied and then confirmed her own chilly perfection. She was the very model of the Nort ice princess, razor-keen and cold enough to burn. The woman allowed herself the brief interlude of a smile, then shut the expression away and entered the room.

Standing to attention by the panoramic window, Volks stiffened as she approached, and that amused her. Poor,

loyal Johann; he lacked the ability to consider any of his
emotions in anything other than a military context, subli-
mating his barely concealed attraction to Schrader into the
need to salute whenever she came near him. She was only
nominally an officer, after all, her rank conferred by the
Nort High Command as a function of her superlative talents in other areas. All those mixed messages she gave off
around him... It had to be confusing for the piteous
Kapten.

Volks glanced at her, then to the room's other occupant.
The second man was tall, wide across the shoulders but
surprisingly slender in build. Schrader saw the close-
cropped hair framing his blunt skull and the dark battle
coat he wore ostentatiously over his tailored chem-suit.
The general had his back to her, watching the play of
clouds and light through the window.

"Ah," he began. "So good of you to join us, Madam
Director. At last."

"The pleasure is mine, general. Welcome to Domain
Delta," she answered with obviously false politeness.
Schrader had already mapped the course of this meeting in
her mind, so she saw no reason to pretend at courtesy. She
settled into a chair and laid the sample case on the table
before her. "I was detained by an important experiment on
the sub-levels," she said airily. "I'm sure you understand."

Volks, seeing he had missed a cue, became animated.
"General Rössa, may I present Kolonel-Doktor Lisle
Schrader, base director–"

Rössa waved him into silence. "I know who she is," he
turned to give her his full attention, "and she knows why I
am here."

Schrader held his gaze for a calculated moment, then
looked away. "The loss of the material." Beyond the window, she could see the trio of parked flyers that had
brought the general and his retinue to them. Rössa's personal guard stood around them in a loose ring, stances
casual and bored. Sloppy, she thought.

"The material," Rössa repeated. "I marvel at the way your kind shake your test tubes and come up with these little words to minimise your gargantuan errors!" He flicked derisively at his beard. "You allowed a live test subject to escape, Schrader! You let it go free to run halfway around the planet!"

Volks swallowed hard. "Sir, it was never expected to survive that long. The gene-markers were designed to begin a process of breakdown the moment it left the sealed environment–"

"I did not address you, Kapten!" Rössa snapped. "Your part in this debacle is well documented and you will be seen to account for all your mistakes!" He glowered at the younger officer. "It is clear to me now why you were reassigned from the Kashar Legion to such a backwater posting as this, Volks. I can barely conscience how an officer so inept could have served Nordland for so long!"

Schrader gave a theatrical yawn. "Oh, General, please. You have blown this entire incident completely out of proportion."

Rössa's face reddened. "I beg to differ, Kolonel-Doktor! Quite frankly, my colleagues and I have never understood High Command's dogged interest in this freakish circus you have out here..." he gestured at the dome with an angry flick of the wrist. "But your cavalier attitude towards protocol has come to an end!" The general produced a digi-pad from his pocket and tossed it on to the table before Schrader. "Endless requests for extra funding, prisoner transfers for unspecified experimental testing, requisitions for weapons and hardware – and yet with all this you find it nearly impossible to submit satisfactory progress reports on your research!" He took a step closer to her. "Domain Delta is not your private little kingdom, woman! You are a servant of the Nordland people!"

She sighed. "I admit the escape of the test subject was slightly problematic, but it is dead now, isn't it? Volks assured me that it had been captured and scheduled for execution."

Rössa sneered. "No thanks to you. You have made your last error, Schrader. By my order, Domain Delta is to cease operations and close down." He gave a harsh smile. "This sick little project of yours has no place in a man's war. It is a waste of time and valuable resources."

"General, thank you for confirming my diagnosis that you are a gutless, short-sighted imbecile. You have no comprehension of the scope of my work. I am unlocking the genetic potential of super humanity; superior physical and mental power, perhaps even extra-sensory abilities, all of it within my reach..."

"I know what you are hiding!" the officer barked. "I know all about the off-book research and unreported testing you have been doing!"

"Yes, your pathetic spies hiding among my staff," she said in a bored voice. "I wonder, has it occurred to you that you haven't heard from them in a while?" Schrader watched him carefully. "They all suffered a terrible lab accident when a seal vented unexpectedly. Quite tragic, really."

The general bared his teeth. "You are relieved of your post, Madam Director," he said with venom. "Both of you are to consider yourselves under arrest! You will accompany me to Nu Nuremburg where I will convene an immediate court martial into your activities here... Perhaps if both of you throw yourselves on the mercy of the tribunal, you may avoid a firing squad!"

"I think not," Schrader gave Volks a shallow nod. "Johann? If you would?"

Volks hesitated for a moment, licking his lips. He looked to the woman for some kind of guidance.

"Kapten..." Schrader insisted, her voice hardening.

Volks gave the smallest of nods and then whispered into a communicator on his uniform collar. "Code one, expedite."

"What−?" Rössa whirled as shapes moved outside the window. Troopers from the facility's garrison emerged to surround the parked flyers and robo-gunners floated into view. Although the armoured plastisteel of the dome was thick enough to turn away a las-bolt, the sounds of gunfire still penetrated. The general watched his personal guard cut down in a storm of laser blasts.

Rössa's pistol was in his hand as he turned to face Schrader. The ornate Rheinmetall SonneHauk was a family heirloom that dated back to the earliest Nort campaigns on the Argentine Moons, and the heavy, blunt maw of the gun yawned before him. "You're insane!" The general squeezed the trigger, but the weapon emitted nothing but a harmless click. Rössa worked the gun fiercely without result.

Schrader pointed up at the ceiling, where a lamp concealed a humming pack of circuits. "Beam polariser," she explained. "Negates all laser reactions within a fifty metre radius." The scientist stood, opening the sample case. "You're a victim of your own vanity, General. That antique you haul around with you like some ridiculous fetish is your undoing. If you had lowered yourself to the indignity of carrying a ballistic handgun like most senior officers, then you might have been able to kill me." She produced a pistol-like device made of plastic and glass. "As it is, your toy is now no more than an elaborate paperweight... Unlike this one."

She pressed the skinny weapon into Volks's grip. "Let's finish this sordid matter now, shall we?"

Rössa snorted. "You wouldn't dare. Kapten Volks, you are an officer and a member of the Nordland Party! You will obey me and surrender your weapon!"

Schrader continued to speak as if Rössa had said nothing. "This is a bact-gun. I've loaded it with some of the less promising examples of my experiments. Show the good general, Johann."

With an angry roar, Rössa launched himself at Volks, his greatcoat flaring open behind him like wide black wings. The Nort officer fired on reflex and the bact-gun spat a viscous plug of jelly into the general's face. Rössa fell back under the shock of the impact and shrieked. The gelatinous fluid burned into the bare skin around his throat and chin, seeping directly into the pores.

Wracked with agony, Rössa crashed to his knees and clawed at his flesh. "What have you done to me? Stak! Nain!" Blood flooded out from his nostrils, mouth and eyes. "Aieeee!"

Schrader stood and watched Rössa collapse to the floor screaming and convulsing; seconds later, he was dead. Volks pushed the bact-gun back into her hands with sweaty fingers. "He... he won't be the last. What will we do when more of them come?"

She gave him a cool smile. "We'll burn that bridge when we come to it, Johann. We're beyond the point of no return now. The location of this dome is recorded in only the most secure of High Command's files. Domain Delta is so secret that even Rössa wouldn't have known exactly where he was going. We'll be safe until I'm ready." Schrader crossed to the window, ignoring the general's corpse. Volks followed her, unable to avoid looking at the dead man. "This place is a graveyard, nothing but desolate wastelands and endless glass." She pulled Volks into a lingering kiss, mentally detaching herself from the physical sensation. "No one will find us here," said Schrader, breaking away. "No one comes to the Quartz Zone."

SIX
REQUIEM IN BLUE

The borders on the map of Nu Earth were never permanent. In places like Nu Kassel or Doomsday Valley, Nort and Souther frontlines moved back and forth on a daily basis. The skies above the planet were worse, with flight corridors seeded by flitter mines and storm generators. Up above, there was no high ground to hold, no places to dig in and fortify. In the footless halls of chem-tainted air, there was nothing but certain death for the inexperienced pilot.

Ferris was anything but that. He had been flying before he could write his own name, and as much as he hated the contaminated world that wheeled below him, Nu Earth's skies were his element. The pilot wrangled the strato-shuttle around the edge of a volcanic plume from the Dust Zones and set it on a sub-orbital hop across the continent.

Rogue glanced at Ferris at the controls, peering through the open hatchway into the cockpit. The man liked to talk to himself as he flew, the GI noted, asking the shuttle questions out loud as if that would somehow make it perform a little better.

Gunnar sensed his scrutiny. "I don't like him."

"Huh," said Helm. "You made that clear enough."

"Synth out, Gunnar. He saved our asses back there," Rogue replied, turning his attention elsewhere. "Like it or not, we're passengers for now."

A low electronic noise like a snort came from the rifle where it lay next to his backpack on the deck.

The GI leaned in closer to the irregular knot of bone-like material on the console in front of him. A set of manipulators looted from a torched medical transport lay spread out near it. Rogue blinked, the muscles around his eyes gently contracting the organic lenses within for close-up work. The surface of the object became clearer to him and he selected a probe to pick at it.

"What is that?" asked Helm. "Looks weird."

Rogue nodded to Bagman. "You thinking what I'm thinking?"

"Affirmative," said Bagman, his optics clicking. "Check it out." The backpack dispensed a digi-pad. The display showed a similar object in cutaway. "It's a bionomic regulator implant, but there's no pattern match in the database."

"In English?" said Gunnar.

"Did you sleep through the medical lectures the Genies gave us?" said Rogue.

"I was awake for the ones where they told us how to kill people."

Rogue frowned. "These things were part of the GI development programme, like an organic monitor unit. The first generation clones couldn't keep their bio-systems in check without them – their bodies would overheat without the implant."

"So what?" Gunnar snorted. "Old tech, old news. GIs like us never needed them. They're obsolete."

"Which begs the question, why did Zero have one?" retorted Bagman.

"We know the Norts had a Genetic Infantry project of their own," added Rogue, "but they didn't have the know-how. Nort GIs use an implant like this."

"Zero wasn't a Nort!" said Gunnar hotly. "He was one of us, blue to the core!"

Rogue shook his head. "That's not in doubt, but you heard what he said. He was regened and his biochip was put into a new body."

"By the Norts?" Bagman was incredulous. "I hate to pop your seal, Rogue, but there's two big holes in your theory. First, why the skev would the enemy regenerate a lethal Souther soldier? And second, if Zero got hit in the Quartz Zone Massacre all that time ago, his chip should have been blank."

"Good point," said Helm. "Sixty seconds after brain death and *pfft*. Gone forever."

The GI rubbed his eyes. Fatigue was setting in. "Guys, I don't have all the answers, I'm just trying to fit the facts."

"We're going a long way off-book for this." Gunnar's voice held a blunt edge. "That trip to the rig, to San Diablo and now back to the Zone... You said after Dix-I we'd concentrate on finding the Traitor."

Rogue gave the rifle a sharp look. "And you said yourself, Zero was one of us. If there's even the remotest chance there were other survivors from the massacre, we have to know!"

"Maybe we should vote on it," said Helm.

"This isn't a democracy," Rogue growled. "We're gonna find Domain Delta."

"Who died and made you major?" retorted Gunnar, before he realised the irony of his words. "Well, what I meant was−"

"Skin outranks silicon," said Bagman. "You don't have to like it, but−"

Without warning, the deck of the strato-shuttle suddenly tipped at a steep angle and Rogue's gear tumbled off the console. "What the hell?"

"Grendels!" Ferris shouted from the cockpit. "They're right on us!"

From the starboard vu-ports a flash of yellow lit the inside of the cargo bay with a brief, brilliant sunburst. The shuttle dropped sharply as it fell into a pocket of turbulent air.

. . .

The Nort flyers were part of the Nordland Aerospace Force's LangJager squadron, pilots trained to operate their Grendel superiority fighters on long, circuitous missions over the edges of occupied sectors. In military parlance it was called CAP duty – combat air patrol – the airborne equivalent of walking a sentry pattern, searching for interlopers idiotic enough to run the blockade. They were on the return leg now, over the glassy plains of the Quartz Zone.

The Grendels themselves were ugly to the eye; fat missiles with stubby winglets, an opaque cockpit on the fuselage like a black bruise. Little more than an engine with weapons, they were still quite stealthy thanks to clever electronic countermeasures circuits wired into their hulls. Sensors on a civilian transporter like the strato-shuttle looked straight through them. The three rocket-fuelled raptors dropped out of cloud cover and tore through the sky towards Ferris's ship.

The lead Grendel had a profile on the shuttle streaming from its onboard war book even as it devoured the kilometres between them: A non-aligned Bravo class sub-orbital, the combat computer told its pilot, a minimal threat; but then a flash alert message from Air Division at San Diablo said something different. "Fugitive aircraft," the advisory screamed. "Terminate on sight."

"He's made us!" Ferris yelled. "That first shot was just a warning, but I'm getting a lidar tone – he's going for missile lock!"

Rogue forced his way into the cockpit. "You got countermeasures? Flares, chaff?"

Ferris jerked his head at the co-pilot console, all his attention on the flight yoke as he desperately tried to jink the shuttle out of the Nort's sights. "Red switch with a white stripe."

The GI tugged the control and a dull thud echoed through the hull as drums of metal tinsel and hot signal flares cascaded into the air behind the shuttle.

In the lead Grendel's cockpit, the Nort pilot swore as his lock-on screen turned into a storm of static. His wingmen were quick to avoid the chaff and accelerated, diving at the ship. The number two aircraft slipped forward, the under-wing railgun humming to life.

Ferris didn't so much see the enemy approaching as *feel* it; what made him such a talented pilot was an instinct for the three-dimensional environment of the air. The acute spatial awareness of his mind's eye told him where the Nort would come from and he slammed his foot into the rudder pedal, making the shuttle groan as it turned sharply. Rogue stumbled against the console.

The railgun shells blasted out of the gunpod and hammered holes in the cargo bay, punching right through the metal and out the other side. Wounded electrics spat fat sparks and a siren sounded. "Chem alarm!" Ferris snapped. "Hull breach!" The second Grendel flashed past the canopy as he cut the throttles and let it fly by.

"Where's your hood?" Rogue asked.

"No time!" Ferris replied. "Get back in the bay. I'll seal myself up here."

"There's three of them," Rogue saw the blips on the sensor holo. "Don't you have any guns on this crate? All the fancy flying in the world won't stop those creeps."

"Hatch in the deck!" said the pilot. "There's a turret on the ventral hull!"

"Got it." Rogue vaulted through the cockpit door and slammed it shut behind him.

The trailing Grendel's pilot matched the speed of the ugly strato-shuttle and kept his aim carefully on the fuselage, tracking as it turned. He hadn't fired a single shot, waiting for the right moment to present itself. The fighter dipped below the ship's midline and the Grendel's war book made a negative sound; something in the shuttle's configuration didn't match the factory specifications of the standard

Bravo class. The pilot saw an irregular glass hemisphere, aft of the cargo ramp. A blurry blue shape moved inside it.

Rogue sprinted down the inclined hull and spun the wheel on the hatch in the floor. The disc slid open to reveal a metal chair with a gunner console dangling over it. The GI slipped easily into the seat and grasped the firing controls. It was cramped, but the weapon was already live.

"There's a wireless interface here," said Helm. "I'm gonna link my sensors to the gun scope."

"Good call," said Rogue, flipping the trigger from "safe" to "arm".

The Grendel pilot realised his mistake as the beam lasers extended from the base of the turret and pulled to port. Rogue saw the ailerons bite into the wind seconds before the turn and fired. The shots went wide, streaks of light narrowly missing the fighter's fuselage.

Helm let out a strident beep. "Two degrees right, elevation four!"

"Firing." Rogue jerked the trigger and the lasers found their mark, shearing off a stabilator. The Grendel wobbled as the pilot tried to get out of the turret's fire corridor.

"Five left and two!" said Helm, but Rogue held back, guiding the cannons on to the fleeing fighter. "I said five left and two! Rogue, hit him!"

"Not yet." He hesitated a heartbeat longer, then unleashed the guns. "Now!" The energy bolts marched up the Grendel's fuselage and tore open the black glass canopy. Rogue watched the Nort flyer flip over and tumble away into the chem-cloud. "Ferris, copy me?" he called into an intercom. "Splash one."

Ferris didn't respond; he had other concerns. Even the few seconds of exposure to the acrid atmosphere that had passed into the ship were enough to make his lungs feel like they had been scrubbed with wire wool. He had a de-chem canister in the shuttle's medi-kit, but that was just out of reach on the wall and there was no way he was going to let go of the yoke with two fighters dogging him.

He wasn't surprised that the GI had aced a Grendel so fast. The guy was bred for combat after all, and the Nort pilots wouldn't have been expecting a dead-eye like his to be behind the las-cannons, but they had just used up their one and only advantage. The remaining ships wouldn't be so easy to mark.

The proximity warning light blinked in the corner of his vision and once again Ferris feathered the shuttle's retro-jets, cutting a haphazard course through the sky. Flying this airborne boxcar against the agile Norts was like a mek-bull running from cybertigers; they were faster, more manoeuvrable and bristled with ordnance, and it was only a matter of time before one made the killing shot. A flash of silvery light blinked up at him from a gap in the clouds. They were crossing into the glass zone now, over the wide expanses of earth fused into brilliant silica plains by repeated heat bomb attacks.

Ferris risked a look at the sensor holo and instantly wished he hadn't. The Grendels were looping around for a strafing pass. Logically, they should have extended out of the engagement and used missiles to bring him down, but Ferris knew the Norts would take the loss of one of their own personally, especially at the hands of a cargo hauler. The Grendel pilots wanted to come up close and tear him apart, so that every moment of his death would be captured on their gun cameras.

The lead fighter turned inbound and came high, avoiding the belly turret and lancing red fire through the chem-clouds. More warning lights bloomed on the console as stray hits found vital components. "Rogue!" Ferris shouted into the intercom. "Hold on!"

He waited a fraction of a second longer than he needed to and then Ferris did something that violated every safety regulation in the strato-shuttle's flight manual. Yanking the steering yoke back to his chest, he slammed open the

brake flaps and toggled the retros; the shuttle's fuselage
moaned like a wounded animal as its airspeed suddenly
bled away. Alert call-outs on Ferris's head-up display went
mad with panic as the ship threw itself into a violent stall.
Instantly, the shuttle flipped up like the head of an enraged
snake, standing on the plume of exhaust flaring out of its
engines. The Grendel pilot panicked and veered away,
almost colliding with the ship as he passed. The insane
manoeuvre bared the underside of the shuttle to the fleeing
rear of the Nort fighter and put it squarely in Rogue's sights.

Ferris didn't see the beams track the target, but it was
impossible to ignore the sudden and bright yellow explosion off the port as the Grendel was cut open.

"Splash two." The GI's voice was gruff; he probably
hadn't appreciated having his head bounced off the canopy
by Ferris's sudden cobra stall.

The pilot let the ship fall back into the pull of gravity and
the wind kissed the wings, buffeting the shuttle as it clawed
back precious lift to keep it airborne. A grin blossomed on
Ferris's face; two down, one left! He started to allow himself
to think that they might actually get through this alive; but
when the third and final Grendel shrieked over the canopy
in a tight reversal, he almost died of fright.

"Oh, shit!" He pumped the rudder pedals, but the strato-
shuttle was lethargic. Perhaps one of those strafing hits
from the second fighter had cut some hydraulic lines or his
crazed stall had busted loose a flap, but whatever the cause,
the hefty atmocraft was wallowing like a bloated ox. The
shuttle flew like a brick on the best of days, but now she was
howling with every input from the stick, fighting him for
each snatch of air beneath her wings. The pilot couldn't see
it from his vantage point, but thin grey streams of fluid were
spitting out of ragged holes in the dorsal hull. The ship was
bleeding to death.

Behind his air mask, the remaining Nort was red with
rage, snarling a continuous stream of hard-edged and

inventive curses about the shuttle pilot's parentage in gutter Nordsprache. He made a yo-yo turn that brought the shape of the crippled ship into his gun cues and turned his las-cannons to maximum yield. With a savage grunt, he pressed the trigger-switch and watched coherent light flay the rear of the shuttle, cutting great divots of hull metal with reckless abandon. Twists of smoke and steel shavings raced past his canopy.

He was bore-sighted on the enemy, his entire world shrinking to the tunnel of sky between the muzzles of his guns and the fuselage of the strato-shuttle. The Nort saw nothing else but his kill and his mouth flooded with saliva at the anticipation of it. The civilian ship would be ripped to bits by his salvoes.

In that second, the Grendel pilot was distracted enough to miss the flicker of his collision warning monitor; a bright white flare came off the shuttle's hull and brought with it a knife of metal the length of a man. The Nort had only a second to register it, to understand that he had brought his own end upon himself, before the steel spar lanced through the armoured glass of his cockpit at the speed of sound. It ran him through, pinning him to his ejector seat through the solar plexus like a bloody butterfly. The Grendel, its pilot choking on dark arterial crimson, dropped away towards a final impact in the glass below.

Ferris should have been elated, but the wall of flashing red alerts from the flight computer dominated his attention. If there was a system on the shuttle that was still intact, the pilot couldn't find it.

"Trooper!" he yelled, his throat raw. "Still with me?"

"Copy." Rogue replied, matter-of-factly. "Should I be concerned by the fact that the ship's on fire?"

"Get up to the cockpit and bring your buddies. I'm gonna eject!" He didn't expect a reply and for the first time since the engagement had begun, Ferris let the flight yoke go, scrambling around for the hood of his chem-suit. He had the neck latches closed just as the cockpit hatch opened to allow Rogue inside. A heavy plug of cold, hard air came with him, battering every loose object in the cabin into a tornado of paper, pieces of stale food and plastic fragments.

The GI fell into the co-pilot's chair and secured his gear in a webbing sling under the seat. "Hull's like a sieve," he jerked his thumb at the ruined cargo bay. "It's only the rust keeping it together."

Ferris saw the green flag in the corner of his helmet visor; full air tanks. He took back control of the ship – as much as he could, anyway – and tried to pull it into a flatter attitude. The mirror-finish of the Quartz Zone's surface made it tough to gauge distance by eye, but he could tell just by the sinking feeling in his gut that they were losing height faster than cash in one of Gog's card games. Ferris gripped the ejector switch and turned it ninety degrees; in reply, the cockpit hatch closed and locked. Explosive bolts all around the strato-shuttle's flight cabin went live.

"Fasten your seatbelt," said Ferris in his best starliner captain voice, "and please extinguish all smoking materials."

"Just do it already!" Helm protested.

Ferris gave the switch another quarter-turn, and the G-force hit them like a fist. The spherical cockpit module blew out from the hull of the atmocraft and tumbled away. Robbed of any semblance of control, the remains of Strato-Shuttle 1138 dived straight towards the ground. It struck the glass with such force that cracks radiated out for kilometres in every direction, jagged fissures appearing to point like arrows back at the point of impact.

The flight pod automatically deployed a parachute ballute, but the ejection height had been far below the recommended minimum. The metal ovoid bounced off the ground, landed, bounced again, landed and then screeched across the fields of fused silica, dragged by the chutes. Rogue slapped at the controls and the balloon detached, allowing the pod to roll to a tottering halt.

He reached over to Ferris. The pilot's breathing was shallow. "We have to get out," said Rogue. "Norts will be vectoring spy-sats into this area to look for downed pilots. They'll mark our landing for sure."

Ferris gave a slow, difficult nod. "Right, right," he managed, unfastening his seat straps with leaden slowness. "I could improve my technique a little, I think..." He stumbled to his feet, dragging a survival kit from a locker that had burst open. "Still, any one you can walk away from, eh?"

"If I had a head," said Bagman, "I'd have a headache."

Rogue saw Ferris recover a snub-nosed slug pistol and stuff it in a suit pocket. "Let's move. You follow me, go where I go and do what I say and you'll keep breathing. Understand?"

Ferris nodded again. "Sure. This is your turf now, right?"

Rogue kicked out the hatch and dropped to the ground, panning Gunnar across the expanse of glassy nothingness. For a long moment there was nothing but silence, the absolute, oppressive quiet of a tomb.

The pilot emerged behind him. The alien landscape gave Ferris the creeps. "Which way?"

None of them wanted to speak, as if daring to utter a word would shatter the miserable stillness and bring black memories rushing back to claim them. At last, Bagman gave a peculiar synthetic cough. "Huh. Nothing's changed."

"We need to find cover," said Rogue in a low, loaded voice.

"Quarter-klick to the north," Helm answered immediately, anticipating the GI's requirements. "A network of crevices. Some shallow nooks in there."

Rogue took off at a jog without looking to see if Ferris was following and the pilot charged after him, giving the pod one last farewell glance. In the distance, in the opposite direction, the plume of smoke from the shuttle coiled up into the clouds, a dark ribbon against an oil-stained sky.

● ● ●

The Quartz Zone was riddled with shallow craters and fissures where the fused surface was cracked and broken, and Rogue's unerring eye for defensive shelter quickly found them a surface cave where they could hide. Ferris sucked plastic-tasting water from a tube in his suit and watched the GI drop his gear.

"Bagman, dispense entrenching tool." The backpack complied and Rogue unfolded a memory-metal spade, walking out to the edge of the crevice. The GI slammed the blade of the tool into the glassy earth and began to dig.

"What's he doing?" Ferris asked.

"Burial detail," replied Helm.

Ferris saw the GI remove Zero's biochip and put it to one side. A sudden, icy realisation struck him. "Skev... This is it, isn't it? This is where you guys... Where you—"

"Died? Bought the farm? Copped it? Got scragged?" Gunnar said. "Yeah, more or less."

The pilot shook his head. "Is there any part of this damn planet that isn't somebody's war grave?"

Helm spoke again. "We're about twenty, maybe thirty klicks from the drop point." The artificial voice seemed distant now. "Mass capsule landing, it was. Seven ships, full compliment of pods. The Norts had been tipped off, see. They were waiting down here with shoulder-mounted rocket launchers."

"Coffin-breakers," Bagman broke in.

"Gunnar... He was hit first," Helm continued, and Ferris felt like the voices from the biochips were not really speaking to him; this was some kind of litany for the dead men, the unwritten memory of their shared trauma.

"I got out, soon as the pod touched down," said the mind in the rifle. "Hammered a hundred of those Kashans. Fed the bastards eighty-eights and gamma grenades like they was goin' out of style." Gunnar was silent for a moment. "Redball and Tagger, they were covering the flank, but then they were gone and I didn't see the Nort with the plasma sphere. Rogue tried to warn me... Next thing I know, I'm bleeding out right there on the glass."

"He put your chip in his rifle," said Ferris.

"*My* rifle!" Gunnar retorted. "It's *my* damned rifle." There was another pause. "I was ghosted but Rogue got me out... I wasn't the last, not by a long way."

Bagman began to speak, picking up the thread of the recollection. "We had no choice. We had to fall back, regroup, so anyone who was left formed up into skirmish units and we splintered. Figured we'd have a better chance of making it to pick-up that way."

"We got to the edge of the zone with five of us left in our team," added Helm. "Bag, Rogue and me, plus Joker and Cowboy. Scopes got popped by a buzzsaw mine on the way and there was nothing left of him. Then we ran into the Kashar Legion... They were sweeping up after the ambush, looking for survivors. They pinned us down in a crater and waited for us to use up our ammo. The map called it Strongpoint Siouxie, but it was just a hole in the ground."

"They didn't wait long, though." Bagman's tone was hollow. "They sent a drill probe in after us. I remember the heat... The smell, like overcooked rations. There was a split in my chest, you understand? Big enough to put my fist in." The chip made a low, guttural sound. "Nnnn. Then I woke up, woke up on silicon. Just like that."

Ferris found he couldn't look away from Rogue as the GI carefully placed the inert dog-chip in its tiny, shallow grave. "What... what about you, Helm?"

"He almost made it," said Gunnar, with a hint of sorrow in his words. "Joker finally got through to Milli-Com on the link and they sent down a chem-strike to screen us."

"Rogue and me took the alpha route," Helm began. "I don't know how we did it, but lady luck had us in the palm of her hand that night. We charged right over the Nort line and just kept on runnin'. Two days later we were on the Oxide Shore."

"No one else?"

"Just the two of us," said Helm.

"Four," insisted Bagman. "Four of us."

"Whatever," Helm became terse. "Anyway, long story short, we wade out into the Orange Sea to get to the shuttle and a bunch of Nort foils pop up and missile the boat..." The synth turned angry. "Those sneaky bastards, we never even got a chance to shoot back! Damn it, they knew! Every one of those Nort goons, they knew where we were every step of the way!"

"There was a traitor." Rogue entered the shelter. "A Souther general sold us out."

Ferris nodded. This part of the story he'd heard, the legend of the lone GI searching for vengeance. "You really think you're gonna find some clue, then? You reckon this Delta place has something to do with that guy?"

Rogue fixed him with a look that was razor-sharp and cold with malice. "We need information. We need to know."

SEVEN
HUNTER HUNTED

They travelled under cover of chem storms and nightfall, with Helm plotting erratic courses across the glass to avoid the footprints of orbital satellites. Rogue navigated by the dark disk of the Valhalla wormhole in the sky above them, the baleful black sun like the unblinking eye of an ancient war God. Ferris did his best to keep up, but the pace the GI maintained left him spent and panting. Rogue never chastised him for his unfitness, just stood by and waited for him to catch his breath before they moved off again.

By the end of the second day, Ferris began to wonder why the trooper didn't just leave him out here to fend for himself. If the circumstances were reversed, the pilot would have been hard pressed to find an excuse not to do otherwise. He was slowing the GI to a comparative crawl. Perhaps it was something in him, Ferris wondered, maybe a kind of genetic imperative wired into the soldier's vat-grown brain? Rogue had to have some programmed bias toward preserving the lives of civilian and allies, otherwise he would have left Ferris sitting in the escape pod and headed out alone.

He watched the GI's back as Rogue walked in front of him, the unchanging, almost mechanical gait of his stride the same as it had been all day. Rogue never seemed to tire and his biochip buddies were always awake, certainly. He had no doubt that Bagman's rearward facing sensors knew exactly where Ferris was at any moment.

They were close to cresting a ridge when Rogue came to a sudden halt and uttered a terse command. "Down!"

Ferris sank to his knees as Rogue crouched and crept forward to the lip of the silica bank. "Trouble?"

The pilot flattened himself and crawled up to the lee of a broken, glassy boulder. Laid out below the ridge was a shallow canyon, pitted with impact craters and broken stubs of rubble. This part of the Quartz Zone had been a settlement, back before the thermal bombardments, and there were some remains of the buildings that once stood there. Ferris squinted. He could see something moving, a handful of vague shapes.

"Southers," said Rogue. "Recon patrol by the looks of their gear."

Ferris could barely make out that the blobs were actually people. "You can see that from here? You got eyes like a hawk!"

"There's raptor DNA in us," said Bagman, popping open his manipulator. "A pinch of tiger as well." The arm produced a pair of field glasses. "Here, use these binox."

Ferris took them and studied the party of troops. Five men leapt into definition through the long-range lenses. "They're moving pretty fast. I wonder why?" The body language of the soldiers was tense and anxious.

Rogue scanned the landscape. "They're being chased."

"By who?" asked Ferris. "Can't see anyone else out–" His words caught in his throat as one of the Southern troopers suddenly spun around in place, a gush of blood exploding out of her chest. Seconds later the cracking report of a single las-round reached their ears.

The other troopers panicked and turned away from the direction they had been running in, instead making for the heart of the canyon and the ruins.

"Stupid," murmured Helm. "They're walking right into it."

Rogue answered Ferris's unspoken question. "There's a shooter out there, herding them deeper into the canyon.

My guess is there'll be another rifleman waiting on the ridgeline over the ruins. One pushes them in, the other picks them off."

"Where's the shooter?"

Rogue pointed toward a tilted fragment of grey glass. "There, see him?"

Through the binox Ferris saw only the shadows cast by the rock; but then something detached itself from the darkness and moved swiftly forward. It had only gone a few steps when the man-shape paused and looked up. The pilot's heart froze in his chest as the figure looked directly at him.

Instantly, Ferris shrank into the cover of the boulder. "Did he see me?"

Rogue shook his head. "No, he's moving on."

The other man swallowed hard. The expressionless face he'd seen through the binoculars was chilling and alien. "He... he had green skin, no mask. Some kinda helmet over his eyes, his head..."

"Not a helmet," said Gunnar irritably. "It's dermal armour plating, fused to the skull. Thick enough to deflect a hotshot from anything less than close range."

Rogue's eyes narrowed. "It's a Nort Genetik Soldat. Our opposite numbers."

"Huh," added Helm. "Not like any kind I've seen before, though. He looks different, bigger."

"Must be the new improved model..." Bagman said dryly.

"You're not just gonna let those men get killed off one by one, are you?"

Rogue dropped into cover. "Bagman, gimme the walkie-talkie." The GI passed the hand-held radio to Ferris. "Take this. Sing out if things start to get hairy."

"Wh-what are you gonna do?" the pilot stammered.

The GI pointed. "I'll double-time it around the lip of the canyon, see if I can't get behind the second shooter and take him out. Reckon he's in the busted tower to the west."

"How can you be sure?"

"It's where I would be, the best vantage point, good fields of fire. You head down the ridge, follow that Nort GI, but stay out of his way."

"Copy..." Ferris gulped.

"Eh," grunted Gunnar. "We just gonna leave flyboy alone? If tall, green and handsome down there gets hold of him, he'll sing like a synthi-vox!"

Rogue shoved his rifle into Ferris's hands. "Which is why you're going to keep him out of trouble." Before Gunnar could protest, Rogue was sprinting away, vanishing into the dark.

Ferris watched him go, staggered by the GI's speed at a full run. He gingerly raised the rifle. "Uh... So, where's your safety catch?"

"Inside the barrel," Gunnar growled. "Why don't you take a look down it and see?"

"Never mind," said the pilot, and he carefully turned the gun's muzzle away before moving off over the ridge.

"A ghost," said Johnson. "It's a ghost! Those Godless abortions, they're phantoms!" In his exertion, the Souther soldier was steaming up the inside of his faceplate.

To his right, Zeke threw him a sharp look. "Knock it off, son. You're wasting oxy panicking."

"Yeah, the sarge is right," added Ruiz, hefting the Blowpipe launcher in his hands. "You keep babblin' and you'll end up ventilated like Taylor back there!"

"She owed me money, skev it!" Purcell said in a snarl. "This is number ten."

Zeke raised a balled fist, halting them all. "Quiet, all of you!" The veteran paused, scanning the canyon. "We gotta find high ground before these Norty freaks flank us."

"Maybe... maybe they already did..." mumbled Johnson.

Purcell stepped closer to Zeke and lowered her voice. "Sarge, this don't feel right. We're walking into an ambush, I can taste it."

The woman's words made the sergeant hesitate; Purcell was a good soldier with excellent instincts, which was what had kept her alive on Nu Earth so far. He glanced around. The wind moaned through the canyon, disturbing drifts of mirror-bright fines where they pooled around the ruins. Zeke's heart hammered in his chest. It seemed like they had been running for days, but it was only hours since things had started to fall apart. The patrol was supposed to have taken them up and away from their unit for a standard reconnaissance sweep, but then the las-fire had come out of nowhere and killed three men in as many seconds, the lieutenant among them. Taylor had only survived because the radio backpack had absorbed the shot meant for her, but now she was gone too and with no communications and not a damn clue as to where they were, the remnants of Zeke's squad were running out of luck. They needed to hole up, try to find their location on the digi-map and return to their unit; but those green monstrosities that had jumped them never slowed. He gave an involuntary shudder. The dead eyes, that bony mask for a face... Whatever the Norts had bred out here, it was a walking horror show.

"Sarge?" Purcell repeated, shaking him out of his reverie.

He pointed to a long, flat piece of wall. "There. Get up and dig in. That's an order!"

She gave him a disgusted look, but obeyed.

G-Soldat NG/442-Sigma had not moved for the past twenty minutes. He was well concealed in the ring of smashed bricks that at one time had been a church's bell tower. The barrel of his weapon, a Mowzer K-Type Stalker, protruded slightly from the cover of his ash-coloured camu-cape. The mimetic camouflage threads in the flexible material matched perfectly to the optical register of the surrounding stones, and with the thickness of his plastiform epidermis hiding 442-Sigma's body heat, there was nothing to alert the Souther prey to his presence. Sigma's designated squad mate for this mission, G-Soldat NG/181-Beta, had already scored two kills on this training sortie and he was eager to claim some for himself.

There was little room for any other kind of emotion inside Sigma's mind. Almost everything but hate and fear had been excised from his intellect; what could be deducted by selective gene-engineering, invasive brain surgery and impulse response blocks was cut away, the rest suppressed and manipulated by chemo-psychological conditioning. G-Soldat NG/442-Sigma understood that he was a weapon, an intelligent field munition with one mission: to kill the enemy.

And yet, deep, deep inside the regimented, programmed core of the Nort GI's psyche there was a tiny, bone-deep centre of aggression and need that craved violence. Had such a thing been part of his make-up, Sigma might have recognised the almost sexual anticipation of murder bubbling away under his iron façade.

The four remaining Southers were well inside his kill zone now and they bobbed up the shallow hill toward him, awkward and afraid as they looked desperately for any signs of enemy activity. Sigma understood fear; it ruled him. Fear of *her*. Fear that he would earn her displeasure and fail, fear that an error on his part would return him once more to the debriefing chambers where additional, painful programming was provided to the Soldats who did not meet the Kolonel-Doktor's stringent mandates. He elected to wait a little longer, so that the Souther troopers would not be able to scatter too far when the moment came to fire. He flexed the finger on the Mowzer's trigger in preparation, then he heard the crunch of boots on glass behind him.

G-Soldat NG/181-Beta would not have dared to approach from the rear, which left only one possibility. The Nort Genetik Soldat tensed and with a grimace of annoyance, he exploded out of cover. The camu-cape fluttered away as he turned to face his new adversary.

Rogue hadn't expected the Nort GI to be so fast – the last ones he fought had been sluggish in comparison – and it almost took him off guard. He leapt without thinking, colliding bodily with the enemy soldier. The fractal-edged combat knife in his right hand sank into the G-Soldat's breast to the hilt as they came together, but the Nort seemed utterly unaware of the wound. The dull white crest of bone on his armoured skull nodded forward and butted Rogue hard on the helmet.

"*ZZzzt!*" spat Helm, the impact rattling his circuitry.

Sigma recognised the form of the Southern gene-trooper automatically; the profiles of this inferior example of his kind had been given to him among the endless indoctrination sessions of his in-vitro training. The prospect of killing a GI kindled the murder-lust in him a little higher and Sigma forgot about the human soldiers for a moment. They were locked for long seconds, the Stalker rifle held between them like a quarterstaff, blue and green hands gripping it, struggling for command of the weapon. Rogue gave a savage tug and in return Sigma pulled the trigger. The shot blazed past Rogue's face, but the nictitating membranes over his eyes cut away any hope of dazzling him.

Down in the canyon, the laser blast echoed through the air and Zeke shouted out an order. "Scatter!"

Ruiz rolled into cover, popping up with the blunt muzzle of the Blowpipe at the ready. "Where? Anyone see the flash?"

"Above..." began Johnson, waving his hand. "I think I saw something."

"In front *and* behind?" said Purcell, her head whipping back and forth. "Skev! I told you this was a set-up, Sarge!"

Zeke frowned, and as if to underline his mistake and prove Purcell right, a couple of las-rounds streaked through the air from the opposite direction. The Nort who had killed Taylor was still with them, dogging them into the canyon. The sergeant would have spat in self-disgust if he hadn't had a hood on; how could he have been so damned stupid? He'd led his men right into a meat grinder.

Grimly, Zeke worked the battery-cartridge slide on his gun and checked the charge. "Pop smoke! Let's make this bugger work for it!"

G-Soldat NG/181-Beta recognised the report of the Mowzer and halted. Something wasn't running according to their tactical plan; it was too soon for 442-Sigma to start shooting the Southers. Sighting through the teleoptics of his own weapon, Beta considered the possibilities. Clearly, there was a third factor in this skirmish that neither of them had accounted for. The Nort gene-trooper reconsidered the moment as he had moved from cover after killing the woman. For just the smallest of instants, 181-Beta had seen what appeared to be movement at the top of the ridgeline. Had there been a third Soldat in their unit, he would have directed him to investigate, but with only Sigma and himself there had been no opportunity. Beta decided that the motion was likely starlight twinkling off glass fragments and nothing more; now he revised his conclusion and weighed the options. If Sigma had engaged a new target, Beta was potentially exposed. That was not an acceptable outcome.

The clone soldier peered into the rolling wall of smoke emerging from the handful of grenades tossed out by the Southers, looking for something to kill. The metallic mist was excellent for baffling automatic sensors, but the organic brain of a living sniper could interpret things no machine ever could. Beta saw a shape change aspect through the smoke and opened fire.

Half-out of his cover, Ruiz yelled in fright as a beam passed within a hand-span of his helmet and another one shrieked off the barrel of the Blowpipe. He dropped to a crouch, the heavy launcher knocked from his fingers.

Beta had his range now, even if he couldn't see him exactly, and his gunsight mind began to estimate the position and angle that the Souther would most likely adopt. He fired a few more probing rounds into the murk. The Soldat did not need to see his target to kill it.

"Do you even know how to use a weapon?" Gunnar asked angrily. "It's a simple interface, pinky, just point and click. Got it?"

"Quit calling me names," Ferris replied in a blunt whisper. "I'm new to this footslogger stuff."

"I'll say. Hold up here and bring me to eye-level."

The pilot did as the gun demanded. "What am I looking for?"

"Muzzle flash." The overlaid multi-spectral display from the rifle's triad optics showed cold stony rubble and grey swathes of smoke, then suddenly a flickering jag of yellow lightning to the right of the picture. "There!" Gunnar growled. "Hold me steady."

Ferris let the barrel dip toward the ground. "Wait, you don't know if that's a Nort or a Souther–"

"Aim me!" Gunnar snapped. "You ain't making the choice here, pal!"

"My finger's on the trigger!" he replied.

"No, it ain't," said the rifle.

Ferris let out a yelp of shock as Gunnar unleashed a full-auto surge of fire into the distance, the las-beams skipping off the glass and hissing through the air. The recoil of the rounds set him back on his heels. "Holy crap."

Out in the smoke, there was the distinctive sizzle of cooking meat as a shot struck bare flesh.

Rogue fought to keep the Nort GI from choking the life out of him; the G-Soldat was as strong as a mek-bull. Automatically he fell into pre-determined combat patterns drilled into him from his youth; Rogue struck out with steely fingers, performing nerve strikes that would have crippled a normal human. The enemy trooper let out painful grunts but gave no other signs of injury. The Nort GI's plastiflesh skin felt uncannily like Rogue's own. The armoured dome of bone-like matter over the Nort's head loomed, filling Rogue's vision; this new variety of Soldat was a lot tougher than he looked.

The GI's hand flapped over the hilt of his combat knife where it remained buried in the Nort's chest and Rogue grabbed on to it. He gave the blade a forceful twist, letting the weapon open up the enemy soldier's wound. Somewhere in the Soldat's chest cavity were the decentralised chambers of his heart, much as they were in Rogue's, and he slashed the knife in drastic arcs as emerald blood shot out like small geysers. The Nort bio-engineers had done their work well; the G-Soldats had ribcages like a tight hex-grid, protecting the more vulnerable organs within.

Sigma felt no agony from the savage wound. A neural shunt conditioned by his creators instantly diverted all impulses from pain receptors, flooding his brain with combat strength endorphins. In such a state, he would be able to march for days on bloody stumps, or beat someone to death with his own severed limb before the eventual fluid loss wore him down.

Rogue saw the green-skinned warrior's eyes widen with the flush of the neurochemicals; he knew the sensation from personal experience. Vision fogging, he tried a last ditch attack and went for the soldat's throat. The GI's teeth bit into the Nort's flesh and tore a lump of muscle away with them.

Sigma dropped Rogue as he clasped at his neck, trying to hold onto the ragged flap of skin, and as he did so, the infantryman spun away and landed hard on the ground. Sigma spat out a mouthful of thick, glutinous fluids. Dimly, Rogue was aware of Helm and Bagman speaking, but their voices shot out like hollow echoes. He shook off the sluggish effects of the soldat's attack. Bagman's arm was pressing something into his hand, a pistol-shaped device.

"Get him!" Bagman cried. "Head shot!"

Rogue realised what the object was just as the enemy GI dived at him, an animal roar escaping from its lips. He brought up the device and caught the Nort in the face. Rogue pressed the coiled flexsteel bit of the hand-drill into the only weak spot on the soldat's head – its eyes – and forced the delicate optical jelly into the Nort's forebrain. Instantly, Sigma tried to pull back, but Rogue caught him in a death grip and rammed the drill deep into his skull.

The enemy trooper made a peculiar, juddering cry and went slack, limbs jerking and twisting as its brain misfired. Rogue let the Soldat slip to the ground and watched carefully as it slowly died.

"A drill?" Helm was sour. "Way to improvise, Bag."

"First thing that came to hand," said the backpack biochip.

"Quiet, both of you." Rogue removed the tool with a pop of wet flesh and then recovered his combat knife. He gave the G-Soldat a brief once-over, then made a couple of quick, deep cuts that severed the Nort's main arteries in its neck. In seconds, G-Soldat NG/442-Sigma had ceased to function, lying in shallow pool of its own synthetic blood.

G-Soldat NG/181-Beta smelled the death scent of its teammate on the cold air and stiffened, the tactical effects of Sigma's killing racing through its brain. The wound on its torso was severe but not crippling. In Beta's regimented mindset, it saw the burnt skin and organ damage like a checklist of plus and minus points: kidney impaired, blood loss increasing, epidermal integrity lost.

The G-Soldat's fight or flight reflex kicked in. The balance of the skirmish had altered radically in the last few minutes, the disoriented Souther soldiers suddenly gaining not one but two allies from out of nowhere – one of which had terminated Sigma without the use of a firearm. The sporadic laser fire from the second new arrival suggested to Beta that the shooter was inexperienced, but the lucky round that had hit him in the gut said otherwise.

All this, the reasoning and evaluation, raced through the warrior mind in a flash. G-Soldat NG/181-Beta's self-preservation protocols rose to the top; retreat and evade, it decided.

"What is that?" Ruiz asked, aiming his Blowpipe at the blue-skinned figure as it walked carefully down the ridge toward the troopers. "He ain't got no mask!"

Rogue tossed away the smashed fragments of the Mowzer rifle; he'd broken it in two after spotting the gun camera lens on the barrel, the transmitter still active. "Who's in command here?"

Zeke frowned behind his chem-hood. "I'll ask the questions. What's your unit?"

Purcell made a spitting noise. "Hell, Sarge, you know what he is! It's the Rogue, man. The Rogue Trooper." She shook her head. "Skev me. In the flesh!"

"Stay away, you monster!" Johnson had his rifle raised and aimed at the GI. "You're no different from those other ones!" He flicked a look at Zeke. "It'll kill us! Just 'cos the skin's a different colour, that don't mean nothing!"

"Stow it!" Zeke snapped.

"Well, that's gratitude for you," said Bagman.

Rogue stood clear of the soldiers, hands at his sides, doing his best to appear non-threatening. The GI had dealt with twitchy types like these on dozens of occasions and he wasn't about to give them an excuse to start shooting. He inclined his head at the broken church tower. "You were walking right into a sniper snare. I dealt with him."

Zeke eyed the splashes of emerald blood on Rogue's chest. "I can see that. There was another one, though..."

"Got away." Gunnar's voice came through the smoke.

Ferris emerged carrying the rifle and jerked to a halt as Ruiz and Purcell swung their guns to bear in him. "Whoa! Easy there! We're all pals here, okay?" He gave a feeble grin. "Southside? Yeah!"

The confederate rallying cry carried little weight with the soldiers, however. "Who the hell are you?" demanded Ruiz.

"He's with me," Rogue answered. "Gunnar, the other soldat?"

Ruiz's eyes widened as the rifle in Ferris's grip spoke in a disgusted snarl. "Flyboy here messed up my aim. I wounded the Nort, but it cut and ran before I could finish him off."

The Souther soldier blinked. "Dead men talking. Now I seen it all."

"Yeah, we're a real freak show," added Helm.

Johnson mumbled a prayer under his breath. Zeke gave him another hard look, then waved down the soldiers. "I suppose we should thank you."

"Yeah, you should," agreed Bagman. "You'd be ventilated like your friend back there if Rogue hadn't waded in."

The GI crossed over to Ferris and accepted his rifle. "How come you're out this far?"

Zeke shifted uncomfortably. "We got cut off from our unit... Lost the radio. Norts didn't give us time to take a breath and get our bearings."

"That's their way," Rogue nodded. "I'm looking for somewhere called Domain Delta, a Nort base hidden in the zone. You heard of it?"

"Inside the zone?" Purcell tapped her mask thoughtfully. "We did get reports of an enemy convoy passing through recently; couple of Nort atmocraft heading out into the wilds. There's nothing out there, though. Seemed pretty strange."

"Could have been supplies for Delta," said Ferris.

"Maybe." Rogue considered the soldiers for a moment.

"We need to get back to our lines," Zeke insisted. "I imagine you won't be following us, though, what with you being a deserter and all..."

The thinly-veiled insult didn't rankle the GI; he'd heard it too many times. Rogue pointed to the south. "That way.

You start walking now and you'll hit allied turf in a day or so. But you better be ready for more of those Nort G-Soldats and their buddies."

"What do you mean?" said Ruiz, failing to keep the fear from his voice.

"I know their kind," Rogue said without irony. "They're not going to stop hunting you until they got all your scalps. It's how the Norts made them."

"You got a better idea?" asked Purcell. Behind, Ferris saw Zeke's expression harden; suddenly the sergeant's troops were deferring to the GI like he was in charge.

Rogue gave a curt nod. "We play their move against them. Set up a fire zone, let them come in and then waste them all."

"Here?" said Johnson, glancing around nervously.

"No, too open. We'll go deeper into the zone."

Zeke was suddenly aware that the other soldiers were staring at him, waiting for him to agree. He fumed inwardly; he couldn't deny that the Genetic Infantryman knew what he was talking about, but instant erosion of his command irritated the veteran. He sure as hell didn't like taking orders from this blue freak – but if the GI was right, they'd never make it back to safe ground.

"Fine," he said brusquely. "You take point, seeing as you know this plate-glass hellhole better than any of us... But any funny stuff and I'll waste you myself."

Rogue didn't acknowledge the order and started off into the glass. Ferris kept pace with him. "You sure this is a good idea, hooking up with these guys? Can't you just give them a digi-map and let them go?"

"They'd be dead in an hour," Rogue replied flatly. "Besides, you saw those Nort GIs. If they're being deployed in the Quartz Zone, then they've gotta have a base nearby."

"You think you could get a live one?"

The clone soldier's eyes narrowed. "We'll see. For now, it's the best lead I got."

Ferris was silent for a moment before speaking. "You're using those dogfaces as bait. What if they're not up to it?"

Rogue gave him a sideways glance but did not answer.

EIGHT
FIRE MISSION

As the elevator rose through the levels of Domain Delta, Kapten Volks nervously brushed stray hair out of his eyes and flicked a tiny speck of lint from the front of his uniform. The hour was late; he had been completing a triple-check of the perimeter sensors in the test range west of the domeplex when the autovox chimed on his communicator.

"Kolonel-Doktor Schrader requests your immediate presence in her chambers," it said. Johann knew from previous experience that such "requests" were not to be taken lightly and returned quickly in a fast fan-jeep. The line troopers and men he passed said nothing as he made his way to the elevator bank. Volks knew that many of them talked about him behind his back, making fun of his liaisons with the director. That bothered the officer; he was afraid that their relationship would erode his authority with the soldiers, making him appear weak in their eyes. Schrader's behaviour towards him did not help the matter. She was frequently critical of him in full view of his subordinates, on some occasions even openly mocking.

Just the thought of it made Volks's jaw clench, his fists tighten. In his darker, more secret moments he wondered what it might be like to strike her, to force the icy bitch to do what *he* said for a change... But then the tiny fantasy of his bravado evaporated as the lift halted and the doors opened at Schrader's personal penthouse at the dome's crown. Volks stepped out into the dimly lit room, the dark of the night through the plastibubble roof casting pools of gloom all around him.

"Reporting as ordered," he said, somewhat redundantly. There was a line of monitor screens glowing in bright actinic hues along a nearby console and one showed the empty interior of the lift. She had been watching him since the moment he entered the dome.

A shadow moved in the dimness and Schrader approached, her ankle-length laboratory coat moving like a cloak around her. She had a digi-pad in one hand and was studying it intently. Volks stifled a gasp as he realised that aside from soft deck shoes, she was nude beneath the lab coat. One glimpse of her lean, strong body made the Kapten's resolve melt and it took a near-physical effort for him to shut away his desire.

She saw the expression on his face and made a show of covering herself up. "Don't stare at me like an addled kadet, Johann. I have something to show you." There was a flash of mischief in her eyes, a certain knowledge of her control over him. "Something *else*." Schrader approached the monitor console and brought up a replay of jumpy vid footage on the largest of the screens.

Volks recognised the coding on the display immediately. "A mission log from the training cadres?" he said. The Nort officer looked to Schrader for confirmation.

She nodded, smiling thinly. "G-Soldat NG/181-Beta and 442-Sigma. Part of the evaluation group set out for live fire sorties."

"Yes, they were sent after that Souther patrol," he said. "They were ordered to track and kill them."

"I changed those priorities," Schrader noted. "I wanted to let the NexGen toy with them a little first." She sighed. "It's important for a good predator to know the pleasure of the hunt before the prey is dispatched."

The Type-K Genetik Soldats – which Schrader had chris- tened the "NexGen" – were the product of two decades of playing catch-up with the Southers in the field of gene

engineering. But they still possessed the flaws of their pre-
decessors, and while the war on Nu Earth had rumbled on,
Domain Delta had been set up to improve Nort bio-science to
a point that would surpass the enemy's advancements. That
had been the dome's mandate, but under Lisle Schrader's
control, what happened in Delta's sealed sub-levels had taken
on a very different purpose. Like everything in the facility, the
G-Soldats were just serving the higher goal that the Kolonel-
Doktor had envisaged, the secret design to which she
ceaselessly worked. Volks felt a weary weight in his chest as
he realised that he was just as much a cog in her infernal
machine as the clone soldiers were.

Schrader was scrolling through the footage from the gun-
camera at high speed. Volks saw flash-fast images of las-bolts
striking Souther troops, figures whipping around and vanishing in churns of splashed red. "G-Soldat NG/442-Sigma was
terminated," she said offhandedly. "A close range melee kill,
it appears."

The Nort officer frowned, confused. The woman's tone
was light, unconcerned. In previous incidents where her precious NexGen had died, she had been positively incandescent
with rage. Moreover, the killing of a Genetik Trooper by a typical Souther was freakishly unlikely. "How could that
happen?" he asked. "Those suds are no match for our G-
units."

"Very true," Schrader demurred. "Soldat Sigma lost its life
to something very different." A new emotion entered her
voice; longing. "Watch."

The gun-camera footage switched to a new view of several
Southers approaching a sniper point, then suddenly the
image went wild, sky and ground flickering around as the
weapon where the camera was mounted flailed around.
Volks got the impression of two muscular shapes wrestling in
the half-light before the view fell away to the dirt. After long
moments, the angle shifted again and a single yellow eye
peered into the lens, followed by a rain of static and the
screen displaying the words: "Signal lost".

"I don't understand. What are we seeing?"

Schrader tutted and used two more screens to display freeze frames from the video. One was the close-up of the yellow eye, the other the two figures. She tapped the first screen. "I ran a comparative ocular scan. This optic does not belong to any of our units or test subjects. The age pattern indicates a far older specimen."

"Another G-Soldat?" said Volks. "Perhaps General Rössa–"

"Ach, you are such a limited thinker, Johann!" she broke in, her irritation rising. "Look here." She tapped a nail on the second screen. "I ran an image transform protocol on this display to clean up the image."

The still picture became washed out as the computer programme artificially added light and shade. Volks watched the two figures gain definition by degrees. One was clearly a Type-K unit, but the other... The other wore a mottled helmet low over his eyes, accenting a grim face locked in angry conflict with the G-Soldat. The helmet bore a circular sigil with the Souther nation's upward facing arrow and two letters.

"GI," Volks read aloud. "Impossible..."

"Is it?" Schrader retorted, barely concealing her eagerness. "The tonal analysis shows a skin coloration variance of more than twenty per cent between 442-Sigma and his killer. Blue skin, Johann! It's *him*."

"Here?" The officer swallowed hard. "Verkammt... The Rogue Trooper."

Schrader's hand strayed to her chest. "I want him. You will assemble a skirmish team of the best G-Soldats from the current crop and go out into the Quartz Zone. Find Rogue and bring him to me."

"Alive?"

She eyed him. "Don't be a fool! Of course! You understand what he's worth to my work? Rogue is the supreme example of a gene-engineered warrior, the toughest of his breed. He's lived through everything that Nu Earth has thrown at him and survived..." Schrader's voice trailed off for a moment. Volks felt unnerved by the sudden change in her manner. He felt as if she were revealing a new side of herself to him and the officer found it disturbing. "He will be most useful for the project," she concluded. "I must possess him."

"As you order, Kolonel-Doktor. But there are... other matters of concern," Volks said tightly.

Schrader's mood changed with the swiftness of a binary switch. "Elucidate. What petty anxieties do you have now?"

"Your dispatch of General Rössa has created unrest among the men. There may be a problem with regard to issues of continued loyalty."

"Loyalty?" she echoed harshly. "If I wanted loyal men, I would breed some." She prodded him with a slender finger. "It is your job to keep the troops in line, Johann, not mine. I expect you to handle your responsibilities with competence, dak?"

He gave a shallow nod. "Dak, Madam Director."

His answer seemed to please her and she smiled slightly. "Just so. Take the search team out at first light and be sure to locate all of the GI's war gear as well. If there are any survivors from that sud patrol, add them to the test inventory."

Volks gave a crisp, parade ground salute and turned to leave, but Schrader caught his arm and held him back. Lit by the cold blue glow of the monitors, she appeared as if her face was sculpted from steel-hard sea ice. "Where are you going?" Schrader said, half-demanding, half-seductive as she let her lab coat fall open. "I have not dismissed you yet."

"I'll say it again," Ferris murmured, "this place gives me the creeps."

Purcell glanced at him and then at the glassy, reflective tree trunks of the petrified forest around them. "Guess I gotta agree with you there."

With Helm plotting a course, Rogue had led them to a part of the Quartz Zone the maps referred to as the "Shard Orchard". The effects of experimental munitions and thermal warheads had turned a dense woodland into a thick stand of ossified trees, their bark transformed into a dull crystalline matter, bristling with sharp slivers of glass. The soldiers moved gingerly through the confines of the orchard, afraid that a single brush against a branch or bole would tear open their suits. The slow, sullen light of a Nu Earth dawn was working its way through the tree line, creeping up on them as the night faded.

Ferris watched Rogue conversing with the terse sergeant, Zeke. The GI seemed utterly unconcerned about the veteran's antipathy toward him as he outlined his scheme for an ambush. Rogue had already had Bagman run up a digi-pad map of the area, posting positions for each of the soldiers to take. With luck, the Nort hunters that followed the escaped Soldat would find themselves drawn into the throat of a lethal crossfire.

Purcell nodded in Rogue's direction. "How'd you hook up with him?"

"Same way as you," the pilot replied. "He pulled my ass out of a fight when I was about to get wasted."

Ruiz looked up from his repair work on the Blowpipe. "We could have handled things."

"Get real," Purcell snapped. "We'd have been sucking chem if Rogue hadn't got that Soldat sniper, you know it as well as I do."

"Huh," Ruiz said. "Rogue, is it? You on first name terms with blue-boy now?"

In a subdued voice, Johnson added, "Not human."

Ruiz didn't seem to notice and smiled at Ferris. "Purcell here, she's got a thing for Special Forces types, ain't ya?"

"Eat glass, you little prick."

He laughed. "Right now, I bet she's thinkin' of what other things about him are 'genetically enhanced'!"

"Maybe... I been around you so long, Ruiz, I forgot what a real man looks like," she replied, then looked back at the GI. "Still, you gotta wonder..."

Johnson made a spitting noise. "How could you even consider such a thing? That creature is an affront to God!"

"Look around," Ruiz said, opening his hands wide to the sky. "This whole skevving planet is an affront!"

The other soldier turned away to clean his rifle, mumbling a prayer under his breath. Purcell gave Ferris a look. "Johnson, he's not what you'd call the most tolerant of people."

"I gathered."

Zeke approached, scowling. "All right, listen up. You saw the map, you know what the fr–" He stopped mid-sentence, looking back at Rogue who stood sentinel on a ridge. "What the Trooper said. Tight aim corridors and fire discipline, people. We draw these Norty buggers in, grease 'em and steal their transport. We're back Southside an hour later."

"Sounds easy," said Ruiz. "It always *sounds* easy."

"Quit bellyachin' and get that launcher ready." Zeke turned on Ferris. "So, what are you good for?"

Ferris frowned. "I'm a pilot," he said lamely, not sure what other answer to give.

"That's no damn use to me," Zeke replied. "Not unless you gotta gunship in your back pocket."

He produced his pistol. "I can hold my own."

The sergeant snorted. "Not with that pop-gun, you can't. Here." Zeke tossed a compact brick of metal and plastic into Ferris's hands. "Autolaser. Just aim it and squeeze the trigger, works just like an old-style machine gun. All you gotta do is make sure there's no friendlies in front of you."

Ferris examined the weapon as if it were a poisonous insect.

"Sarge," said Ruiz. "I volunteer to stand behind the flyboy."

"Yeah, me too," Purcell added, giving Ferris a wan smile. "No offence."

Up on the slight ridge, Rogue studied something through the scope on his rifle. "Nort hopper in the air to the north-west," he said, his voice carrying through the eerie stillness of the glassine glade. "They're coming for us."

Ruiz swore and frantically began to reassemble the Blowpipe.

"Confirmed, residual heat traces located at grid reference L-113 by T-235."

The Nort pilot's voice crackled in Kapten Volks's ear. He frowned behind the full-face hood of his chem-suit, eyes narrowing. "Copy, Air Five. How many targets?"

"Hard to say, sir," the pilot replied. "The zone has unusual properties in this region... The landscape is riddled with fallout and ferro-particle dust."

"Very well. Prepare for an airborne deployment. Circle around and signal when we are on station."

"Aye, Kapten. Thirty seconds to green."

Volks turned away from the vu-port and looked back into the troop bay of the transport hopper. A handful of regular soldiers from the dome garrison were conducting last minute checks of their weapons and chem-gear, some of them swapping ribald comments in gutter Nordsprache. He stood up and grabbed one of the ziplines dangling from the ceiling, fastening it to a connector on his belt. "Stand by for drop deployment!" He snapped out the order, "Lock on!"

The other troopers scrambled to follow his command. At the back of the bay there were four G-Soldats, two pairs of green-skinned warriors sitting opposite one another, immobile and silent. All of them already had the ziplines latched to their gear. They seemed like dark, muscular statues – carved jade idols rather than living, breathing beings.

Volks felt his gut tighten as the hopper came about in a fast, wide turn, shedding speed as it came to a halt over the skeletal crystal trees. An indicator lamp on the cabin wall blinked blue-blue-green and the hopper pilot spoke again. "On station."

"Deploy, deploy, deploy!" shouted Volks, and the floor of the troop bay yawned open beneath his feet. The whole ventral hull of the hopper split and the men on board leapt free, the ziplines singing as the monofilament cables played out behind them. Inertia reels kept the Nort soldiers from dashing themselves against the hard ground, and the cables deposited them gently on the surface.

Volks had done this a thousand times, slapping his gloved palm against the release switch just as his boots touched dirt. The dangling ziplines reeled back into the hopper, spider web filaments hissing through the air. "Set down beyond the search zone and await further orders."

"Air Five complying," came the pilot's voice and the hopper powered away, staying low over the glassy treetops.

The kapten switched comm channels and addressed the men on the ground. "Sweep teams, forward. Watch your suits on those obstacles."

One of the korporals indicated the quartet of G-Soldats. "What about them, sir?"

As the soldier spoke, the Nort GIs exchanged an unspoken communication and moved off into the Shard Orchard without waiting for an order. "Stay out of their way, Korporal."

"Go to ultraviolet," said Rogue, and the view through Gunnar's optics changed to a blue-white palette of images. Furry, ill-defined shapes moved through the solid angles of the crystal growths, edges blurring as they merged and split.

"Still no good," Gunnar replied, the synth from his chip slot a faint electronic whisper. "You're gonna have to rely on eyeballs for this, Rogue."

"Not a problem. Give me standard scope, mag two." The display returned to a normal image and the GI let the view fill his mind.

The shoulder of a Nort appeared for a brief instant. "Come on, Norty..." whispered Bagman. "We got a surprise for you."

"I hear a mess of footfalls and heartbeats on the audio pickup," said Helm. "A whole bunch."

"Not yet," said the GI. His finger rested lightly on Gunnar's trigger and he watched as the enemy soldiers began to emerge from the tree line at the edge of the clearing. He'd chipped off a section of petrified branch from a trunk at the one o'clock position – the idea was that none of Zeke's men would let off a shot until at least two Norts had walked past the tree.

The soldier on point stepped around the marker, unaware that he was under six sets of gunsights. "That's one," murmured Helm.

More Norts appeared, moving in careful formation; like the Southers, they were afraid of snagging their suits. "Rogue," Bagman said quietly. "They're just regulars... No Soldats."

The GI had just come to the same conclusion when the Nort point man's boot broke a piece of fallen glass with a *crack* like a pistol shot.

Purcell heard the noise and pulled the trigger on her laser rifle by reflex.

"No! Skev it!" Rogue growled, but it was too late. The Southers opened up on the Nort sweep team with a punishing exchange of energy fire and the point man was ripped apart, body parts flying in all directions.

A voice on the Nort side shouted something indistinct and the enemy troopers scattered, diving for cover wherever they could find it, firing shots back at their concealed adversaries. Although the ambush had been tripped early, there was still little to favour the Norts and Zeke's unit began a bloody storm of payback for the deaths of Taylor and her squad mates.

Rogue put a trio of rounds into the torso of a Nort with a belt-fed heavy stubber, opening him up from gut to sternum in red-orange blasts of light. Fat ballistic shells from the enemy trooper's gun went wild as he collapsed, chewing out chunks of glass from the crystal trees around him. The broken shards were tiny jewelled shuriken that hissed through the air.

Ferris fumbled with the safety catch on the boxy auto-laser, squeezing the trigger without success. A Nort saw him and charged, the stiletto bayonet on his assault rifle lancing toward his head. A switch clicked beneath Ferris's gloved fingers and the autolaser went hot in his grip. The pilot savagely yanked the firing bar and a fusillade of beam shots spat from the weapon. They were high, too high to strike the Nort's chest and vitals, but not too far that they couldn't remove the top of his skull. The soldier died instantly, collapsing out of his run into a ragged, bleeding heap as if his spine had suddenly turned to water.

"Pour it on!" Zeke demanded. "Don't let them regroup!"

Ruiz held his Blowpipe launcher close to his cheek plate and pumped the firing button; there was a split-second pause, just enough for him to start wondering if he had reassembled the weapon correctly, but then the electric ignition caught and the tube cannon shot its load with a flat thump of compressed air. One hundred tungsten carbide needles, each one the length and diameter of a man's finger, spiralled out of the muzzle on spin-stabilised microfins. Many of the bolts impacted in the glassy trees and lodged in their cracked surfaces, but dozens more tore straight through chem-suit material, through armour and into the soft meat they protected.

"Spike you, Norts!" Ruiz bellowed, opening the Blow-pipe's barrel; the gun was usually a two-man weapon, one firing and one loading, but Ruiz's team mate Eastman had been killed in the very first attack by the G-Soldats. He caught sight of Johnson, pressed up against the bole of a broken tree, rocking back and forth. Las-fire cut bright streaks through the air around him, leaving purple stains on Ruiz's retina.

"Johnson!" he called. "Quit that skev and shoot back! Cover the flank!"

The other Souther didn't seem to hear him, the blank look in his eyes speaking volumes. Ruiz called into his throat mic. "Sarge! Johnson's lost it!"

Elsewhere, Rogue heard the soldier's angry words. "What the hell? We have to keep the pressure up from all points or this ambush will fall apart!"

"Pink meat, nothing but weak through and through!" Gunnar said sourly.

"Forget that," Bagman broke in. "I got a twitch from the lateral sonic track – there's someone else out there aside from the Norts..."

Rogue reloaded quickly, slamming a fresh GP magazine into his rifle. "Where?"

"Close!" Bagman replied. "Real close!"

The ear-splitting reports from the guns were like nails boring into Johnson's head, each one hammering pain into him. He bit down on his own lip so hard that he could taste blood, warm and metallic. The Souther felt the shakes coming on him again and this time there was little he could do to resist them. His suit air was foul with chemicals and urine and each breath was like razors against his ribs.

None of the other men had seen the small rip in his chem-suit, the thumb-sized tear he'd taken when the Soldats first appeared. In a panic he had injured himself and by the time he had managed to press a patch to the damage, his lungs had been made vulnerable to Nu Earth's stinking atmosphere; it began to eat away at his body and internal organs. At first, Johnson had thought he would be all right – there had been no immediate effects, so perhaps he had only taken a small dose – but then little by little his mind had begun to fog and he realised that it was no simple poison that had entered his bloodstream. The miasma of psychogen gas shredded the last pieces of reason in

Johnson's mind and drove him over the edge. He looked and saw nothing but men with blue and green skin around him, their clawed fingers reaching for his face.

Johnson screamed and bolted from his cover, the rifle in his hand spitting laser fire in every direction. Beams skipped off the boles of glass trees and hit reflective surfaces, bouncing them back and forth in a web of deadly fire.

Ruiz caught a rebound in the shoulder, burning a tight hole through his forearm. The Blowpipe fell from his hands, still unloaded, and the Souther was punched back by the shock of the blast it. Breathing in laboured gasps, Ruiz tried desperately to reseal his suit.

Beam fire from Johnson's maddened attack struck Nort and Souther alike, ripping into Volks's sweeper teams with wild abandon. Nort soldiers flailed as they were hit, guns discharging and adding more random rounds to the lattice of laser shots cutting back and forth over the clearing. Johnson took a glancing hit but kept on running, fuelled by madness and an overload of adrenaline.

"He'll kill us all!" Ferris shouted, and Rogue knew instantly that he had no other option.

The GI swung the rifle around and took a snap-shot at Johnson's head; the engineered reflexes of twenty plus years of Souther innovation enabled him to kill the maddened trooper with a single bolt through the back of his skull. Johnson's pain ended as his cerebral cortex vaporised.

"Rogue!" It was Ferris's voice again and the warning tone turned the GI on his heel as dark hulks came racing through the trees toward him. Four G-Soldats, each armed with a powerful electrostunner, launched themselves at the Rogue Trooper in a concentrated attack. The GI had no time to bring Gunnar to bear; he simply dodged, marshalling every last flicker of energy in his muscles. The closest Soldat – each was the mirror of the others – punched out with the stunner and struck empty air where the GI had been a split-second before. Rogue extended away and delivered a sharp blow to the first Nort's neck with the broad butt of Gunnar's stock, getting a high-pitched snap of breaking cartilage in return.

Seamlessly, he turned the pivot toward the first Soldat into a spin kick, his leg coming up to strike the next clone soldier in the gut, staggering him backwards. The third Soldat grabbed at him as he passed, missing the chance to pull him into a bear hug. Experience and speed were paying dividends against the brute force of the G-Soldats, but the fourth had held back a moment to gauge his enemy.

It now lunged with the rod-like stunner, hot sparks spitting from the tip. They wanted to take the GI alive. Rogue saw the blow coming, telegraphed by the bunching of the Nort's muscles under his webbing vest. He tried to step sideways, but his opponent feinted, then slammed the stunner into his chest.

Rogue yelled as a burst of high voltage tore into him and by reflex he brought Gunnar up in an arc. The biochip in the rifle unloaded a point-blank shot into the Soldat's torso, punching a huge burst of superheated flesh from its back. The corpse of the Nort GI dropped away, but Rogue stumbled, the effect of the stun bolt screaming in his ears.

The Soldat with the broken neck was still in the fight and from its fallen position, it snagged Rogue's ankle and pulled. The GI, already off-balance, dropped to his knees.

Automatically, Rogue forced himself up from the dull, glassine earth, but two electro-stunners were there to meet him, and they fell in a rain of punches and blows, flaring blue lightning numbing nerves and propelling him towards the blackness of unconsciousness.

Against one NexGen G-Soldat, Rogue would win; the odds lengthened with two, but his superlative skills gave him an edge over the vat-grown Nort clones; but three...

Three would tip the balance. Three, four even, and the Rogue Trooper would not survive.

Someone shouted his name from very far away. It sounded like a ghost out there, a ghost from a place made of glass and razors, a place deep down in the core of his memories.

NINE
DOMAIN DELTA

Pain brought Rogue back from the blood-warm darkness, dragging him up from the depths of unconsciousness like a hook to his heart. The GI's head lolled backwards and forwards as a fierce windstorm tore over his bare skin, the rough abrasive fines of the atmosphere burning with friction. He tried to open his eyes; one was swollen shut.

His body was a map of agony, islands of bruising across his chest and torso tightening the plastiflesh into knots. His arms were above his head, the wrists secured together in manacles, his entire weight hanging on them. Rogue tried to focus. There was nothing beneath his feet but a blurry carpet of shiny grey, shifting and moving. He looked up, ignoring the pain from the bones in his neck and saw where the manacles were strapped to cables trailing off the side of a bullet-shaped hopper. With a sudden lurch of understanding, Rogue realised where he was.

The Norts had captured him, Ferris and the other Southers, and hung them like the corpses of hunted animals from the skids of the flyer. The hopper was moving quickly, the wind buffeting and turning the prisoners as it flew on. Rogue glimpsed Ferris's limp body flapping like a loose flag from the opposite skid; he couldn't tell if the pilot was alive or dead.

The razor-edged wind changed direction as the Nort ship turned and Rogue's head bounced off the landing ski. He was without his gear, Gunnar, Bagman and Helm either destroyed or secured somewhere inside the flyer. The latter was more likely, he decided; if the Norts had gone to all the trouble of taking him intact, they would want the biochips of his fellow GIs and the storehouse of special technology his war gear represented.

Rogue gave his knees an experimental flex and was rewarded by fresh jolts of pain from his joints. He let out a bark of annoyance and the wind tore it from his lips. A plan was forming in his mind, something desperate and daring.

The landscape below him was changing; the flat glass expanse of the Quartz Zone proper was thinning out and beneath his feet Rogue saw a wide natural arena marred by old bomb craters, the wrecks of meks and scar-lines of trenches. The formations of the decrepit barricades and broken pieces of cover seemed uncoordinated, built without any single defensive purpose – but then it came to him. He was looking at a firing range, or some sort of training ground, not an actual fortification.

The real thing emerged from the low mists beyond the open canyon. Camouflaged in the same drab shade of old, burnt bone as the Quartz Zone itself, the dome rose like a shallow mountain. Rogue remembered the Nort prison camp Glasshouse-G; this was a similar construction, a huge sealed bubble of thick armourplas fortified with spars of steel. Rings of automatic guns and manned missile pods girdled the hemisphere, open muzzles turned to the sky. There were smaller satellite bubbles arranged around the perimeter and one face presented a flat ferrocrete landing dock with hopper pads and gunships on launch cradles. A low-visibility grey-on-grey version of the Nordland Forces emblem dominated one face of the dome, next to a thick black triangle that designated the building's identity; the Greek symbol for *delta*.

The GI grimaced; this wasn't how he'd wanted to arrive at the Nort bio-lab. He flicked a glance at the ground below. How high were they? Above tree top level, perhaps a couple of hundred metres – certainly nowhere near a survivable fall, even for him. Rogue exercised the muscles in his arms and made ready, and when the flyer changed tack again, he used the gusts of wind to help him.

With a flick of his legs, Rogue swung his weight back then forward in a snapping movement. With a speed and grace that belied his broad form, the GI reversed his position and wrapped his ankles around the undercarriage of the hopper. Only a simple latch secured the manacles around his wrists and after a hard twist they came free. With his hands still pressed together, Rogue's options were limited, but he had never let that stop him before. He pulled himself up onto the skid and caught sight of sudden movement through the hopper's vu-port – the Norts inside had seen him and they knew what he was going to do.

He had seconds; the hopper dipped sharply toward the pads, desperate to make a landing before Rogue could reach the cockpit. The GI scrambled across the hull and slammed his hands, manacles and all, down on the canopy. The impact cracked the plastic and inside the Nort pilot reacted with sudden violence. Stamping down on the rudder, the pilot made the hopper tilt wildly to one side and Rogue felt his balance flee. He lost his grip on the hopper's fuselage and there was a sudden, stomach-churning moment of freefall. He dropped away from the ugly little aircraft, spinning and turning with an automatic feline grace.

Rogue fell to the landing pad and hit hard, the shock making his feet skip off the ferrocrete, throwing him to the ground. Every instinct in him screamed to get back up, to run or fight, but the concussion echoed through his bones, hobbling him. He forced himself to a slump-shouldered stance as the hopper landed close by. Norts boiled out of an airlock, rifles at the ready. With angry acceptance, Rogue realised that at least for now, there was nowhere he could run to.

A figure in a Nort Kolonel's chem-suit – a woman judging by the kinetics of her stride – emerged from the knot of soldiers and studied him carefully. Rogue could only see the blank eyes through the goggles of the Nort suit and the predatory glimmer in them made his innate danger sense ring like a struck bell. Even though he was under the muzzles of dozens of enemy guns, Rogue knew instantly that she was the most serious threat on the pad. He recognised distinctive rank flashes on her epaulettes, the snarling winged snake of the Nordland Special Medical Korps.

"Even on your enemy's doorstep you attempt escape. Always the soldier," said Schrader, unable to take her eyes off the GI. "I expected nothing less."

Favouring his bruised side, Rogue at last drew himself to his full height. "Glad I didn't disappoint you."

"Bio-subject GI: 3627218/R2," she said, using Rogue's batch code identity number. There was a smile in her voice. "Welcome to Domain Delta. I have waited so long to meet you."

On the pad, the G-Soldats unhooked the rest of the prisoners and dragged them into a ragged line. Rogue saw Ferris stumble, but keep his balance. For now, at least, the civilian was still breathing. Volks approached with the hopper pilot and a line trooper at his side.

"Your report, Kapten Volks?" she demanded.

Volks gestured at the GI. "Success, as you can see, Kolonel-Doktor Schrader. We lost a number of men and a single G-Soldat unit."

"That was to be expected," the woman said with a nod. "Have the corpse taken to Lab Six for organ harvest." She looked at the pilot. "You. Explain what you were doing just before you landed."

The Nort pilot hesitated; he hadn't expected to be addressed. "Uh, Kolonel-Doktor, I was just... uh... That is, I was attempting to defend the hopper from the GI−"

Schrader silenced him with a dismissive wave. "You understand the worth of this prisoner, yes?" She pointed at Rogue. "His value to me greatly exceeds yours, or your aircraft. You could have killed him."

"Kolonel Schrader, I–" the pilot turned to indicate the hopper so he did not see the shot that ended his life, as Schrader drew her pistol and put a round through the back of his skull.

"I will have discipline from my subordinates," she said, in a flat voice that carried across the landing pad. "My tolerance of incompetence only stretches so far."

Rogue watched the events unfold, his expression neutral even as he took in every motion and impression from the Norts around him. The woman looked at him again and the GI heard Zero's words ringing in his mind. "You have to stop her…" In that moment, he had absolutely no doubt that Schrader was who his dead comrade had been describing.

"Process the prisoners," she was saying, "and take Rogue to holding room three. Have someone clean up that mess." Schrader turned and walked back to the airlock.

Volks gave the GI a hard shove and brandished his pistol in Rogue's face, irritation flaring in his voice. "Move it, blueskin."

Rogue saw an opening and decided to probe it. "Easy there, Norty. You heard her, the kolonel won't like it if I get damaged…"

"Move!" Volks snarled. "I won't tell you again!"

There was an undercurrent of tension between the kapten and the kolonel; it was clear as day to Rogue's keen eye. He had been trained to watch for weaknesses in the enemy, equally able to spot a deficient piece of plating on an armoured vehicle as he was to see a psychological flaw in a human being. The GI filed this piece of information away, keeping it safe for the moment when he would be able to exploit it.

He saw Ferris and the other Southers vanish through a broad loading hatch in the deck and with them, a cargo lifter carrying a dead Soldat and Rogue's GI equipment. Volks forced him through a different airlock and into the depths of the bubble dome.

. . .

The floor of the steri-shower was cold under Ferris's bare feet and he hugged himself to keep warm. The Norts stripped them all at gun point, bundling their chem-suits into a pile and feeding their fatigue undergarments through a vat of de-chem solution; from there they were shoved into an ultraviolet chamber that blasted them with a flash of radiation. Ferris covered his face with his hands, but the blurry after-light still dazzled his vision. Everyone stood shivering and red raw, as if they'd been frost-bitten.

Ferris choked out a cough and glanced at Purcell. She saw him looking and turned to face him full on. "Take a good look, flyboy. This is the last piece of ass any of you dinks is going to see."

He ignored the comment. "Ruiz is hurt."

Purcell took the soldier's arm, examining the laser wound. The shot had cauterised the injury, but the flesh was still swollen and livid with colour. "You need a medi-pack on this, pal," she said.

"Yeah," Ruiz bit out the words though chattering teeth. "I'll ask Norty for one along with the wine list and a silk cushion for your fat ass."

"Quiet!" snapped a guard through a grille on the wall. "No talking!"

Purcell was going to add something sarcastic, but a jet of acrid water blasted them from the nozzles set in the walls of the decontamination shower. Ferris stumbled and almost fell over under the punishing deluge.

After several seconds, the chamber door opened. "Out!" ordered the Nort. "Get dressed!"

They did as they were told, each of them silent and sullen, the dehumanising effect of the cleansing regimen beating down their spirits. More guards were waiting for them, bored looking men with the tattoos and top-knots of the Nordland infantry cadres. The largest of them, a Nort with a face like a clenched fist, gave Purcell an appraising look. "Plenty of meat on this one."

"Skev you, needle dick," she replied with a snort.

The Nort laughed off the insult. "Always the same with you Suds, all full of yourselves when you come through the gate." He smiled, and it was an ugly sight. "Just wait a while and you'll change your mind. Once you see what the ice queen's got planned for you, you'll beg to be my little doggie." The soldiers marched them down into the dome, through ranks of cage-like cells. "She likes to have live ones, dak?" said the guard in a languid voice. "Tries out her new toxins on you." He shook his head in mock concern. "It's a very poor way to die."

"I'm a civilian!" Ferris blurted out, his nerve breaking. "You can't do this to me, it's against the War Compact!"

Zeke gave him a hard look. "You ain't got no rights here, kid," he said grimly. "None of us have."

The holding chamber resembled a cross between an interrogation cell and a medical examination room, with a table and chairs mounted on retractable rods and a spidery device in the ceiling that concealed arms ending in probes and las-scalpels. A cluster of sensors above the door tracked Rogue's movement as he examined the perimeter of the room, looking for anything that might be useful as an escape tool. Schrader had obviously prepared Volks for him. On the way in, the kapten covered the GI's head with a hood that masked all sound and vision, leaving Rogue with only his sense of direction to map the route that had taken him from the airlock to the room. If the opportunity arose, he would be able to flawlessly back-track, but he doubted that the kolonel would allow him the chance – not after his failed attempt to flee on the landing pad. The GI contented himself by shifting to a passive mode; he was gathering information with every passing second, assembling it into a framework that he could manipulate.

In fact, escape was a secondary consideration to him now; the Genetic Infantryman was exactly where he wanted to be, deep in the heart of Domain Delta. It was only the manner of his arrival that was problematic. His circuit of the room complete, he considered the spider-mek in the ceiling; any one of its limbs might serve him well as a makeshift weapon, but that was a card he didn't want to play just yet. He sat and waited. The next move was Schrader's.

She did not disappoint; little time passed before the woman entered the room with Volks and a hovering orb-drone.

The robot drifted toward him and Rogue eyed the fan of needles in the machine's manipulators.

"I'm not going to torture you," Schrader said, anticipating his thoughts. She gave a mirthless smile and sat opposite him. "The droid will give you something for your injuries."

"I'll heal just fine on my own," said Rogue.

"I insist." Her smile froze and Volks let his hand drop to the gun in his hip holster.

The GI said nothing and let the robot do its job; with quick, insectile movements, it shot a stimulant-biotic cocktail into his bloodstream and then applied a salve to his swollen eye. It didn't escape Rogue's notice that the machine also took a blood sample and a skin scraping. Once it was finished, the drone floated away and out of the door.

"Now then," Schrader began, "here we are." Her scrutiny made Rogue feel like something on a microscope slide. "I'm very pleased to finally meet you, Trooper. I've studied your career with great interest." She produced a sheaf of digi-pads and document files. Rogue saw indistinct reproductions of Souther paperwork among them, no doubt the copies made by some backroom spy concealed in Milli-Com. "I'm going to enjoy working with you."

He nodded at the papers. "Would you like an auto-graph?"

The woman's face twitched in a poor approximation of a smirk which spoke volumes to Rogue. Schrader was some-one to whom emotion was a dislocated concept, a cold personality that exhibited responses only because it was expected of her. He glanced at Volks, wondering about their relationship.

"How about you?" Rogue addressed the officer. "Are you a fan of mine as well?" He nodded in the direction of Volks's rank tabs. "Kashar Legion, right? Maybe we met before, out in the Zone?"

"Speak to me, not to him!" Schrader snapped, and Rogue smiled inwardly. Good, a flash of the Kolonel-Doktor's real self. Obviously, there were some things that would get a rise from her. Schrader's voice returned to a conversational tone once more. "We have to discuss your future, Rogue."

He flexed his hands absently in the cuffs around his wrists. "Becoming one of your lab rats isn't on my agenda, Schrader. I know what you're doing here."

She shook her head. "I don't think you do, but don't worry, I'll tell you all you want to know in good time. No, I have an offer for you, Rogue. An opportunity."

"And what would that be?"

Schrader leaned a little closer. "Help me end the war, Rogue. Once and for all."

The GI's face twisted in a sneer. "I'll die before I see a Nort flag rise over this planet."

"Nort, Souther..." she shook her head. "I don't care about nations! Just lines on a map, names for fools who send others to their deaths. I said 'end the war', Rogue, not win it. Neither side deserves to take Nu Earth for themselves, they've done nothing but squander life and turn this world into a charnel house. The time has come for a new order to be created."

"With you in charge?"

Schrader's gaze was hard and intense. "I am the visionary, Rogue, but you..." She reached out a hand and touched him. "You are the catalyst."

Something about the look in her eyes revolted him and the GI drew back from her. "Yeah, well let me know how it goes with that."

The woman smiled again. "Of course you have your doubts. I would not have expected otherwise... But I can offer you something in return."

Questions were churning inside Rogue's mind like a hurricane: questions about Zero, about the Traitor General, the Quartz Zone. "I don't think so," he said.

She tapped a slender finger on a bio-schematic of a G-Soldat. "You've seen my creations first-hand, you know they're vastly superior to anything Clavel or the Southers created–"

"Not so superior that I couldn't kill two of them without breaking a sweat," Rogue interposed.

Schrader continued, ignoring the interruption. "There are new crops in the tubes as we speak. Your comrades entombed on those pathetic slivers of silicon, I can give them life again. Do you really believe that Milli-Com will regen them when you finally turn yourself in? They'll be erased, cancelled like the rest of the GI programme." Her eyes flashed. "I can make them whole again!"

"No one's going to collaborate with you, Schrader," he replied, a little too quickly. Rogue hid his thoughts with a scowl; in truth, he couldn't be sure that Gunnar, Helm and Bagman wouldn't be swayed by the offer of a new life after an eternity of artificial non-existence.

"I think you will, Rogue." The scientist nodded to herself, a chilly certainty crossing her pale features. "Because only I can provide you with the single thing that drives you, the object of your quest..." Schrader selected a digipad and pressed the activation stud; on the screen the faces of four men scrolled past in quick succession. Each was a Souther general, one of a contingent of officers stationed aboard the Milli-Sat known as Buzzard Three – and one of them was the traitor who had caused the destruction of the GI platoons at the Quartz Zone drop.

Rogue's expression turned to stone as he remembered his showdown with the men on Buzzard Three, the attack that had destroyed the station and the flight back to Nu

Earth in a sabotaged escape pod. Only one other lifeboat had made it down – and on board, the man he knew as the Traitor General.

Schrader saw a change in the GI and knew she had put the hook in him. She touched another switch on the digi-pad and a voice, thick with distortion and static, spoke in low, urgent tones. "Buzzard Three agent-in-place, debrief session nine. Subject, Souther Special Programme two-two-eight. It is my opinion that the development of the Genetic Infantrymen is the single largest threat to the Nort domination of Nu Earth–"

She silenced the playback. "The voice of your Traitor, Rogue, from my data files. His intelligence on the creation of your kind was quite extensive." The four faces continued to flicker across the screen. "Which one is it? That's the question. You've stared at these faces for hours, haven't you? Searching their eyes for some glimmer, some clue that could reveal which of them was your betrayer... I can give you that knowledge. I can tell you where to find him." Schrader's voice dropped to a hiss. "I can give you justice!"

"You're lying."

Schrader shrugged. "He's a traitor, worthless to your side and to the Norts. His life is a pitiful price to pay for your goodwill, Trooper."

Rogue's eyes never left the digi-pad. After a long silence, he asked, "What do you want from me?"

The kolonel-doktor's milk-white face blushed with genuine excitement. "All in good time, Rogue. I need you to rest first. I want you fit and well."

"What about my buddies?"

"They're being held in the armoury," she replied, then tapped a communicator tab on her collar. The door slid soundlessly open to reveal a pair of Nort troopers. "These men will take you to your quarters. You will be monitored, so please do not attempt anything rash."

Rogue said nothing and followed the guards.

When the door sealed behind him, Volks turned to the scientist. "This is a dangerous game, Lisle. If the GI suspects you are misleading him, he'll kill you."

"You will address me by my rank or as madam director, Kapten Volks," she said without pause, "and while your juvenile concern is touching, it is misplaced. The identity of the Traitor is only the lure that will bring Rogue closer to me." Schrader licked her thin, blood-red lips. "He'll understand soon enough. You all will. I'm going to change the face of Nu Earth forever."

As he walked, Rogue mentally ticked off his checklist of observations about Kolonel Schrader's personality; she was insane. He could see it in the motions of her eyes, the shallowness of her character, voice and manner. The icy heart of a sociopath beat in the scientist's chest and the GI knew that she wouldn't hesitate to burn him or anything else to get what she wanted. He needed to get off the defensive, and fast – but he couldn't do it alone.

The two guards hustled him into a cylindrical elevator. With a slight jolt, the lift began a quick ascent. Rogue glanced up; in the middle of the elevator roof was an unblinking camera eye.

He waited until the lift had passed the second level and then hit out, fast as lightning. With his manacled hands he punched into the camera and shattered the mechanism inside; at the same instant he kicked with his leg, breaking the knee of the Nort to his left. The first guard was still falling as his elbow came down and shattered the other trooper's nose. Wet crimson exploded from his nostrils and he yelled.

Rogue was on him, forcing the manacles into the soft meat of his throat. There was a sickening crack of breaking bone and the Nort died choking on his own blood. The GI turned in place; hand-to-hand combat inside the confined elevator was an exercise in the controlled application of force. He flicked the emergency stop switch and the lift ground to a halt just shy of the third level. The Nort with the smashed leg tried to prop himself up on his rifle and failed, slipping to the floor. Rogue took a handful of the Nort's chem-suit and hauled him up, bouncing the soldier off the wall. The guard landed a couple of hard punches to Rogue's ribcage, but the GI shrugged them off. With the economical motions of a thousand combat kills, Rogue hit the Nort again and he went limp in his hands, dangling like a rag doll.

His guardians dealt with, Rogue reached up to the hatch in the elevator roof and tore it open. Above him, the lift shaft extended away to the upper floors.

TEN
TURNCOAT

The guards had their weapons trained on the doors as the elevator arrived, the emergency override automatically returning it to the lower levels. The body of a trooper toppled forward and landed in a heap and from inside a second figure in Nort battle gear gave a weak wave.

"The hatch..." he coughed. "The blue-skin went up through the hatch..."

"Verkammt!" swore the korporal in charge of the unit. "Get to the upper tiers, seal off the shaft!" His men, used to following his orders without question, broke apart into two-man teams and headed to their assigned positions. The soldier glanced at the injured man. "Are you all right, comrade?"

"Dak..." wheezed the trooper. "I'll be fine." He got to his feet and pushed past the korporal and into the corridor.

The other soldier accepted this with a nod and then climbed into the elevator, using his rifle's torch to illuminate the shaft. Higher up, he could see a vent cover torn open and a shadowy shape in the dimness. Someone was up there. The korporal began to climb and called back over his shoulder. "You there! Come with me!"

The guard from the lift didn't acknowledge him and continued to walk away. It was then that the korporal realised the other Nort trooper was wearing his chem-suit hood up.

He should have recalled his men. He should have approached the figure with backup; instead he strode over to the guard and spun him around. "I gave you an order–"

The korporal's words died in his throat as he matched gazes with the reptilian yellow eyes staring out at him from the goggles of the full-face hood. "GI!"

"Mistake," replied Rogue, and buried a stolen vibro-dagger in the Nort's chest. He held the korporal towards him in a deadly embrace, watching life leave the soldier's eyes. Acting quickly, Rogue recovered the knife and threw the Nort's corpse into the elevator along with the dead guard. He glanced up through the vent in the roof; he wouldn't have long before the Norts who were searching the levels above discovered the body of the second guard stuffed into one of the vent shafts. Sealing the lift door shut, he turned on his heel and made his way toward the armoury.

The voice was muffled as it came through the heavy hatch. "There's been a prisoner breakout on this level! The Genetik Infantryman is loose!"

Master Sergeant Kolt gave his subordinate Lars a sharp look. "The equipment!" he snapped. Kolt raced over to the holding area where the GI-issue helmet, rifle and backpack were lying. "He might try and recover his gear–"

Kolt turned and saw Lars keying in the code to open the hatch. "What are you doing? He didn't give the password!"

Lars had the door half-open before he realised his error, but by then it was too late. He tried to slide the heavy hatch back, but a muscular arm shot through the gap and grabbed a handful of his tunic. Lars was pulled straight into the doorframe with a bone-jarring impact. Rogue curled his thick fingers around the edges of the hatch and pushed, his enhanced musculature widening the gap against the whine of the automatic servos. The GI dived into the armoury, tucking and rolling; behind him, the hatch slammed shut and resealed.

He barely had a moment to get his bearings before a laser bolt skipped off the floor near his head. Rogue scrambled into cover behind a cluster of ammunition cases.

Kolt yelled out across the room. "Lars! Lars! Are you all right?"

"He's out for the count, Nort," Rogue replied, glancing at the unconscious trooper. "Just you and me."

"Good!" snapped the sergeant and fired again. "I won't have to share the kill, then!"

Rogue weighed the vibro-dagger in his hand; he'd have to get closer if he wanted to use it. But there was something that rang a wrong note in his mind, something familiar about the report of the gun that the Nort was using. He chanced a quick look over the top of the crates and glimpsed the sergeant sweeping the room with a GI rifle in his hand.

"Come on!" Kolt said, as if he sensed Rogue's scrutiny. "I'll take you down with your own weapon!"

"Gunnar!" shouted Rogue. "Trigger lock!" The GI leapt from his cover and sprinted through the lines of gun racks.

But Kolt didn't react; he drew a bead and – impossibly – fired again. Rogue saw it coming and twisted aside behind a cargo pod, but he was too slow to avoid a glancing burn as the beam lanced over his shoulder. The Nort swore and he heard him shifting position.

Rogue examined his injury. Could the Norts have done something to his weapon? The command to the biochip in his rifle should have automatically engaged a safety catch that only he could override, but that clearly wasn't working. "Gunnar! Helm! Bagman! Sound off!" he called out. No reply came in return.

"Not so cocky now are you, gene-freak?" said Kolt. "You know, this is a nice gun. Too good for the likes of a blue-skin. I think I might keep it."

Rogue said nothing, listening to the Nort's voice, trying to pinpoint where he was standing. Silently, he ran his fingers over the equipment cases in the cargo pod, looking for anything he could use. He had to move quickly;

although the gunfire wouldn't carry through the armoury's soundproofed walls, it wouldn't take Volks long to figure out where Rogue had gone.

"Nothing to say? No matter, I can still find you." Kolt raised the rifle to his face and squinted down the target scope. With a flick of his finger, the Nort switched through the sight's vision modes. "You can't hide from eyes that see in the dark..."

The GI's hands closed around a rod-shaped device and he gave a cool smile.

Kolt swept the gun over Rogue's position and saw the faint trace of warm flesh; even though the Genetic Infantryman's engineered skin was designed to give off an extremely low heat signature, at this close a range it was still enough to target him. "Now I see you!" the sergeant grinned.

"Now you don't," Rogue snapped and threw the rod into the air; it burst into a brilliant glare of orange light. The signal flare alone would have been enough to flash-blind a man, but peering through the enhanced infrared scope on the rifle made Kolt's eye burn with a sudden, terrible agony. The Nort clawed at his face and reeled away.

The nictitating membranes over Rogue's eyeballs protected him and he easily disarmed the sergeant, clubbing the flailing Nort unconscious with the rifle. "Mine, I think." The GI flipped over the weapon and his blood ran cold; the reason for Gunnar's failure to obey his order became clear. The chip slot on the rifle was empty.

He felt tightness in his throat. The air in the armoury seemed to be getting thinner. Ignoring the sensation, he scrambled to the rostrum where his helmet and backpack were secured. Both Helm and Bagman's dog-chips were missing from their slots as well.

"What the hell?" Rogue wheezed. He was finding it hard to breathe and his vision was fogging. The air! He strained to listen and heard a faint hiss of escaping atmosphere. Volks had found him, but instead of sending in more men, the kapten had sealed off the armoury and evacuated the air. Rogue fumbled at his backpack. "Need... oxy-bottle..." he said aloud, but without a biochip in the pack's slot, the manipulator arm remained inert.

The GI opened the pack, but his sight was now turning grey, tunnelling. Reasoning became difficult, each thought as slow and heavy as a glacier. Every movement of his lungs seemed like a colossal effort; Rogue's kind could breathe anything in the mess of poisons that made up Nu Earth's atmosphere, but he still needed some amount of air to survive. He fumbled through lazooka shells, aerosol canisters, chem-tone tubes, his desperation increasing. "Can't... Bagman, help..."

Rogue collapsed, dragging the backpack off the stand as he fell. The contents spilled out across the armoury floor in a confused scatter, the emergency oxygen cylinder rolling to a halt close to his outstretched hand, too late to save him from oblivion.

Kolonel-Doktor Schrader entered the command centre and the duty officers parted before her automatically, like flights of birds startled from trees. She didn't spare any of them a glance; until they had some purpose to fulfil, they were beneath her notice. In the middle of the circular room, Kapten Volks stood on the observation dais, elevated above the duty stations so that he could keep a watch on all of them. He came to attention as she approached.

"Madam Director, I apologise for disturbing you at this early hour."

She silenced him with a glare; Schrader had been awake since well before the dawn, unable to sleep, eager with the possibilities that her new acquisition represented. "I have been reviewing the GI's bio-sample results. Most interesting."

"Indeed." Volks had taken the opportunity to let Schrader's tek-droids perform a number of other "examinations" while Rogue was unconscious, before placing the clone in a secure holding cell guarded by a las-web. "Has he recovered?"

Schrader nodded. "How many Nort soldiers do you think he has killed since they decanted him, Johann? Hundreds? Thousands? He's a fascinating specimen."

Volks looked away. "Was it necessary to let him run loose through the facility? He could have done anything..."

"Don't second guess me, Kapten," she replied. "I understand the mindset of these gene-troopers better than you ever will." Schrader nodded to herself. "I must break him, do you see? He must come to understand that I alone control his fate. When he does, Rogue will give me his loyalty willingly." She paused. "He's down there in his cell, unable to think of anything else but what has happened to his biochip comrades."

Volks glanced up at a monitor screen displaying the interior of Rogue's cell. The GI was carefully performing a series of unarmed combat exercises, swift katas blending the most lethal elements of a dozen martial arts. He seemed none the worse for wear after his asphyxiation a day earlier.

"The Southers programmed that into him," Schrader continued. "Loyalty to his fellows, obedience to authority, the need to protect the innocent..."

In spite of himself, Volks gave a low snort of derision. "He doesn't seem that obedient to me. He's a deserter, after all."

"Only because his morals have given him a higher dictate to adhere to. I'm going to use that to my advantage." She turned away from the monitor, the ardour for her pet project cooling. "I hope you did not summon me here to hear more of your trivial worries, Johann."

Volks let the insult pass and indicated the main screen. A sector map of the Quartz Zone was displayed there, focussed on Domain Delta's position. A quartet of dart-shaped targets was approaching the base. "Long-range sensors detected a formation of Vulture-class atmocraft on an convergent vector. IFF signals match those of hoppers from General Rössa's command." He faced her. "The lead ship has been transmitting a hailing code on the general's private frequency and they've broadcast repeated requests to speak to you."

"You have not replied?"

"No, as per your standing orders."

Schrader considered this for a moment then snapped out a command to one of the other officers. "Have the Rogue Trooper brought up here, quickly."

Volks was startled. "Kolonel, are you mad? You would allow the blue-skin to simply walk into the heart of our operations?"

"I see an opportunity to use this to my advantage." She gave the kapten a loaded stare. "I do not need to explain myself to you, Johann. For your own good, I advise you to never question my sanity again." Schrader turned and summoned another officer. "You. What is the position of the flyers?"

"Uh, passing over the outer perimeter of the test range now, Madam Director,"

"Excellent. Activate area effect countermeasures and ready the dome's defence batteries."

Volks saw what Schrader was planning and lowered his voice to a harsh whisper. "Kolonel, this will only escalate matters! Perhaps, if we allow them to believe that the general was killed by an enemy attack, or—"

"You're second-guessing me again," she said, her voice deceptively light. "If you make a habit of it, you will displease me."

"Repeat, this is Falkon Two on secured channel, Internal Affairs Apparat code gamma. General Rössa, respond please." The atmocraft's co-pilot threw a glance over his shoulder at the kommander standing behind him, clasping a digi-pad. The Nort officer bore the IAA badge over his left breast, a Nordland lightning bolt capped with an unblinking blue eye; the Apparat were the police force of the military machine and their unswerving dedication to the letter of the party law was known and feared by all line troopers. "Still no reply, sir."

Kommander Yest grimaced. "Ach, this is all wrong. Do you have the general's personal locator signal?" Yest had served as Rössa's adjutant for two tours on Nu Earth and he had developed a gut instinct for a bad situation.

The co-pilot shook his head. "No, sir. We are certainly close enough to pick it up now."

"Then he's dead, or worse." Yest tapped the atmocraft's senior officer on the shoulder. "Pilot, you have a tight-beam laser for ship-to-ship communication?"

"Of course, kommander."

"Use it," Yest insisted, "and send a message to the other craft in the flight. Tell them to go to weapons-free status and stand by to open fire."

"Sir?" the pilot's eyes widened. "But this is a Nort facility!"

"Do as I say." He turned to the co-pilot. "You, get me a satlink to High Command."

The co-pilot tapped his headphones in confusion. "Standard communications are inoperable, sir! It just happened – all I hear is static!"

"They're jamming us?" said the Nort pilot. "Why?"

"Verkammt!" Yest spat. "Break formation, quickly!"

A strident alert tone blared from the cockpit console, overlapping the kommander's orders. Threat lights blinked on in rapid sequence; radar and lidar-guided weapons were locking on to the aircraft.

The command centre doors parted to allow Rogue to enter, flanked by not two but four armed Nort troopers, each one watching the clone soldier for the slightest hint of movement. All of them had heard about the guards he'd killed in the elevator and none of them were going to take any chances with the blank-eyed devil.

Schrader gave a little clap of amusement as he came closer, a disturbingly childlike gesture for someone so malevolent. "Perfect timing," she said, "I want to show you something, Rogue."

The GI took in the screens, the tactical map of the Zone and the Nort ships. "What's this? More of your friends, Schrader?"

The woman's face soured. "Hardly. Associates of the late General Rössa, formerly of Nordland's internal investigation division."

Rogue remembered the name from the communiqué in the Vok-IV datacore but said nothing, letting Schrader play out her little performance for him.

"The General took issue with my... my research, and so I was forced to take certain steps." She gestured at the flyers. "These are the consequences."

"Falkon One and Four are veering off," said Volks. "Falkon Two and Three moving into attack postures."

Schrader never took her eyes off Rogue. "Eliminate them."

"Missile batteries, fire on all targets." The kapten glared down at the weapons officer below him, an unmistakable threat in his eyes. "Now!"

Monitors fixed on the outer walls showed plumes of yellow fire belching from honeycomb launcher pods dotted around the dome's equator. Slender surface-to-air missiles leapt away, leaving corkscrew trails as they spiralled towards their targets.

Schrader turned to study the monitors. "Target view," she ordered.

One of the screens switched to a nose camera mounted in the leading missile and Rogue saw a Nort Vulture appear in its crosshairs, expanding from a black dot to a shape that filled the view; there was a fraction-of-a-second impression of a screaming face framed in a vu-port and then the screen turned into static.

Rogue saw long-range telemetry of the other missiles streaking through the air; two more hits and positive kills, the warheads impacting the atmocraft directly in the engines. The fourth and last missile looped around, temporarily baffled by a burst of chaff and flares from the surviving ship. Switching to a proximity fuse, the smart munition got as close as it could to the fleeing atmocraft and then detonated.

On the screen, the Vulture flipped over as if an invisible hand had slapped it from the sky.

Aboard Falkon Two, the missile blast turned the cockpit into chaos. The explosion threw Yest to the deck, his arm snapping under him as he fell. The pilot's head ricocheted off the inside of the canopy and lolled, as blood streamed from his nostrils. Electrical short-circuits skipped across the console in trails of blue sparks, spitting streams of acrid smoke from burning components.

"Master alarm!" cried the co-pilot as the broken ground of the test range rose up to fill the cockpit window. "Lifters are gone! Fire in the engine spaces!"

"The nose, bring up the nose!" Yest managed, dragging himself to a kneeling position.

"We're going down!"

Kommander Yest stumbled and found himself face-to-face with a portrait of Domain Delta's base director, displayed on his fallen digi-pad. "Bitch!" he swore, the instant before the Vulture struck the top of the ridge.

The camera followed the stricken atmocraft down into the hills of the no-man's-land and watched it collide into the ground in an orgy of smoke and shattering metals.

"Three confirmed kills," Volks said in a tight voice. "One probable, pending confirmation."

Schrader gave a sullen nod. "No one would be able survive a crash landing like that. Domain Delta is safe again, for the present."

Rogue studied her carefully, keeping his blunt features perfectly inert and emotionless. He could see it in her eyes; the kolonel was about to make her play for his co-operation. No one dared to speak in the command centre; the room was silent but for the soft sounds of the working consoles.

"Do you understand what I have done?" Schrader said, after a long moment. "I'm like you, now. We have both turned against our own commanders. I too have become a rogue." She looked away, as if the pressure of it all was almost too much to bear. "I have turned my back on Nordland and embraced my own path. I choose my own destiny from now on, like you!"

"You're nothing like me," he said flatly.

"Don't be so quick to judge, Rogue," she retorted. "Look at all you've done, and you were just one man! I have this facility under my guidance – together, there's so much more we can achieve!"

Rogue glanced at Volks; a storm of conflicted emotions exploded on the kapten's face as he tried to comprehend the orders he had just received. "I'm not sure the rest of the men here will share your vision."

Schrader made a dismissive gesture. "I have the loyalty of the men that I need and the fear from the others. Don't concern yourself with those matters." She paused and drew closer to him. "The Nort High Command tried to shut down this dome – don't you want to know why, Rogue? Don't you want to know about poor Zero or the NexGen? What about all the other GIs who died out there in the Quartz Zone?" The scientist waved at the walls and the glass plains beyond. "Don't you owe it to them?"

Rogue's jaw hardened. "What I *owe* them is to find and terminate the Traitor who betrayed us." His voice was like steel.

A flicker of fear crossed Schrader's face for the briefest of moments, but then she swallowed it down like some rare delicacy. "And you will, with my help."

The GI sneered. "You seem pretty convinced that I'm going to buddy up with you. Let me tell you, my experience with Nort dames ain't exactly making me partial to your charms, Kolonel."

"I think you'll see the merits of working with me soon enough."

"Convince me, then," Rogue demanded. He held his hands up in front of her; there were still lines of bruising around the wrists where the manacles had been placed. "Taking off the cuffs and putting me in a room with a comfortable bunk... If that and a bunch of empty talk is all you've got to give me, you're gonna fall a long way short."

She frowned. "Some areas of the dome are restricted but you're not a prisoner here–" Schrader began.

"Only because you know you couldn't stop me if you wanted to," Rogue broke in. "You want to earn my trust, you tell me where my friends are, right now!" He stepped closer to her, baring down on the woman.

To her credit, Schrader did not flinch or back away and she waved off Volks as he drew his weapon. "Gunnar, Helm and Bagman? You want to see them?" She smiled. "You only had to ask." The kolonel beckoned him with a hooked finger. "Come with me."

It was too generous to call it an exercise yard. The rectangular area was surrounded on all sides by three tiers of cage-like cells accessed by metal steps, and it resembled more a fighting pit or gladiatorial arena than a prison. Ferris learned the rules of the place quickly; when night fell, they were locked in the cages and in the day they were herded into the yard. They fed them at noon and other than that, the Norts left them to their own devices. For strength in numbers, the pilot automatically gravitated to Zeke and his team, but all of them soon realised that there was hardly anyone among their fellow prisoners that were interested in rousting them. There were perhaps twenty, maybe thirty men and a few women. Most of them were Southers, but there was a handful of Nordlanders in the mix too. They varied from the hollow and malnourished to ragged, wild-eyed types who were little more than human wreckage.

Ruiz sat quietly and watched, his face pale and sweaty from infection. Zeke used brackish water from a feeble standpipe to tend his soldier's wound, while Purcell and Ferris watched their cellmates like hawks.

"This ain't no POW camp like I've seen," the woman said. "Look at these poor bastards. This is a death pit."

Ferris nodded as a figure approached. "Company coming."

It was a man; he'd been olive-skinned once, but now he was pallid and drawn. "Specialist Sanchez, Savanna Battalion. You?"

"Rangers, One-fifty-first," answered Purcell automatically. "How long you been here, Sanchez?"

The soldier sat down, but not too close to them. "Since the push for Dix-I. Got captured on day one, they shipped me here. I lost count of the time—"

"Dix-I only fell a few weeks back," said Ferris.

"Lost count," repeated Sanchez. "It's bad here, you know? The ice queen, she treats us like animals." He pulled up a sleeve to show a series of laser burns. "Tests," he said, as if the word would explain everything.

Out in the middle of the yard, one of the other prisoners stumbled and dropped to his knees. Without warning, he pitched back his head and began to scream.

"Skev!" Purcell bolted to her feet. "What the hell?"

"No!" Sanchez waved his hands in front of her. "Back, stay back, sister!"

The prisoner was clawing at himself, ripping his tattered fatigues away, tearing red streaks in his dirty skin and still screaming. On the observation balcony above, Norts were moving to investigate, and down in the yard, a guard pushed his way into the open.

"What's wrong with him?" Ferris gasped.

"Got the rips, man. He's cold meat," Sanchez shook his head.

His eyes wide with the madness of agony, the prisoner writhed and Ferris heard the cracking of bones. Blood flooded from his nostrils and his skin rippled like water. The pilot was horrified but mortified curiosity got the better of him; he could not turn away.

The prisoner staggered to his feet, his arms flapping and contorting; he broke into a run, clawing at the air as he saw the Nort guard in the crowd. The enemy soldier aimed at him and fired. Shots tore into the ragged figure, casting off bits of flesh, but still he ran on, screaming his pain.

The Nort fired again and this time all the other guards in the gallery joined in. The combined las-fire reduced the man to a scar on the yard's soiled floor.

Ferris fought down the urge to vomit.

Sanchez gave a solemn nod as the stink of burnt meat washed over them. "Tests," he repeated.

Schrader led Rogue into a section of the dome fitted as a drill area, with exercise gear, a sparring ring and other items of training equipment. Volks followed him in with a pair of troopers, his eyes nervous.

The GI's face soured as he recognised the room's other occupants; green-skinned NexGen were hard at work pumping iron and running on treadmills. Rogue threw Schrader a disgusted glance; he knew what would come next. Volks would force him into the ring at gunpoint and put him up against the Nort GIs. He'd barely recovered from the beating in the Shard Orchard and now the sick witch was going to have him battered all over again for her perverse amusement.

Schrader gave him a quizzical look. "Is something wrong? Don't you recognise them?"

One of the Soldats stood and swaggered toward him. "Eh," it said. "Never realised how puny you looked, pal. Like last year's model."

"Gunnar?" The GI's face creased in confusion.

"In the flesh," he tapped his chest, "so to speak."

"It's a kick, huh, Rogue?" said a second clone soldier. "Like I said before, 'new and improved'."

Rogue shook his head. "Bagman, you too?"

"All three, actually," the last of the G-Soldats spoke, this one with Helm's voice. Each was a deeper, harsher variation on the synths he had carried with him for months.

Rogue turned on Schrader. "What did you do to them?"

The scientist smiled. "I made them better."

ELEVEN
DEATH AND REBIRTH

Every warning instinct in Rogue's brain tugged at him as the implications of Schrader's words became clear. The trio of Nort-created Genetik Soldats standing in front of him were the vessels for the minds of his long-dead squad mates; it was an astonishing thing to comprehend and the GI felt a wave of conflicting emotions wash over him.

The three figures were nearly identical, mottled green skin covering broad torsos packed with engineered brawn; hard, hairless faces with cowls of cultured bone-armour over their skulls. Rogue found himself automatically scanning them for weak points, for places to land a nerve strike or knife stab. His hands reflexively balled into fists as he struggled to take it all in. On some basic level he couldn't shake the sense that these things were the *enemy*.

Schrader watched him with faint, lofty amusement. "Quite an improvement, don't you think?"

Rogue showed his teeth. "You had no right!"

The scientist raised an eyebrow. "Really? Who are you to determine the fate of these men? Surely you wouldn't think of denying your comrades a new lease on life?"

"You stole those biochips!" he said hotly. "You plugged them into your toy soldiers!"

"I admit, there was some resistance from your teammates at the outset," Schrader allowed, "but that quickly passed once the capacities of the G-Soldats became clear. I told you, Rogue, I no longer serve the Nort military." She waved a hand at the three figures. "I did this as a gesture of good faith."

"I never thought I'd feel like this again," said Helm, studying his own hands. "Man, I didn't realise how much I missed just breathing in and out!"

Rogue ignored him and pressed on Schrader. "You're just using them as lab rats! That's what you did with Zero, right? You just want some GI meat for your slab!"

"Oh, come now," she said. "You cannot deny the great gift I've given them! Life, Rogue, true life – not some synthetic silicon analogue of consciousness, but a real existence." Her eyes narrowed. "Far more than your own people ever gave you."

"They would have been regened once we went back to Milli-Com," Rogue denied. "That was the plan. Once the Traitor was dead, I'd go back to the Genies."

"And do you really think that they would have accommodated you? Just welcomed you back like the prodigal clone-son and decanted new bodies for your friends?" Schrader shook her head, giving him a pitying look. "The GI programme is an embarrassment to the Southern Command, a costly failure – and you are a living, breathing reminder of their mistake."

"They never would have regened us," growled Gunnar. "I always knew it."

"No–" Rogue began, but Schrader cut him off.

"Be realistic, GI! No matter what you've done, dead Traitor or not, the moment you stepped back into a Souther gene-lab your life would be over! Your dog-chips would be drained of every useful byte of data and then thrown on the scrap heap... The last chapter of the GI legacy would be ended."

Rogue gave her a steady glare. "I refuse to believe that." The tension in the room came to an edge and for long seconds no one spoke.

The passion on her face melted away. "I'm disappointed. I expected better, Rogue, but perhaps I was wrong about you. All this time it seemed like you had the best interests of your fellow GIs at heart, but perhaps it is only your demands that were being served."

"What the hell are you saying?" he growled.

"This quest of yours to find the Traitor General," Schrader replied. "Did it never occur to you that four GIs searching for him would have been better than one? You survived, you had the opportunity to return to Milli-Com, but you didn't take it. If you really thought that Gunnar, Bagman and Helm would be regened, why didn't you at least turn them over to your own side?"

"We stick together," Rogue said tightly. "We're a team."

"Only because *you* commanded it," said the woman, "but now I've given your friends the chance to decide their own futures."

Rogue looked back at the three G-Soldat faces. They were all expressionless masks, unreadable and impassive.

Schrader sighed. "I can see that you will not accept any answer I will give you, Rogue, but perhaps you will listen to your fellow troopers." She dismissed Volks and the guards with a look. "There will be men outside to escort you back to your quarters when you are ready."

Rogue then looked up and he was alone with the Soldats. They stood in a semicircle around him, all of them a good half metre taller. It took every bit of his self-control not to tense into a combat stance.

Bagman broke the silence. "It's really us, Rogue." He tapped the back of his neck. "She re-implanted our biochips."

Rogue stepped backward, extending the distance between them. "You'll understand I'm a little sceptical." He paused for a moment. "Helm, what was the name of that loudmouth Souther who led the breakout at Glasshouse-G?"

"You're testing me now?" Helm retorted. "You don't trust us?"

"Answer the question."

The NexGen's face twisted. "Rogue, it's me–"

"Answer it!" the GI snapped.

"Helm wasn't there," Gunnar replied, "and neither was Bagman. It was just the two of us. The guy's name was Mac-Inrow."

Rogue glanced at Gunnar. "So, you'd remember how we aced that master computer in Veygas City, right?"

Gunnar frowned. "We ain't ever been to Veygas. Norts wiped it off the map with a dust-storm bomb."

"It was Nu Hamelin," said Bagman. "You jacked me and Helm into the computer and we took it out from the inside."

"You convinced now," Gunnar demanded, prodding Rogue in the chest, "or do you wanna play 'pop quiz' some more?"

"I had to be sure. You would have done the same."

Helm glowered. "Thought you'd be pleased to see us whole."

"I am," he said, not really believing himself, "but it's a little hard to take." He eyed Helm's biceps; like all the G-Soldats, he had the faint tattoo of an ident code and a Nort symbol there.

Bagman saw what he was looking at. "That don't mean nothing, Rogue. It's what's inside that counts." He smiled. "We're a real team again!"

"Yeah..." Rogue breathed. "But where do we go from here?"

"Schrader knows about the Traitor," began Gunnar. "She's willing to spill what she's got about him. Reckon we could use her connections to track him down and pinpoint the creep."

Rogue sneered. "She's real generous. That's a new wrinkle for a Nort."

"You heard what she said," Helm shook his head. "Schrader's out for herself now, just like us. The Norts want her head on a spike."

"The enemy of my enemy is my friend," added Bagman.

"We don't have any friends," Rogue broke in. "Sounds like you guys are sweet on this ice queen."

"Grateful, maybe," admitted Gunnar, "but that's all."

"She says she's got a way to end this war. I reckon we

should hear her out. It's the least we can do." Helm sat and began lifting a set of weights again.

"No, the least we could do is walk outta here," Rogue replied. "And don't forget she's holding Ferris and those Southers down below somewhere." The GI's wariness wasn't receding; if anything, the alarm bells ringing in his mind were getting louder as his team mates talked.

"That ain't gonna matter if the war is over." Gunnar said. "Schrader says she can do it and I believe her."

"They didn't just make us to fight, Rogue," added Bagman. "They made us to *win*. If she can bring peace to Nu Earth, it's our duty to help her."

Helm nodded his agreement. "This could be the biggest thing we've ever done. No more run-and-gun, no more hiding in the chem scavenging for scraps of intel..."

"What is she planning?" the GI demanded.

"It's big, Rogue," said Gunnar. "Real big."

Bagman laid a hand on Rogue's shoulder and the contact made him go rigid. He felt the strength of the G-Soldat's grip, even at rest. "She could upgrade you too, Rogue. It wouldn't be hard to get Schrader to remove your biochip and implant it in a new body like ours."

"I like the skin I got just fine," said the GI. The thought of surrendering himself to the kolonel-doktor's mercies on an operating table made Rogue's blood run cold.

"Are you in or out?" Bagman finished.

Rogue's mind raced and his eyes caught something familiar as Helm glanced away. There, on the back of his neck just below the skull, there was a slight distension in the flesh. A bony object was lying underneath the skin, in exactly the same place as the device he had pulled from Zero's corpse.

He heard himself say, "I need to think about it. It's a lot to take in."

Gunnar nodded. "Make your mind up quick, Rogue. We're decided already. We're gonna see where Schrader's plan takes us."

Bagman smiled. "We want you with us, buddy. The four of us. The whole team."

Helm looked up at him. "You want to be on the winning side, right? Forget the Southers or the Norts, this is it."

"Right." Rogue gave a wary nod and left them behind. His expression did not change as the guards shadowed him down the corridors, but behind his war-mask face, the GI was divided.

Bagman. Helm. Gunnar. They had fought alongside each other for so long that he knew them as well as himself, and he had no doubt that the intelligences inside the G-Soldat forms were those of his friends; but their words, their manners and ticks of personality were warped somehow, off-kilter. It was crystal clear to him; Schrader hadn't simply given them new bodies – she had twisted their loyalties as easily as she altered the DNA of the NexGen.

He couldn't be sure what kind of game Schrader was playing. Perhaps she was relying on his innate pack instinct to bring him into line with the others, or perhaps this was some kind of warning to him, a display of what the scientist was capable of. Whatever Schrader was intending to do, the ante had just been raised. Rogue stood silently in the quarters assigned to him and wondered. With cold clarity, he found himself more alone than he had ever been before. The GI was unarmed, in the heart of enemy territory, with no one to watch his back.

Rogue stood sentinel by the plastibubble window and watched the sky turn dark as the night approached; gradually, tactics revealed themselves and a plan began to form in his mind.

In his fitful sleep, Ruiz moaned and tensed. Ferris eyed his cellmate from across the enclosed, cage-like space. The sparse pallets on which they lay were little more than plastic benches, cushioned only by thick, coarse blankets that stank of stale sweat and fear. The pilot wasn't sure how much sleep he had got; he drifted off into moments of mental deadness but never seemed to actually go under. Each time he closed his eyes, he saw the man in the yard and the strange ways his bones and skin had been moving, just before the Norts shot him dead. He watched Ruiz twitching, favouring his wound. Ferris wondered if the soldier would last another day; the Souther was tough, but even he would have his limits. Perhaps, he thought, it would be a mercy if Ruiz quietly died there; better to perish in the depths of a feverish sleep than to expose yourself to whatever was waiting in the experimentation chambers below.

Sanchez was a talkative fellow. Once it was clear that none of the new arrivals were going to roust him, the trooper laid out the pattern of life in the camp for them. He talked about the tests, over and over, as if speaking their name would ward them off like some arcane demon. Ferris saw the burn marks all over him and shuddered. A humourless smirk came to his lips as he thought of Pitt City with something approaching fondness; suddenly, running from the Milli-Fuzz and crossing swords with Gog didn't seem so bad.

He heard the Norts before he saw them, their heavy boots ringing on the punched metal stairs as they ascended to Ferris's level. He drew the ragged blanket up to his neck in an unconscious gesture of protection that harked back to childhood, pressing himself into the wall as the guards approached. Some of the prisoners awakened by the intrusion made catcalls and kicked at the bars and in return the Norts hammered back with stun-rods.

The pilot's heart leapt into his throat when three dark figures crowded outside his cell. Wide-eyed with terror, Ferris met the gaze of the ugly guard who had taken a shine to Purcell and the Nort showed him a smile of blunt teeth. "Here," said the guard, and spoke into a collar microphone. "Open twenty-three."

Ferris scooted along his bunk until the corner of the cell was at his back. There was nowhere for him to hide in the tiny metal cage.

The guard shouldered into the room and gave Ferris a sneering once-over, then turned to Ruiz. The Souther trooper was awake and trying to prop himself up without success. "Whuh?" His voice was thick with fatigue.

Ferris hated himself for the relief he felt when he heard the guard's next sentence. "Take this Sud down for testing." One of the other Norts reached for Ruiz and the soldier made a weak attempt at resisting.

The words spilled out of Ferris before he was even aware of them. "Leave him alone!" The ugly guard rounded on him, his tattoos dark and demonic in the half-light. A voice in Ferris's head screamed at him to be silent, to let Ruiz be taken instead of him, but his mouth was working on its own accord. "He's hurt!"

A Nort yanked open Ruiz's uniform shirt and peered at his injury, considering the livid purple and yellow spreading across his arm. "Is true," said the Nort.

The ugly guard nodded. "Can't have that." His hand shot out and grabbed a handful of Ferris's shoulder-length hair. "This one, then."

"No, no!" The pilot's skull burned with pain as he was dragged out across the metal decking. A boot stuck him in the kidneys and he coughed up thin, watery bile.

"Get him out of here," the Nort said, and Ferris's vision blurred and swam.

Domain Delta was a complicated creation. The dome had teeth and claws in its missile batteries and roving robo-gunners. It had myriad eyes and ears in its monitors, and like the animals that had once lived on the desert plains where it now stood, Delta had a protective camouflage. By day, the photoreceptive cells in the dome's outer skin adopted the colouration of dusty grey glass of the Quartz Zone, and when night fell, the hemisphere became a featureless black pearl concealed in a landscape of shadows. Only in the deep core sections did the facility never sleep; in the reinforced bunker levels, Kolonel-Doktor Schrader's experiments progressed regardless of Nu Earth's day-night cycle.

The darkness was like a second skin to the Rogue Trooper; he made short work of the soldier covering his door, putting a nerve punch in the Nort's spine that would leave him unconscious but still erect, propped up in an alcove across from Rogue's quarters. Judging by the guard's body mass, the GI would have ten, perhaps twenty minutes before he came to. Plenty of time for what he had in mind.

He slipped through the places where the guards didn't look, the puddles of unlit ground between the security sensors and the gaps in the camera footprints. Rogue had the measure of the men stationed at Delta; they hated the posting, partly because it was remote and dull, but mostly because they were afraid of Schrader. The Norts here would be more concerned about their own safety than that of Domain Delta and that bred a climate of negligence he could exploit.

The labs were split over several levels of the dome and it appeared that the more sensitive the work, the deeper underground they were. Rogue nodded to himself. It made sense; the protected lower levels would be far more likely to survive any assault that would wipe out the upper dome.

The Genetic Infantryman was no stranger to brutality; he'd been born into it, and the innumerable faces of the war dead he'd seen blurred into one soulless barrage of ruined corpses and empty eyes. But in the chambers he passed as he progressed through the labs, he glimpsed things that turned his stomach. Outwardly, Schrader's base was clean, pristine and clinical – but inside, the flawless white plastisteel rooms held horrors that no soldier would ever dare to imagine. There was little screaming; most of the subjects opened to the mercies of the auto-teks were already dead.

Rogue faded into a shadow as an elevator deposited three Norts and a struggling figure. The guards each had a limb, dragging the man toward an open door where another operating table lay waiting. Metal probes sprouted from the sides like the legs of an inverted steel spider.

The prisoner planted a hard kick in the crotch of the largest of the Norts. The big man recoiled and barked out a string of swear words. The other guards returned the defiance with a beating of their own and Rogue caught a glimpse of the captive's face as he went down.

Ferris.

The GI evaluated the situation in a nanosecond. For stealth's sake, it was in Rogue's best interests to let the Norts take Ferris to his tortures and avoid any confrontation that might raise the alarm, but the genetic imperative in his brain flared with a hot surge of adrenaline. A civilian was in danger and Rogue was duty-bound to save his life.

The injured guard, the big one, was recovering from his pain, and in one hand the Nort had drawn a vibro-dagger with intent to cut some good manners into Ferris. Rogue exploded from his hiding place. His first punch landed in the small of the Nort's back, shattering vertebrae, even as his other arm snaked around the guard's neck and twisted it. The dagger skittered away from nerveless fingers. A second crack of bone announced his death, and Rogue was on the next guard even as the first sank to the floor. His reflexes firing at speeds that even the most highly trained human couldn't hope to match, Rogue struck the second guard and propelled him into the waiting room. The Nort fell face first on to the operating tabled, and the robotic device instantly locked him in place with thick flexmetal straps. A series of arrow-sharp manipulators fell on the guard, cutting into him though chem-suit and flesh.

"Get off me!" Ferris was shouting, his flailing hands finding the combat blade by sheer chance. The pilot tore the vibro-dagger around in a punishing arc and buried it to the hilt in the last Nort's chest, stabbing him again and again in mechanical fury.

"Ferris!" Rogue barked, arresting his arm. "Stop it!" When the young pilot didn't respond at once, Rogue slapped him.

Ferris staggered under the blow, the manic flash in his eyes suddenly fading. He let the blade drop to the floor. "Oh shit." The pilot felt his gut clench.

Rogue gathered up the guard's corpse and tossed it into the room. "Help me with this one." Ferris, pale and shaken, took the legs of the ugly Nort and dragged the other body into the chamber. He glanced up; the man on the table was already dead, a forest of needles bored into his back.

The GI ripped an identity card from the senior guard's uniform and examined it. The pass key encoded into the card's memory was enough to get into the next level of the labs, but not high enough to access all the areas; it was a start, though. He looked over at Ferris; the pilot was wiping blood from his hands and he looked as if he were about to throw up. "Hey," he snapped, grabbing a pistol. "With me."

Ferris sealed the door behind them as they returned to the corridor, pinning his hopes on no one checking inside the torture chambers until he and Rogue were long gone. He spoke in a rush. "There's gotta be a hopper or something on the pads upstairs. We get there, I can fly out of this death-trap before they know we're gone..." Ferris wasn't thinking about Ruiz, Purcell or any of the others now – he just wanted out. "Come on!" he urged, blinking away fear sweat.

Rogue coolly worked the code lock in the elevator. "No. I have to find out what Schrader's doing in this place. I can't leave without getting into the labs."

"Are you insane?" Ferris barked. "Who knows what kind of twisted skev that mad bitch is doing down there?"

The lift doors opened. "You coming?" Rogue asked. "It's your choice, but I figure you have a better chance staying alive if we stick together."

Ferris's frenzied manner ebbed away as the cold, hard logic of the GI's words hit home. The pilot knew that his life expectancy would be measured in minutes the moment he parted company with the trooper. "Ah, skev me," he grated with heavy finality, and he followed Rogue into the lift.

They descended as low as the dead guard's clearance would take them and Rogue frowned when the elevator stopped several floors above the main sub-levels. They emerged into an enclosed glass corridor that split off into numerous work rooms and lab compartments. Many were sealed tight with biohazard airlocks and las-cage security barriers barred others. Like much of the base, the sub-level was on a night time mode with subdued lights and a minimum of activity. No humans were visible, but several varieties of auto-tek droids were working in a precise robotic silence.

"What are we looking for?" Ferris whispered.

"I'll know it when I see it," replied Rogue, moving quickly from door to door, peering through the armoured glass walls. In some of the chambers there were thick glass tubes swimming with oily fluids and inside them the shapes of human-like things, green-hued flesh growing from tiny foetal clusters of skin and bone.

"Schrader's got a whole clone farm down here..." The pilot gave a low whistle.

"That's not all." Rogue tapped on a window. In another chamber there were caskets wreathed in white wisps of cryogenic gas and through their frozen lids the GI could see the bodies of dead prisoners, many of them sporting distorted and discoloured flesh. Portions of necrotised skin coloured blue-green by some sort of viral infection were being carefully dissected by the scientist's tireless droids. Ferris thought he caught a glimpse of a familiar face in one of the tubes – a prisoner he'd seen in the exercise yard on the day they'd arrived. He recalled the man being dragged away by the Norts; now his fate was clear.

"In here." Rogue ordered and Ferris followed him into a chamber where a large console faced a series of circular depressions on the floor. One of the hatches was open and extending up from below was a slender tank filled with preservative fluid. A maintenance drone was at work on the device, ignorant of their presence. Rogue worked the console, bringing screens to life. "Looks like storage."

"For what?" A central display screen illuminated and pages of text scrolled across it, too fast for Ferris's eyes to follow. "Can you read that?"

The GI nodded. "These are files from Milli-Com's Bio-Division. Records copied from the Genetic Infantry programme." Rogue recognised the ident tag keyed to the file; it bore the Buzzard code name. "That worthless traitor... Even before he set us up, he was feeding the Norts everything he could on the development of the GIs."

Ferris watched him work, noticing the tension in Rogue increase. "Makes sense. The Norts steal the bio-tech, make their own clones and have the traitor wipe out your battalions."

"That's not it." Rogue said flatly. "Schrader's not just breeding G-Soldats. There's more to it than just making super-soldiers for the Norts..." His voice trailed off as he came across a panel on the console. "Stand back," he warned.

The pilot glanced around nervously and stepped away. Rogue's hands danced over the controls and with a hissing gust of ice-cold vapour, the rest of the storage tanks emerged from the floor, presenting their contents. Ferris's breath caught in his throat as he realised what he was looking at.

In the closest tank there was a shoal of blank yellow eyes, each in a wire cradle trailing thin optical nerves; another sported a shrunken humanoid arm, the turquoise skin pale and decayed; a grinning skull, half of it still coated with burnt blue-black flesh bobbed in a third. The worst sight was in the middle of the tubes, in the largest of the storage tanks. It was a corpse, missing its right leg in a stump of sheared bone and meat, drifting with its hands pressed against the glass as if attempting to communicate a last dying message. The body was the exact twin to Rogue, from the rough aspect of its face to the cue of white hair on its head. The GI gave the dead man a name. "Zero..."

"Where...?" Ferris managed. "Where did these come from?"

"The Quartz Zone." There was a menace in Rogue's voice that Ferris had never heard before and it made him afraid of the soldier. "They couldn't even let us die in peace. Those Kashar filth, they must have picked the ambush clean. Gathered up the corpses like skevving hyenas. That bitch is nothing but a grave robber!" Rogue stabbed a finger at the display. "The Nort clones have a high mortality rate. Schrader's ripping DNA from dead GIs to solve the problem."

Ferris felt a chill as the weight of their discovery hit him. "And now... she's got a live one."

TWELVE
GODS AND MONSTERS

Ferris followed Rogue through the darkened camp as closely as he could, his head bobbing as his heart jumped at every shadow they passed. The Genetic Infantryman's composed, static face had changed with the sights they'd seen in the laboratory and the pilot could see a smouldering anger building up behind those blank yellow eyes.

"We have to get out of here," Ferris insisted for the third time in as many minutes. "Rogue, come on! You can't take on a dome full of Norts on your own!"

"Wasn't planning on it," the trooper replied. "I've got to warn the others. If they know, maybe they'll see all that Schrader is offering them is a lie."

Ferris grabbed his arm and pulled him to a halt. The GI's stormy expression gave him a second's pause, but he swallowed hard and pressed on. "Look, you're a soldier. You understand all about acceptable losses and all, right? If we stay in this madhouse one second longer than we have to, we'll both wind up like your buddy in the tank back there! Your pals have thrown in with Schrader! Cut them loose and we can make a run for it."

"Acceptable losses." Rogue said the words like they left a sour taste in his mouth. "There's no such thing. If I believed in acceptable losses, I would have left that surgical droid to cut you up and use your organs for spare parts." Ferris blinked, for once at a loss for words. "I wouldn't expect you to understand, but you're right about one thing. I am a soldier and I will not leave my comrades behind. Not Zero and not Gunnar, Helm or Bagman."

The pilot found his voice again. "Even if it could get you killed?"

"Every second we're still breathin', there's a chance we'll find a way to shut this place down." He turned away. "You want to keep running, then you go right ahead. I'm not leaving until the job is done."

"Guess I'm with you, then," Ferris gave a heavy, resigned sigh and nodded. "I'm going to regret this."

"Look on the bright side," the GI said dryly. "With the odds stacked against us, you probably won't regret if for long."

Volks felt a chill on his shoulders and turned over under the bed sheets, instantly returning to wakefulness with the trained rapidity of a seasoned warrior. A wistful smile crossed his lips as his hand snaked across bed in search of warm flesh, but the expression faded when he found nothing but a cold emptiness next to him. He propped himself up and found Schrader standing over a nearby console, working at a display. Once more, she wore her lab coat over her naked form.

Johann slid out of bed and padded over to her, navigating by the light of the flickering screen. He brought a hand around her waist and allowed the other to travel up the coat to her breasts. Schrader brushed him away with the same indifference she might have shown a bothersome insect. "Don't touch me," she said with icy disinterest.

Volks withdrew, his face tightening as if she'd slapped him. "Of course, Kolonel-Doktor." His hands drew into fists of their own accord.

Schrader gave him an arch look of slight amusement. It was plain as day on her face; she enjoyed the little humiliations she forced Volks to endure, almost as if she were more excited by the possibility that he would turn violent towards her than by their mechanical, passionless lovemaking. "Are you growing weary of your duties, Johann?" she asked, masking the moment. "Perhaps you would prefer to remain in your own quarters?"

"I am your loyal subordinate," he replied, heavy with irritation.

She gave a hollow chuckle and studied him with contempt. "Of course you are."

Volks watched her return to the screen, where images of the Rogue Trooper scrolled by, along with biometric read-outs and DNA scans. Schrader absently licked her lips as she paged through the files, a desire apparent in her eyes that the kapten had never seen directed at anything else.

An abrupt electronic chirp sounded and the officer crossed to the discarded pile of his uniform clothing. He recovered his communicator and spoke into it. "Volks."

"This is the officer of the watch, sir. Four men are late for check-in and security sensors have registered an unauthorised access in laboratory nine. One of the overdue troopers was guarding the Genetik Infantryman's quarters."

Volks gave Schrader a sharp look. "Mobilise a sweep team and lock down the base perimeter! If that blue freak escapes, I'll have your head!" He angrily snapped off the transmitter and began to dress. "Your new pet seems to have slipped his leash again, Lisle. Perhaps this time I may be forced to damage him before he can be recovered."

"You will do no such thing!" the woman snapped. "Your jealousy disgusts me, Kapten! Show some backbone. You could learn much from the GI."

"Your... attraction to that blue-skin is repellent," Volks said. "Every moment he lives, he is a danger to us!"

Schrader's mood shifted, melting from cold and unyielding to an icy allure. Volks hated himself for it, but he couldn't take his eyes from her. She took Volks's head in her hands and kissed him. "My dear Johann," she breathed, "you must trust me. Rogue's value is incalculable. With him, I will be able to accelerate my

plans and achieve my objective in days, not months!"
The scientist nodded at the computer screens. "These
initial test results are the most promising I have ever had.
Just promise me your patience and the project will be
complete!"

"You always speak of 'the project', always your secret
design..." The officer's anger drained away at her touch.
"I have done much for you, Lisle. I have betrayed my oath
to the party and crossed lines beyond my own morality. I
have never asked anything of you, but now I must. I am
not sure I can go any further without knowing where this
course will lead us."

"Morality is for the weak, Johann, not the concern of
the bold." Schrader looked at him with a clear, steady
gaze. "You have given me your faith and perhaps it is
time I rewarded it with the truth." She discarded her coat
and began to put on her clothes. "Come, then. I will show
you."

"But I must recover the GI—"

"Do not trouble yourself," she smiled. "I know where
he is. He's like you, Johann. The Rogue Trooper is a slave
to fixations that he cannot overcome."

The need for sleep was one of the first things the genetic
engineers targeted when the technology to manipulate
clone DNA matured; the tissues that produced the
fatigue poisons to stifle the muscles and the organs of a
man were reconfigured and altered to increase the waking functionality of the gene-soldiers. Nort and Souther
scientists both found ways to allow their creations to
operate for days on end with only minimal downtime for
deep REM sleep. On the open dais of the training deck,
Bagman, Helm and Gunnar were testing the limits of
their new bodies. They had been sparring non-stop for
hours, each one tackling the other two in a three-way
unarmed combat. None of them felt sluggish or
exhausted.

Gunnar had slipped into his new organic sleeve like he had been born in it, working out the kinks and quirks of the G-Soldat body as if it were a finely tuned machine. He stepped into a judo move, one of a million hand-to-hand tactics drilled into him as a tube trainee and tossed Bagman to the mat. "Ah!" he said. "Just like riding a grav-bike. You never forget how to do it."

Gunnar expected a dour comeback, but Bagman's attention was elsewhere, as was Helm's. The other two troopers had dropped their guard. Gunnar turned and felt mild surprise. "Rogue?"

The GI approached, with Ferris tagging close behind. Gunnar saw the fierce look in Rogue's eyes and instantly knew that trouble was brewing.

Bagman got to his feet; he missed the subtle cue in his comrade's expression. "So, Rogue. You decided then?" He pointed at the GI's chest. "Gonna turn that blue model in for a green machine?"

"Schrader's been lying to you," Rogue said without preamble. "Nort or not, she's using you."

Helm frowned, his hand straying to the back of his neck. "Now, hold on, buddy. Whatever gripes you got against her, she–"

"Damn it, Helm!" Rogue snapped. "All of you, can't you see what's going on here? You think she decanted you new flesh just out of the goodness of her heart?"

Gunnar curled his lip in a sneer. "I'm sure you got an explanation, right?"

"Tell them what we saw," Ferris broke in.

"You keep out of this, pinky," Gunnar growled at the pilot. "Go ahead, Rogue. Tell us."

"I found Zero," he said flatly.

Bagman's face wrinkled in confusion. "Zero's dead, we saw it happen. You vented the corpse over the swamps."

Rogue shook his head. "Not that Zero. I'm talking about the *original*. The one who died in the Quartz Zone, or at least what's left of him. He's floating in a tank like some cut of preserved freezemeat! Schrader's hoarding GI body parts down in the bio-lab levels, pieces of our dead buddies laid out for her to cut up and screw around with!" His outburst hung in the air, poisoning the room.

"I don't understand..." said Helm.

"Then let me explain it to you," Rogue replied with disdain. "Your new girlfriend, Kolonel-Doktor Schrader, is using the bodies of men we fought with for her little science project!" He stabbed a finger into Gunnar's bare torso. "We all know those Nort G-Soldats are a poor imitation of us... But now these NexGen come out of nowhere and they're faster, stronger. It doesn't take a Genie to figure it out, Schrader's cut up our dead to make those meat bags you're wearing!" Rogue met Gunnar's hard-edged gaze. "For all you know, she could have shreds of skin from *your* blue hide down there in a tank of formaldehyde!"

"You've gone section eight!" Gunnar replied. "There was nothing left after the zone wiped us out!"

Helm sat heavily, massaging his neck. "But what about the Kashar Legion?" He was sweating and his brow was knotted with tension. "There were always rumours that they looted the battlefields..."

"You can bet your dog-chips that the Nort Bio-Directorate wanted every last scrap of GI meat for salvage!" said Rogue. "Schrader's got it all down there and she's using it to breed a better Nort Soldat!"

"Or worse," murmured Ferris. "She's experimenting on the prisoners here, as well."

"You expect us to buy that?" Gunnar shook his head. "Man, I didn't want to believe it, but she was right about you. Schrader warned us that you'd go against us once we were regened. It makes me ill to see you turn on your own kind."

"What the hell?" Rogue demanded. "My own kind? Gunnar, it's me, Rogue! You know me! All of you do, we fought together, we–"

"Died together?" Bagman broke in, frowning. "All of us except you, Rogue. I always thought it was weird that only you made it out of the zone alive."

Gunnar prodded Rogue with a thick finger, menacing him. "None of us ever had a chance to make our own choices before now and the moment we do you're bucking to get us back in a chip slot again! No way, Rogue. No more of that 'skin outranks silicon' skev!"

"No," Rogue said, "that's not it–"

"We never had a vote when we were chipped, but that's changed." Bagman rubbed a hand over his neck. "You were the one who sent us off on that wild goose chase across Nu Earth, Rogue. *You* made all the decisions for us. All I ever wanted was my life back. You don't know what it is like living like that! Having your soul sucked into a piece of plastic, never resting, reliving the blood and the pain of dying over and over. That ain't a life, its hell! I'm not going back to that!"

Rogue saw Bagman's face tense as he stroked at his neck again; he glanced at Helm, who had fallen silent. Both of them kept reaching for the same spot, as if they were rubbing at an ache. "Bagman, your neck–" Rogue extended a hand, but the other man knocked it away.

"Don't touch me!" Bagman hissed. "Just back off!"

Gunnar unconsciously mimicked the motion as well; each of them was probing the skin above the bio-implant below their skulls.

The GI felt control of the situation slipping away from him. "Guys, focus! Schrader is the enemy here, not me. She just wants you for her experiments." Rogue heard the hatch sliding open even as he spoke and like the starring actress coming on stage as her cue was uttered, the scientist entered with a grim-faced Kapten Volks and a group of Nort troopers at her flanks.

Schrader shook her head sadly. "Oh, Rogue. How little you understand my work. I'm distressed by your suspicion. There was no need for you to kill my men or break into my labs. You only had to ask and I would have given you access. It is important that we have trust in our relationship."

"You're nothing but a Nort quack with delusions of grandeur," Rogue retorted. "You're a jackal preying on the bodies of dead men."

She pouted. "I see we still have a long way to go." From the corner of her eye, the scientist saw Ferris's hand dart toward the stolen pistol in his belt. She gave Gunnar a sharp nod and the soldier struck him with a hard cross that knocked the pilot to the floor. The weapon skittered away across the deck. "Thank you, Gunnar," she added. "Perhaps you can return Mister Ferris to the cell block for me?"

"Sure," said the G-Soldat, eyeing Rogue.

Helm spoke in a quiet, tight voice. "Is what Rogue said true? Have you really got the corpses of our brothers on ice?"

Rogue expected a lie to leap from her lips, but instead Schrader gave a hollow sigh. "Yes, it is true. But I want you all to understand why." She took a breath to steady herself, and Rogue watched her performance with a cold eye. "I used my connections at Nort High Command to have the... the material transferred to Domain Delta where I knew it would be safe. If the Norts kept hold of the bodies, there would be no telling what they could do with them. I know they were trying to develop a pathogen that would destroy GI bioengrams, based on a fungal form discovered in the Polar Zone. I knew I had to stop them before they wiped out the last of you. Without you, my research will count for nothing."

Rogue covered his surprise at Schrader's last words; at least she was speaking the truth. His suspicions were confirmed; she needed him alive.

She looked directly at him for the first time since she entered the room. "I won't keep anything from you anymore, Rogue. Come with me, and I'll show you the future of Nu Earth."

■ ■ ■

Rogue watched as Schrader removed a key card from a pocket on her tunic; it was similar in size and shape to the one he had stolen from the guard, but the thin slab of plastic was a featureless black all over. The elevator hissed open and she punched in a code. "No one has visited the heart of my operation before," she told Volks and the GI as they followed her in. "Every aspect of my work is conducted by a crew of auto-teks directly under my control."

"But there are other scientists working here, other geneticists," Volks noted.

She nodded. "Only on the higher tiers. The tasks I give them are low priority, the unimportant matters involving the NexGen development program."

Rogue watched her carefully. "You're not just breeding a new strain of G-Soldats here, are you? I was right."

"Yes," the scientist admitted. "I was foolish to think I could conceal anything from you." Schrader pressed a button and the lift began to sink. It descended past the level Rogue and Ferris had visited, past the highest security lockouts and at last into the deepest core of Domain Delta. The elevator halted and with a chime the doors opened. "Welcome to my vision," Schrader said.

The layout differed little from the upper tiers – Nort military design was hardly the most innovative in the galaxy – with a central corridor extending out to a series of branching laboratory chambers and holding cells. The woman paused at a security door where the deadly glitter of a laser web prevented any access.

"Recognise: Schrader, Lisle," she said to the air. "Password: Prometheus." The net of energy dissipated and the hatch irised open.

Volks was on edge, his right hand never more than a fingertip away from the heavy calibre pistol on his belt. "This level does not appear on any of the dome's security grids," he said carefully.

"Of course not," said the scientist. "I made sure of that. After the base was constructed, I had all record of this tier deleted from every plan and schematic of Domain Delta. The facility's central computer was programmed to conceal the power and atmosphere usage. Like a thirteenth floor, it doesn't exist."

They passed by compartments that resembled zoo cages more than laboratory spaces and Rogue's breath caught in his throat as he saw the misshapen forms that moved within them. Behind thick shields of clear plastisteel there were things that shuffled on malformed limbs, creatures that perhaps had started out as men but now were little more than living organic mutations. Rogue heard Volks curse softly under his breath as some of the man-shapes came out of the depths of the chambers to look at them. In the cells, the GI saw grossly distended forms, warped flesh that might once have been human distorted into death-grey abnormality; mutated grotesques studied him with milky eyes and broken spirits.

"What are these... things?" Volks asked.

"Errors," said Schrader. "I keep them alive to remind me of how far I have come."

"They almost look human," said the officer.

"They were, once upon a time." She glanced at the GI and beckoned him over to a different chamber. "Look here, Rogue. Perhaps you might see a family resemblance."

Inside the other cell there were dozens, perhaps hundreds of hulking, crippled figures and Rogue knew instantly what they were. They sported abnormal, crooked limbs, bloated torsos and monstrous faces. The poor, pathetic creatures looked like some hideous parody of a human body, moulded out of dull green clay by someone with only a vague concept of what a man should look like.

"My first attempts at a new breed of Genetik Soldat," Schrader had a hint of perverse pride in her voice. "Sadly, the mixture of recovered GI DNA and the original Nort Soldat templates had some unfortunate side-effects."

One of the largest of the freakish NexGen pressed up against the glass and studied Rogue, some semblance of confusion on its disfigured face. He realised that the thing recognised him on some bone-deep genetic level and unbidden he raised a hand to touch the glass.

"Keep away!" Schrader barked suddenly. "They are unpredictable."

After a moment, Rogue broke eye contact with the creature and walked on, his mind spinning back to a similar encounter in his twelfth year, when he and Bagman had stumbled upon a collection of similar genetic rejects aboard Milli-Com. He shook off the memory. "How does Zero fit into all this?" he demanded of the scientist.

She nodded to herself. "Ah yes, Bio-Subject GI: 3530972/Z4. My one and only viable decant using recovered material."

"Recovered?" Rogue repeated. "You have his corpse!"

"Yes. I wanted to clone a Souther pattern GI and Zero seemed like the most suitable candidate. His body had been excellently preserved, thanks to the ministrations of the Kashar's salvage operatives. After six attempts to copy him, I was finally able to accelerate a blank adult body for reanimation, although the life span was severely shortened." She shook her head, as if she were perturbed at the outcome. "Despite all the data your traitor provided, I was never able to duplicate the Souther process exactly... And Zero proved far more resourceful than I ever could have anticipated."

"He escaped."

"Yes," Schrader smiled at him, her eyes flashing, "but now I have you."

Rogue ignored the implication and pressed the point. "You may have been able to make a clone of Zero's body, but how did you clone his mind? His biochip was destroyed! After sixty seconds outside a support frame or an organic host, every GI personality matrix becomes useless!"

Schrader threw him a condescending look and halted outside another security hatch. "Oh, my poor, poor Rogue.

That is what your creators at Milli-Com told you," she pressed a control and the hatch yawned open, "but you'll find the truth is much different."

The door folded back into the wall to reveal an oval room pulsing with muted energy. On a wide central platform there was a vertical wall of translucent plastic extending to the ceiling; the vast panel was compartmentalised into grids, each separate pocket linked into a network of glowing power nodes. On every node there was a GI biochip, each a twin to the one that lay buried in the soft flesh of Rogue's cerebral cortex.

It was as if he had walked into a war memorial for the troopers who had perished in the Quartz Zone; there were hundreds of chips pulsing in the slots, some of them bearing code letters and numbers from men he had fought and trained with. Rogue approached the panel, his steps leaden. He felt heavy and hollow all at the same time, as if the gravity in the chamber had suddenly increased.

On closer inspection, he could see that most of the dog-chips were ruined, blackened by laser fire or had melted. Some were shattered like broken glass, held together by twisted meshes of fine wire; others were dry remains where their organic protein matrix had been leached away. A cascade of emotions thundered through him; anger, disgust and terrible sorrow.

Volks watched the play across the GI's face and felt a curious surge of empathy for the clone. As a soldier, he understood only too well what Rogue would be feeling as he took in the enormity of Schrader's revelation. On some level, he pitied the trooper; his creators had never granted him the human release of tears.

Schrader's voice was low and reverent, as if she were in a church. "It is true that after one minute the biochip matrix begins an irreversible process of decay, but under certain conditions that decay can be retarded. Even after months, some tiny elements of the original pattern imprint remain. Zero's biochip retained almost thirty per cent of his mental engrams and I was able to enhance the rest using splinters recovered from the other, less well preserved specimens."

"You gave him a patchwork mind," Rogue moaned. "You put him in a body that fell apart."

"I saved him," she insisted and gestured to the chips. "I saved them all, don't you understand that?"

Rogue ran his hand over the panel. "How many of them are still... still aware of themselves?"

"You must understand, none of the personalities stored here are whole," Schrader insisted. "These are just fragments, less than ghosts."

"Show me!" Rogue turned on her, his face thunderous.

With a slow nod, Schrader tapped in a command. Suddenly the room was filled with a chorus of voices, some of them babbling, some screaming, an incoherent flood of pain and anguish.

"Can you hear me?" the GI shouted over the din. "It's Rogue! Do you understand?" The rush of yelling synths grew in volume until he finally shook his head. "Enough!"

Schrader silenced the voices of the dead. "I have had no success in my attempts to recover them, but perhaps with your help, I could do more."

Rogue crossed the distance to Schrader in a flash, his hands tight in hard fists. "Help you? I'm a heartbeat away from killing you!"

She waved Volks away as he went for his gun. "Rogue, please. We want the same thing, you and I. An end to the war and a future for your kind."

"What future?" he demanded bitterly.

"You are unique, Rogue. In the entire galaxy, you are the oldest surviving genetically engineered life form. No other clone has ever come close to you. Perhaps it was by design or some random chance, but you are the most superior artificial being mankind has ever created." She gently touched him. "Within your genetic code, you have the key to a creation that will irrevocably change the face of this planet and this war!" Schrader removed a small canister from her pocket; inside was a vial of clear liquid, swirling with flecks of blue. "This is an early generation of a synthetic retrovirus. It is my life's work. Any human infected with this solution will instantly begin a process of controlled genetic mutation. DNA will be rewritten at the molecular level and a new form will arise!" Her eyes were bright and shining.

"What do you mean, a new form?" said Rogue.

"Like you," she smiled. "It will change a normal person into a NexGen, a mixture of human and GI!"

"Nain..." Volks shook his head, unable to comprehend the scope of Schrader's vision.

"Think of it," Schrader whispered. "An army of enhanced soldiers unfettered by toxins and human weakness! Nu Earth would fall beneath their heels in weeks!"

"You are insane," said Volks. "This is monstrous!"

She sneered at the officer. "Your fear disgusts me, Johann. This is the chance for greatness, the chance to become more than human! I will begin the next stage in our evolution and this planet will be the first step in a campaign that will shake the stars! Your petty human concerns are worthless in comparison."

Schrader turned to the GI and ran her hand over the rough plastiflesh of his hairless chest, enjoying the sensuous thrill of the contact. "I need you, Rogue. And there is so much I can do for you in return."

THIRTEEN
WAR GAME

Schrader's heart was racing; she felt giddy at the prospect of what was about to happen and unfamiliar, uncontrolled emotions welled up inside her. She leaned into Rogue; he was so close now that she could taste his scent on her lips. It wasn't the dry musk of a human male nor the poor perfume of a weak, ordinary man like Volks, but something darker, more reptilian. She felt the undeniable thrill of primal and animalistic sexual arousal.

With perfect clarity, Lisle suddenly understood that everything in her life had been leading up to this very moment, preparing and moulding her. The child of a career military family, Schrader's youth in Nordland's Niebelung protectorate had been a clinical affair. She saw little of her parents, both of them serving on different fronts in the colonial wars, their contacts limited to brusque vid-messages on her birthdays, rare visits and more often than not, severe letters to underline their disappointments when she performed poorly in the Youth Cadre. Despite the expectations of her parents, it was clear from the start that Lisle would never be a soldier, but her intellect grasped the rudiments of biochemistry with the ferocity of a steel trap and the ever-watchful party instructors selected her for the science directorate. If her childhood had given her anything, it was a loathing for the weakness of emotion in any form and Lisle went into her new life determined to never give any of herself to anyone ever again.

In the hothouse climate of genius she excelled. Where other students dickered over insignificant concerns like morality and ethics, Kadet Schrader used her talents to conceive of horrific new methods for the Norts to kill their enemies. She opened up avenues of research in gene-manipulation, striving to find ways to excise the deficiencies of men through the application of controlled mutation. When other students got in her way, she found it easy to arrange fatal accidents for them in the laboratories. Her ruthlessness earned her an officer commission on graduation and the army took her to Nu Earth, the playground of a billion bio-weapons and man-made toxins. By then, Lisle's mother was dead, killed in a sortie on Horst, but her father had risen to a division command and with pride she contacted the old man to tell him of her accomplishment. General Kurno Schrader, a man to whom only cold steel and the absence of mercy were weapons, suggested instead that his daughter stop toying with her silly test tubes and become a real soldier, perhaps on the frontlines where her life might have some actual value to the Fatherland.

Lisle hated herself in that moment, hated her own weakness, her pathetic need for his approval – but she hated the old bastard even more, so she carefully organised the delivery of an untraceable packet of the agent magenta nerve bane to his private quarters.

Then she was free, but with her parents dead and buried she found herself adrift. Without her hate, her need, Lisle's life had no focus. Like Nu Earth itself, forever tidally locked into orbit around the Valhalla singularity, Schrader craved a dark star of obsession to hold her in place. Her work began to suffer and eventually High Command shifted her sideways into what most of the science directorate considered a dead-end posting; the costly and unproductive G-Soldat program.

It was there that she first saw Rogue, his cerulean face staring up at her from a grainy security vid-feed. He was frozen in the middle of a kill, ripping the mask from a soldier in some nameless Hellstreak bunker. She studied the picture for hours, examining every line on his countenance, absorbing the controlled energy of his personality she glimpsed there, daring to wonder how it would be to touch him. All her life, Lisle had been searching for a way to expunge the fragility that she saw in herself, in her species, her nation – and she found it in the Rogue Trooper.

The GI was the perfect embodiment of her ideals; heartless and inimical, bred for strength, trained to feel no pity or remorse. An organic machine designed only for killing and superiority. Lisle found a new goal in Rogue's eyes. She wanted to possess him, and even more, she wanted to *become* him.

And now he was here, in her grasp, ready for her. Schrader ran her hand over Rogue's chest. The skin was cool and dry like a snake and beneath there wasn't an inch of wasted flesh, not a single pocket of useless flab. He was all hard muscle, a statue cut from blue steel. The scientist licked her lips, savouring her excitement. Schrader allowed herself a tiny gasp of delight as she toyed with the idea of engaging in other activities with the GI...

She cocked her head to kiss Rogue, to touch her perfect azure icon, and with a look of utter loathing and disgust, he turned away. "Don't ever touch me again," he said in low tones loaded with antipathy.

"What?" she choked, an abrupt heat rising on her cheeks. "What did you say to me?" Her eyes fluttered, she must have misheard. She and Rogue were alike, couldn't he see that? He would never, ever reject her... "You must–"

This time he forced her away with the flat of his hand. "Get away from me, you demented witch! You're out of your mind!"

For the first time since her childhood, tears sprang to Schrader's eyes. "No, no. You don't understand! You and I, we will be gods, mother and father to a new order–"

"You're insane if you think I'd ever help you unleash something like that," he stabbed a finger at the retrovirus vial, "on the galaxy!"

Anger flooded into her, a brilliant, searing hate hotter than anything she'd ever felt before. "Fool! You cannot defy me!"

Schrader grabbed Rogue's arm and then he did the unthinkable. The GI slapped her across the face. He pulled the blow, but it was still hard enough to send her tumbling to the ground. Volks, the pistol still in his hand, watched the pair of them. The moment seemed unreal, disconnected from reality.

The scientist came to her feet, ignoring the trickle of blood that seeped from the corner of her lips. Schrader's whole body was tense with a white-hot fury, every muscle in her body vibrating like a struck chord. "You worthless blue bastard!" she bellowed. "You have betrayed me like everyone else! How could I ever have loved you? You're just like every other man. You're wretched, useless!" She spat at him. "I don't need you! I've taken what I want from your flesh, raped you while you slept!" Tears streamed down her face. "I could have given you immortality, but instead I'll watch you die screaming!"

Volks's hand tensed around the gun. The Nort wasn't sure which of the two people in the room represented the greatest danger.

With trembling hands, Schrader wiped at her face, making a vague attempt to regain her composure. Black kohl smeared over her cheekbones. "Take... take him to the test range!" she snarled at Volks. "We'll see how well he can survive against his three friends!"

Rogue shook his head. "I won't fight them."

"You will!" she shouted, her hand jerking an electrostunner from a pocket in her coat. "They will give you no choice, trooper! I control them now, it is my conditioning that drives them!"

"The implants..." he breathed.

"I will watch you die!" Schrader cried, her voice breaking. "The myth of the Rogue Trooper perishes here! I will build a new world from your ashes!"

Too late, the GI saw the bright blue flash of discharge from the teeth of the taser. The scientist buried the stun rod in his chest and triggered a massive surge of electrical energy. Darkness rose up around him.

Rogue floated in a foggy, blood-warm nothingness, images and sensations passing through his mind like light through a warped lens. He saw the faces of his fellow GIs melting and changing, distorting into the mutant forms glimpsed in Schrader's hidden laboratory. He saw Ferris, Zeke and Volks with blue skin and yellow eyes, all of them reaching out to him in some terrible agony.

He heard a voice calling his name, over and over and over.

"Rogue? Rogue! Snap out of it, trooper!"

The clone soldier opened his eyes and felt a fuzzy pressure all across his skull. "Who...?"

A hand gripped his arm and pulled him to a sitting position. "It's me, Ferris. You okay?"

There was a constant humming in the GI's skull. "What's that sound?" He blinked; they were inside some kind of moving vehicle.

Ferris jerked a thumb over his shoulder. "We're in a Nort cargo hopper. They just chucked us in here and set off."

"Us?" Rogue looked around and saw a ragged handful of figures in Souther chem-suits, Zeke and the others among them. "Schrader said something about a test..."

"Aye," Sanchez nodded, "the test range. It's the ice queen's little playground for her green toy-boys, comprende? They say if you can find a way out, you can go free."

"Has anybody ever done that?" Ferris asked quickly.

The soldier shrugged. "Nobody has ever come back from the range, if that's what you mean."

Rogue felt a change in the speed of the flyer and glanced around the enclosed cabin. The Nort guards watching them from the far side of the bay readied their guns. "We're slowing down."

Zeke pulled Ruiz to his feet. "Here we go." The other soldier looked pallid and weak behind his breath mask, but he managed a vague nod.

The hopper dropped into a hover mode and the rear door of the cabin opened. Rogue saw broken ground outside.

"Get out!" snapped one of the Norts, waving his gun to underline the point. When the prisoners hesitated, he let off a three-round burst into the chest of a kneeling Souther, killing him instantly. "Die here or die out there, it's your choice!"

They needed no encouragement and with a disordered rush the troopers jumped out the door. The ground was several metres below the ramp and some of the Southers landed badly; a second man died, impaling himself on a tank-trap projecting out of the earth.

Rogue dropped into a cat-like stance as his boots hit the dirt. Like everyone else, he was unarmed, stripped down to just his battle fatigues. Then a flurry of objects fell from the hopper, tossed out by the Norts and the GI instinctively rolled into cover.

Ferris cowered as a kit bag flopped into the mud at his feet. "Whoa! What the hell is this thing?" A dozen bags, one for each of the prisoners, lay scattered on the ground.

With a shriek of jet noise, the hopper vectored away and was gone.

Purcell examined the dead man's body and found a packet of suit patches in a pocket. She tore it open and distributed them among the others as far as they would go. "Don't touch that sack, flyboy," she began. "You've got no clue what's in it."

Sanchez dropped into a crouch and began to rip open one of the bags. "No, no. It's part of the game, see? To make it sporting."

Ferris gingerly opened the pouch at his feet and found a pair of Nort-issue binox. "Huh? I was hoping for a mini-nuke, at least."

"The ice queen, she gives everyone a piece of kit," Sanchez continued. "Up to you how you use it."

Rogue accepted this with a nod and found a bag, ripping it down the seam. Inside was a revolver with a couple of extra reloads. He glanced at Sanchez; the prisoner had an assault rifle gripped in his trembling hands. "Here," Rogue offered him the pistol. "Trade with me."

"Nuh, I'll keep this," said the other man.

Rogue shook his head slowly. "I wasn't asking you."

After a moment Sanchez nodded and took the revolver in exchange. "Aye. Guess you'd be a better shot with those GI peepers of yours, right?"

The clone soldier gave the Nort rifle a quick once-over. Satisfied, he studied the lay of the land around them. Where the Quartz Zone proper was a maze of razor-cracked glass crevasses, spires of fused rock and plains of silicon, the test range had been bombarded so many times that it resembled more the crater-pocked surface of Nu Earth's airless moons. Burnt-out frames of dead tanks sprouted from pits of thick grey mud, trenches snaked back and forth with no obvious pattern, and broken porta-domes lay cracked open all across the barren landscape. Once more, Rogue was in his element.

"What do we have?" said Zeke, studying the bandoleer of grenades he held. "We need to pool all the kit, maybe figure out who would be best with what—"

"You ain't the sarge no more!" snapped another prisoner, who sat cross-legged on the dirt, fumbling at the collar of another bag. "This ain't some exercise, bucko, this is every man for himself!" Something made a clicking noise and the sack gave an explosive splutter. The Souther tumbled backwards, a fleshy knot of red skin and white bone where his head had been.

"Griswold grenade," said Rogue grimly, recognising the telltale discharge of the fist-sized anti-personnel weapon. "Better watch the rest of those sacks."

Sanchez nodded in agreement. "She usually booby-traps one piece of kit each time."

Zeke gave him a hard look. "Thanks for mentioning that in advance! Is there anything else we should know?"

The prisoner shrugged and opened his arms to take in the whole vista of the test range. "We'll probably get a five, maybe ten minute start on the Soldats."

Ruiz eyed Sanchez. "You seem to know a lot about this set-up, pal. How do we know you ain't in it with the Norts? A spy in the ranks?"

Rogue watched the interplay between the two men carefully. Sanchez seemed unconcerned. "You wanna tear me?" The prisoner nodded at the combat knife in Ruiz's hand. "Go ahead. Now or later, here or there, I'll be dead. You too. I watched this happen a hundred times from the cellblock."

"To hell with that," snapped Purcell. "I say we double-time it to the perimeter and take a gamble getting over the barriers. If we can make it into open country outside the range, we got a chance."

"Never happen," said Zeke. "You saw this place on the way in, all bunkers and ferrocrete walls. You'd need a tank-mek to crack them."

Ferris gave a cough. "Uh, I got an idea..."

"Go on," said Rogue.

"Yesterday, those Nort atmocraft that got shot at... Well, uh, there was one that went down to the west. There's a chance it could still be airworthy... The Norts build them tough, see."

"You could fly it?" Zeke said. "Get us out of here?"

The pilot shrugged. "No guarantees, but it's a chance, right?"

Rogue hefted the rifle and checked the ammunition pack. "Let's do it."

"Movement," said one of other prisoners. "I see movement back at the dome."

The GI grabbed Ferris's binox and trained them on Domain Delta a few kilometres distant to the point where they'd been dropped. Three hawk-like shapes were lifting away from the landing pad, climbing into the sky and turning toward the range. Rogue caught sight of a figure leaping aboard the last hopper as it took off; a hulking form with dark green skin. "They're coming for us. Three squads."

"We gotta move," said Zeke. "If one of them catches us in the open, the other two will be on us in seconds."

Rogue nodded. "Affirmative. Make for the atmocraft but take an indirect route. We don't want them figuring out what we're up to."

"Just one thing," said Sanchez, drifting over towards Purcell, "what if that ship is wrecked? Then what?"

Rogue handed Ferris back his binox. "Then we'll have to stand and fight."

"Where is he now?" Schrader demanded, scanning the map of the test range from the command centre dais. All trace of her earlier emotional outburst had vanished as if it never happened. She was her clinical, calm self once more, focussed and controlled.

Volks traced a circle with a laser pointer. "In this sector, I believe. Seismic sensors registered a grenade detonation."

She nodded. Another dead Souther. It would not have been Rogue who was caught by the bag trap; he was too smart to fall for something so crude. Such a death would be without artistry or panache and she wanted the GI to perish in a far more meaningful way – at the hands of his former comrades.

A signal blinked on the monitor. "Detection from a static munition test grid," Volks reeled off the information. "Multiple footsteps, westerly direction."

Schrader glanced at the arrow shapes indicating the hunter flyers; they were too far away to converge on the location and besides, to bring them in all at once would ruin the game. She turned her attention to Volks. "What kind of munitions are buried there? Pulse mines, rot-spray nozzles?"

Volks checked a display. "Puffball packs."

A smile crossed her face. "Set the trigger to fire on the last man in line."

"As you order, Kolonel-Doktor."

There was a momentary pause before the indicator for the buried weapon went red, signifying a successful detonation. Schrader visualised the moment in her mind – the instant when the foamy ball of artificially cultured organic muscle inflated into a sphere as large as man's head. It would erupt from its shallow hiding place under the ground like a fast-forward fungal growth, the bio-weapon releasing a deadly shot of fine bone needles in a tight swarm. As a distraction from her main duties, the scientist had cultured the puffball from a class of Nu Earth plant life that had survived into the early years of the war, making it tougher and more resilient, and breeding in a chemical trigger that turned it from a harmless fungus into something far more dangerous. The weapon was ideal for anti-infantry operations, spitting out spines that lanced right through armour weave and chem-suit material.

"Sensors register kill probability, one casualty, ninety-seven per cent," said Volks. "Other targets moving out of the grid's detection range."

She could have used the puffball to kill more of them; but where would the sport be in that? It would be far more enjoyable to cut down the prisoners one by one until only the GI remained.

"Detonation, section four." Schrader recognised Gunnar's voice over the radio from the lead hopper. "What's the situation?"

She tapped the communicator controls on her console, speaking aloud as she manipulated the microwave sub-channels that broadcast alongside the voice band. "Target proceeding toward western sectors of the range. Englobe and attack."

"Say again, Delta?" From the second hopper, Helm's voice was hesitant. She would have to watch his loyalty index closely.

"Units one through three, use your own discretion and attack. Weapons are free, all targets to be considered hostile."

"Please confirm," Bagman joined the conversation. "We are *not* to apprehend targets? What is the order?"

Volks looked up at her from the operations level. "The conditioning is weakening, I think. They should not be questioning your commands so soon."

Schrader brought up the sub-channel controls and increased the gain. The bio-implants in the G-Soldat bodies were one of her finest pieces of work. The complex knots of vat-grown neural matter and calcium-silicon circuits inside them gave her a window into the minds of her clone soldiers. It had taken months of research, trial and error, but now the current generation of her NexGen carried in their heads an organic receptor designed to accept certain frequencies of microwave radiation. She had conditioned their brains in the gestation stages with cues tied to pre-programmed pulse cycles; at the push of a button, she could make them obey her, as easily as a tug on the leash of an attack dog.

Schrader sent the obedience signal into the minds of the reborn GIs. "The order is to locate and terminate all targets."

"With pleasure," Gunnar growled and his hopper peeled off from the formation. She nodded to herself. Trooper G's innate ambivalence had made him the easiest to manipulate, playing on his rivalry and resentment of Rogue. She doubted that the GI would survive a one-on-one confrontation with the enhanced Gunnar.

• • •

"Ferris, come on," said Rogue, placing a hand on his shoulder. "She's dead."

The pilot couldn't look away from the dead Souther's body, the woman's chem-suit riddled with dozens of glistening spikes as long as a human finger. "Who was she?" he asked quietly. "What was her name?"

"Rossi," said Sanchez. "Don't know what unit. She came from the Neverglades front."

"She took my place on the line," Ferris said quietly. "Swapped over with me. I'd have been dead if she hadn't done that." He had not seen Rossi's death; rather, he'd heard it, the hissing thud of noise and the slice of bone skewers through the air.

"Lucky for you," said Sanchez. "Lucky for us. No pilot, no escape, eh?"

"Tell that to Rossi," Ferris replied and followed Rogue.

Strung out in a loose line, they crested a low ridge. Below them, cradled in a shallow valley, the Vulture-class atmocraft rested half-on and half-off a slight incline. The pilot's trained eye instantly saw a dozen pieces of damage, any one of which could mean the ship was beyond saving.

Zeke gave him an expectant look, but then the sergeant looked away. "Trooper!" he called to Rogue. "You hear that?"

The GI nodded, pointing back toward Domain Delta. "Hopper grav-engines, closing fast. Can't see them, they must be coming in low."

Zeke barked out orders. "Ruiz, with me! Purcell, Sanchez, take the others and spread out! We'll draw them off from the wreck." He looked back at Rogue. "You think you can get the flyboy down there in one piece?"

"Count on it." Rogue brought up his assault rifle. "You just keep them outta my hair."

Ferris spoke in a low voice. "Rogue, that ship's worse off than I thought..."

The soldier rounded on him and the pilot was startled by the controlled anger in his yellow eyes. "Ferris, don't quit on me now. You fall to pieces here and I swear I will shoot you myself, got it?"

"Uh, okay."

Rogue sprinted down from the ridgeline as the noise of thruster jets grew louder behind them.

Gunnar looked at the other G-Soldats in the hopper and grimaced; it was like staring into a mirror, but it still turned his gut on some deep, instinctive level. These creeps were still Norts, after a fashion, never mind what Schrader told him. Old habits died hard and his finger was twitchy around the pistol grip of his GI-issue rifle. It was in excellent condition, as well maintained now as it had been on the day that he'd drawn it from stores aboard Milli-Com. It fell easily into his grip in the same way it had since he'd first laid hands on such a weapon, when he was ten Earth-standard years old. Gunnar felt a churn of animosity, another surge in the slow burning fury that directed itself at Rogue. Why had it been him that had to die first in the Quartz Zone? Why not Rogue or Helm or one of the others? They lost six hundred men in the first wave of landings and Gunnar had only made it a dozen metres from the place where he put down, before the blast from a plasma sphere opened him up from thigh to shoulder. He should have lived. It should have been Rogue's dog-chip inhabiting his rifle, not Gunnar reduced to a rectangle of plastic and rage, jammed into the frame of his own damn gun!

His free hand rubbed at a spot on the back of his neck where a bloom of heat was making his muscles bunch. Damn Rogue and his bloody-minded quest for revenge! Gunnar was sick of him making all the choices, running their pitiful excuses for lives. He held the gun in his hands and gestured to the hopper pilot to bring the flyer low. Things had changed now, though. Schrader had given them all the chance to live again and as usual it was Rogue who laid down the law, trying to tell them what to do, to go back to that synthetic hell. Gunnar slid off the safety catch and checked the ammo counter. The rifle was full and ready.

Rogue would have to learn the hard way, Gunnar decided, his eye twitching as the warmth in his head reached forward. The only way Rogue would give up his self-centred quest was if he saw it from their point of view; if only he could know what it was like to walk around in one of these NexGen skins, he would understand how they felt. Gunnar sighted through the rifle's scope as the hopper drifted low and the other clone soldiers leapt out. He saw a crumpled corpse in a chem-suit and held the crosshairs over its heart, imagining he saw blue skin.

If Rogue wouldn't submit to taking Schrader's upgrade willingly, Gunnar would have to force his hand. One shot, then sixty seconds to recover his biochip. Once he was regened, Rogue would be thanking Gunnar for doing it.

The rifleman swung himself out of the Nort hopper and landed in the dirt, his weapon scanning the horizon.

FOURTEEN
COUNTER STRIKE

With Gunnar and the first G-Soldat team on the ground, the lead hopper thundered over the landscape in a wide, low turn.

"Down!" shouted Zeke and the Southers threw themselves into whatever cover they could find; all except Ruiz, who stumbled and fell short of a crater where Purcell and Sanchez had hidden.

"Ruiz!" shouted the woman, peering over the lip of the pit, beckoning. "Come on, man. Get over here!"

The soldier tried to push himself up from the dirt and failed, slipping. Like a fast-moving bird of prey, the hopper was sweeping up behind him, nose dipping downward to present a barbed chin turret.

Purcell bunched her muscles and hauled herself up over the edge of the crater, holding her arms out as far as they would reach. "Ruiz! Get off your ass and run!" Her feet scrambled against the burnt earth. Shots from the hopper churned the ground as the Nort pilot marched the laser bolts toward Ruiz's crawling form. "I'm going to get him!" she snapped, vaulting over the rim.

Sanchez caught her by the straps on her oxy-filter and pulled hard, dragging her back into the crater. "He's already dead."

"No, you son of a bitch!"

Purcell saw Ruiz get to his knees just as the hopper strafed over him in a blare of thruster noise; the shadow of the Nort ship swept by and was gone.

The soldier wobbled, hands coming up to touch the fist-sized hole in his chest, then Private First Class Ruiz fell back into the dirt and died.

Sanchez's chem-hood rang as Purcell backhanded him across the visor. "Bastard!" she spat. "I could have got to him!"

The other trooper rolled up and over the crater edge, throwing her a look. "Maybe I should have let you. Then you'd have been ventilated too." Sanchez dropped to a crouch and took the combat knife from the corpse's grip. "This guy, he was injured, he was slowing us down, aye? Better he bought it now than later, when it cost one of us?"

"Skev you. He was a friend of mine."

Sanchez looked around. "That don't count for nothing out here." He drew his revolver. "Those greenies will be here any second. Move it."

They raced down the steep incline of the valley, half-running and half-falling as the loosely packed earth crumbled around them. The dirt in the test range had been reorganised so many times by bombs and artillery that it resembled a thick layer of dead powder, settling in drifts and dunes. When the winds roared in off the Quartz, there were dust storms thicker than thunderclouds. Rogue was sure-footed and quick, while Ferris flapped his arms trying to keep his balance. The pilot almost collided with the grounded fuselage of the atmocraft as he skidded to a halt.

Rogue panned around with his ersatz rifle. "Do your thing," he ordered.

Ferris hesitated; he now wished that he hadn't said anything about the Nort ship. His suggestion had led them here and if the flyer turned out to be a total loss, it would be on his head. Ice water flooded his gut as he examined the Vulture. There were the signs of massive fire damage around the engine bells and the odour of spilt thruster fuel even managed to penetrate the chem-filters of his air mask. One of the wings was crumpled against an incline and the cockpit glass was white with shatter lines. "Oh man, this thing isn't going to touch sky ever again."

Rogue gave him a hard stare. "Be sure."

"I *am* sure!" he retorted, pulling at a hatch that had popped open on impact. "Trust me, don't you think if I could get the hell out of here, I would?" The door fell open and a figure came with it, tumbling out on to the ground. Ferris jumped back in surprise.

"Nort officer," Rogue said, turning over the body. "A kommander, by the rank pins." He tapped the sigil on the dead man's chest. "Internal Affairs. Must have been out here to shut down Schrader's GI stud farm." Rogue looted the body of a handgun and gave it to the pilot. "Take this. We may not be able to get this wreck airborne, but there's gotta be gear on board we can use."

Ferris nodded. "Copy that."

They scrambled into the dim interior of the atmocraft. Sooty deposits from smoke blackened the inner walls of the fuselage and fittings dislodged by the crash dangled like trailing vines. In some places, entire pieces of the hull were missing where curls of plastisteel were folded back in peels. "It's a wonder this thing never went up in a fireball," said the pilot.

"There's still time," Rogue noted. "Get up to the cockpit, see what you can salvage. I'll look for weapons."

Gunnar moved silently, flashing between slabs of cover, ducking into trenches to pass unseen around the Southers. His enhanced hearing picked up the rasping breaths of Purcell and the others and in one moment Zeke dodged by him without ever knowing he was there, hiding in the shadows of a spent fuel tank. He listened to Zeke's thudding heartbeat as he faded away; it would have taken no effort at all to just reach out and kill the veteran. The warm patch on the back of his neck throbbed as the thought crossed his mind. It was a curious sensation, part of him excited at the idea of murdering the soldier, another part sickened at himself for even considering such a thing.

Gunnar shook the thoughts from his mind and approached the downed atmocraft. Two sets of footsteps echoed through the warped hull and the rifleman dropped into a crouch. Gunnar's GI weapon was an extension of his own senses, a magnifying lens on his uncanny abilities. Before, in his old blue skin, Gunnar had known he was more than equal to any soldier on Nu Earth's blighted battle zones; now, in this impressive G-Soldat regeneration, he was the ultimate. The tingle returned as he sighted down the rifle scope. Through holes in the fuselage he saw a dark shape moving through the wreckage, picking at broken hardware, pausing and moving on. For a brief second, the watery daylight caught a flicker of mottled blue flesh.

Rogue. He was in Gunnar's sights, the black cross of the target scope tracing down the line of his neck, crossing his biceps. The sniper knew exactly where to aim, marking the spot where the nerve plexus of the GI's decentralised heart lay. The dull heat was consuming Gunnar now, as his finger curled around the pistol grip. It would only take one shot; just one.

His finger tightened on the trigger.

Ferris reached the cockpit and retched, holding down bile. What was left of the Nort co-pilot had spread itself across the control panel in a mess of flesh, bone and blood. The atmocraft's pilot was also dead, his comparatively intact corpse hunched over a side console. Gingerly, Ferris pulled the body away. Several of the panels were lit, indicating that some of the systems still had power.

He couldn't read Nort, but Ferris recognised some of the symbols. The pilot must have been trying to activate the Vulture's automatic defences in the final seconds before the missile hit them. The atmocraft had a two-tier countermeasures system that used self-targeting anti-missile lasers and a broadband jammer that blanketed the air around the ship with a microwave signal disrupter.

Ferris grinned and completed the dead man's actions, bringing the system online; it would be a nasty surprise for any hoppers trying to strafe the wreck when the las-gun turret shot back at them.

In Domain Delta's command centre, one of the desk officers screamed and ripped his monitor phones from his head as a bloom of red colour suddenly appeared in the middle of the test range map. The disc blinked on, instantly covering the cluster of dots representing the first group of G-Soldats and the suspected positions of the prisoners.

Schrader slammed her hands down on her panel. "What is this?" she demanded.

"Microwave disruption field," Volks read the answer from a sensor relay screen. "Something is generating a jamming broadcast in there. Hoppers two and three are still outside the range of the effect."

The scientist stabbed at her communications array and spat. The new signal was filling the airwaves with an incoherent garble on all frequencies – including the subliminal microwave band. "Silence it!" she demanded. "Do it now!"

"Must be the wreck of that IAA ship," Volks was saying. "They still have power."

"Rogue." She said the name like a curse. Schrader let out an angry, bitter laugh. "He's lucky, I'll give him that. We shall see how far it gets him."

The Vulture's jammer worked by cycling random pulses through the microwave radio bands that Souther missiles operated on, hoping to confuse and baffle them into self-destruction. As a side-effect, any microwave communication sources at close range found themselves caught in a shower of disordered static. For Gunnar, within a few feet of the transmission antenna on the atmocraft's hull, it was like a steel spike being buried in the back of his head.

The bio-neural implant was flooded with searing, razor-edged white noise and every muscle in the NexGen body went rigid. Gunnar twitched and jerked the trigger of his rifle; the las-round went high and splattered into the hull of the ship.

Rogue spun away by reflex, bringing his assault weapon to bear. He caught a glimpse of a green-skinned figure convulsing in pain, shooting wildly.

Gunnar's roar of distress went up and down as the agony from the implant rose and fell in time to the random bursts of energy from the jammer. Instinctively he knew that the ship was the source of his anguish and pain and he raked the hull with laser fire. "Rogue... Aaah! You son of a tube!"

The sniper glimpsed movement in the wreck's cockpit and turned his weapon on it, going to full auto-fire. His vision went red with rage as he tore ragged chunks of plastic out of the canopy.

Inside the cockpit, Ferris recoiled as laser bolts punched through the spider-webbed plex and bored holes through the dead Nort still strapped in the pilot's chair. Wild rounds hit the console and the jammer fell silent. He tried to get out of the way, but in the cramped bridge of the atmocraft there was nowhere to hide. A deflected shot tore through the corpse's throat and spent the last of its energy in Ferris's right leg, melting flesh and bone just above his kneecap. The pilot went down with a scream.

Rogue heard the cry and ignored it; Gunnar was his main problem. The sniper ducked out of sight, shaking off his pain. The GI closed his eyes, concentrating; he realised that he had become too reliant on Helm's sensors and Bagman's detector grids. The scanners in his GI-issue helmet and backpack would have detected Gunnar's approach long before he had the chance to shoot.

There was the click-snap of metal against plastic. Rogue knew the sound too well – Gunnar was reloading the GI rifle, slamming a fresh clip of las-rounds into the magazine.

Gunnar would not miss a second time. Rogue vaulted forward through a rent in the atmocraft's hull, flipping over into a tuck and roll that brought him up at the foot of the valley wall. In the same instant, Gunnar rose from his cover with the rifle in his hand and opened fire.

Rogue did the same; the Nort assault weapon was no comparison to the smooth, perfectly machined GI rifle, pulling up and to the left as it discharged. Rogue instinctively compensated and ran the shots up the hill and across Gunnar's chest in a line of burning darts. Capacitor cartridges spat from the ejector port in a stream of hot plastic as the gun emptied its one and only clip. A brief, brilliant web of laser light filled the air between them.

Gunnar's snap-shots were grouped closely, one cutting the air with a crack near Rogue's right ear, the other two gouging trenches in the meat of his shoulder. He had always been the better killer of the pair of them and perhaps at any other moment the victory would have belonged to him, but Gunnar's new flesh was still untested and that tiny factor of unfamiliarity tipped the balance.

Rogue's weapon clicked empty and Gunnar collapsed in a twitching, palsied heap. The GI swarmed up the side of the shallow valley to his comrade's vantage point. Thick, sticky blood gummed his hands where he touched pools of the emerald fluid. He recovered the rifle where it lay undamaged on the ground.

"Ruh... Rogue." Gunnar spat out the words between gasps of air through a wheezing chest wound. Oily sweat wreathed the G-Soldat features. "Gotta... kill..." he croaked. "Must die... Schrader made me... kill. Kill you!"

The GI cradled his dying friend for the second time in his life, watching the spirit in Gunnar's eyes flickering out. "Easy. I got you," he said. "I'm sorry," he added. Rogue had shot back on reflex, the muscle-memory of a thousand skirmishes taking over. It was only now as Gunnar bled to death in his arms that he realised he had made a lie of his vow to Schrader not to fight his friends.

"Rogue..." Gunnar's voice was thick with torment. "Help me. The pain! Skev, what did she do to us?" The GI felt the back of his skull. Around the implant, the green flesh was feverish and inflamed. "My guh-gun... Not again! Aaah!"

A groan of poisoned air escaped the NexGen and Gunnar's body went limp. Automatically, Rogue began to count back backwards from sixty. He rolled the body over and ran a hand over the spot where he would need to make the incision. The GI drew the rifle on to his lap, the weapon's open chip slot ready and waiting.

Rogue glanced around. When the Norts had disarmed him, they had removed the slender commando-pattern combat knife in his boot and he had no idea if the atmocraft's medi-kit would have a laser scalpel in it. He would have to improvise. The soldier's gaze fell on a piece of airfoil that had been sheared off in the Vulture's crash landing, torn by chance into a rippled blade edge. It would have to do. Gathering the scrap of metal in his hand, Rogue set to work.

Bagman felt his gut lurch as he dropped from the open hatch of the hopper. Genetic Infantrymen never succumbed to motion sickness but for long moments his vision swam and the ground felt fluid beneath his boots. The pair of Nort G-Soldats that accompanied him said nothing, watching expectantly. The wave of nausea faded and Bagman reached up to massage his neck; the motion had become a reflex now, as if running his fingers over the implant would somehow regain him his equilibrium. The soldier felt sluggish, the weight of his GI pack pulling him off-balance. For the first time since he had opened his new eyes on the operating table, Bagman felt like he was out of place in the green flesh of the Soldat form. His thoughts were fuzzy, the edges blurring into one another.

"Team two, move out," Schrader's terse voice spoke over the communicator loop over his ear. "Proceed on foot and locate the GI. All resistance is to be met with lethal response."

When Bagman didn't reply straight away, the scientist spoke again. "You have your orders! Execute them!"

"Yes..." Bagman managed and walked on, away from the grounded hopper. With every footstep, the confusion in his mind increased. He had his orders, yes, and those were to be obeyed... But the pain from his neck was lighting up splinters of memory in his psyche, moments from his trek across Nu Earth and the instant when Bagman's life had ended at Strongpoint Siouxie. Gunfire and shouts drifted over the landscape; the Southers had engaged the other Soldats. In Bagman's mind, the sounds merged with those of the past.

"Not right..." he mumbled. "I shouldn't be here..."

The two Nort GIs with him exchanged glances; his behaviour confused them.

"This is wrong."

Ferris helped himself to the contents of a speed-heal pack in the atmocraft's surgical kit and limped from the downed ship, his looted pistol held tight in one hand. He spotted the GI and hobbled toward him. "Rogue! I heard shooting..." His words trailed off as he recognised the shape of the rifle in the trooper's hands, and the verdant bloodstains on his forearms. "Holy skev, what happened to you?"

Rogue held the rifle as if it had never been taken from him. "Gunnar's with us now."

"But he... They, they threw in with Schrader!"

"I had a wake-up call," grated the synthetic voice from the weapon. "I felt it, right there in my skull, like a buzzsaw through the brain. Something from the atmocraft, like razors..."

Ferris glanced back at the ship. "Whoa, that was me!" He nodded to himself, understanding. "The countermeasures system on the Vulture, I turned it on."

"I don't follow," said Rogue.

"Microwave disrupters, man," the pilot pointed at the antenna. "Norts use them to spoof missile seekers, but maybe they work on GIs too."

Rogue shook his head. "I never felt a thing. Those signals don't affect organic matter, even stuff grown in a tube."

Ferris considered this for a moment. "You don't have one of them implants, though, right? Your buddies do."

"Razors," Gunnar repeated. "Just for a second, it all went red. I could hear Schrader there, in my head, tellin' me to ice you, but Rogue was there too, pulling me back." The synth made a disgusted noise. "That psycho witch. What kinda games is she playing?"

"Conditioning," said Rogue. "I knew it. Those meat bodies she gave you were straight out the vat, Schrader didn't have the time to programme them to be loyal. She's gotta be reinforcing the indoctrination through the implants."

Ferris nodded. "The gear took a hit from trigger-happy here, but I reckon I could get it back online. Give your pals a headache, maybe?"

"Watch the lip, pinky," Gunnar snapped.

"Do it," Rogue demanded.

The pilot gave the rifle a long stare. "So... he's back on our side now, right?" The dull pain of the shot Gunnar had put in him was pushing through the numbness of the no-shock syrette he'd injected into his wound.

"More or less," rumbled the dog-chip.

The gamma grenades detonated with a hollow thump of noise, blasting another crater in the pockmarked wilderness of the range. Zeke watched it happen from his hiding place, afraid to look away from the hasty tripwire he'd set up in case his worried glances were the only things that were keeping it in place.

As he expected, the sharp eyes of the G-Soldats caught sight of the wire instantly. Zeke had seen them drop from the hopper with the sniper and break off, sweeping down towards the Southers like a pair of hunting dogs. Without a single spoken word of command, the two clones disconnected the wire and rendered the makeshift booby trap inert; but in the process, one of them stepped on the plastic contact switch that Purcell had improvised out of her torch and triggered the actual booby trap. Four grenades tied together by a lanyard chain-fired and ripped into the Norts.

Zeke grinned. These green-skinned clones were a different breed to the GI. Where the Rogue Trooper moved with the skill and composure of a veteran soldier, the G-Soldats were still green. Oh sure, they were fast and they were sharp as a sabre-cat, but they were just book-trained. None of them had been in the thick like Zeke, Purcell or the GI. "Move, move!" the sergeant called, beckoning to Purcell and the other survivors. "The other teams will be on their way!"

"Wait a sec," said Sanchez, walking forward with his revolver drawn. "'Fore you pat yourself on the back, let's make sure. I seen these greenies get up from more than your little love tap." The ragged soldier found the bodies of the G-Soldats close together and to Zeke's surprise they were still clinging to life. Sanchez used the large calibre pistol to put a bullet through each of their optic sockets. He indicated his own forehead. "Too tough to punch through their skull plates with ballistics," he noted. "Gotta shoot 'em in the eye."

Purcell jabbed a finger at the sky. "Hopper incoming."

Zeke threw Sanchez a look. "I said move."

A spark spat out of the cockpit console and Ferris cursed. "I think that's it. Wait. No. I got it."

"This isn't gonna work," said Gunnar irritably.

Ferris glared at the biochip. "This wouldn't be necessary if you had checked your fire."

"I've had a bad day," Gunnar's synth was acid. "So sue me."

The pilot said something under his breath and forced a connection into place. "There. The secondary bus was fried, so the signal strength is way lower than it was and patchy, but the range will be greater."

"Is it going to be enough to screw with Schrader's transmitter?" said Rogue.

Ferris flipped the power switch. "Only one way to find out." He handed the GI a microphone salvaged from one of the dead crewmen. "You're on the air with Radio Norty."

"Helm, Bagman, if you can hear me," Rogue said into the mic. "I'm not the enemy. It's Schrader; she's using your bio-implants to control you!"

"Schrader." The word cut into Helm like a knife of fire, bringing with it a cascade of hurtful images, a thousand subliminal cues that were designed to make him bow to every command the scientist uttered. He could hear Rogue speaking through the earpiece he wore, but the voice seemed like it was coming from everywhere at once. Rogue was all around him, in his mind, tearing at him, forcing him to see what he had become. Helm twitched; it was like emerging from a waking dream.

He looked down at his hands, at the dark emerald skin. "No," he said to himself. "Oh, no." Only the sensation of the GI-issue helmet on his head felt right; every other element of his self was like a mosaic of jigsaw pieces hammered into the wrong picture.

The other G-Soldats in the hopper studied him with mute suspicion, hands moving toward their rifles.

The hopper pilot turned in his seat to face Helm and the other troopers in the open cabin behind him. "There's a jamming signal being broadcast from inside the test range. Something is wrong."

Helm was just a hand's length away from the Nort. "Yeah, you're right," he said, a crystal clarity descending on him. With a lighting fast motion, he slammed his head forward and used the GI helmet to butt the pilot on the nose, cracking the bone and tearing open the front of his chem-mask. The Nort shrieked and clawed at his face, the hopper controls out of sight, out of mind.

It all happened at once. Unguided, the hopper dipped sharply to port and began a spinning dive. The two G-Soldats collided with Helm, grabbing at him, tearing at toughened skin, and then the cabin slipped away under them as Helm's tether snapped. He was falling through the air, caught in a knot with the G-Soldats, the twisted earth rushing up to embrace them.

"Schrader!" The name was a block in Bagman's path and he stumbled over it. Heat, crippling and constant, washed over his chest and head from the burning brand in his neck. His fingers picked at the edges of his bony skull armour, as if ripping it off could bring some relief from the fire flooding through him. He staggered like he'd been gut-punched, one hand whipping out to keep his balance, the other clutching at his backpack.

Strong fingers gripped his wrist and pulled him off-balance. Bagman blinked away the agony behind his eyes and saw his G-Soldat chaperones watching him. Without orders, they were falling back into their usual operational patterns; kill anything that exhibited behaviour outside the parameters set by the kolonel-doktor.

"You are impaired," declared the one that was holding on to him.

Bagman touched the dispenser slot on the back of his pack and tapped an item code on the touch pad there; he knew the numbers like he knew the names of every GI that had died in the Zone. Item four-six-three dropped obediently into his palm.

"Desist," said the other Soldat, drawing a combat knife. "We are to locate and terminate the GI. You must follow the kolonel's commands."

Heat lanced through his chest and arms, radiating out from the epicentre of the bio-implant, cramping every one of Bagman's muscles. "I gotta get this outta me..." he hissed through clenched teeth. "Nnnnnn! I ain't one of you no more!"

The las-scalpel in his hand blazed into life, the blade beam extending to its full magnitude. Bagman swept it around in an arc of yellow light, cutting cleanly through the wrist of the first Soldat. The second trooper should have ducked backward – that was what a seasoned soldier would have done – but instead he tried to turn inside Bagman's reach. He was ready and the las-scalpel tore open the other Soldat's throat. Green fluid spattered all over Bagman, burning him like acid.

He reached up to wipe the blood away and realised that some of it was his own; the G-Soldat's knife jutted from Bagman's ribcage. How had he missed that?

He stumbled onward, leaving the disarmed clone to bleed out in the dirt.

FIFTEEN
WILDFIRE

The pain in Ferris's leg was growing worse and he tried to put all thought of finding more no-shock ampoules out of his mind. As much as they would help, he wanted to stay sharp and focused. He wasn't about to accept Rogue's dead buddies back into the fold as easily as the GI did.

"Definitely a hopper," he said. "What's left of one, anyhow." Through his binox, Ferris could see a wing poking up from the twists of wreckage in the near distance. He glanced at Rogue; the GI had spotted the aircraft spiralling down out of the sky. "Did you see a missile?"

"Negative," said the GI. "But the pilot of that thing was dead before it hit the dirt."

"You think Helm or Bag were aboard?" said Gunnar.

"Can't be sure." Neither of them said what they were thinking. If their comrades had been in the hopper, they would surely have been killed and with no one around to save the biochip, they would stay that way.

"There's still, uh, bad guys out there," said Ferris. "You got a plan?"

Rogue gave a shrug. "I'm making this up as I go."

Gunnar gave a guttural snort. "Nothing changes."

A voice echoed down from the ridge. "Trooper? Sound off!"

"It's Purcell," said Ferris.

The Southers were tired but wary and the ragged group emerged over the top of the shallow valley with their weapons primed. Purcell had salvaged a gun from one of

the G-Soldats and she held it like she was itching to use it.
Zeke, Sanchez and three more men came with her into the
embankment cut by the crashed atmocraft.

Sanchez surveyed the wreck and made a spitting noise.

"What's going on?" Zeke demanded of Rogue. "I saw a
hopper go down. You do that?"

The GI looked back, impassive. "Threw a spanner in the
works. Right now Schrader's realising that the rules of her
hunt have just changed."

"With all due respect," Purcell broke in, "that psycho
blond can go chew on a torpedo for all I care." She looked
at Ferris. "Forget Schrader, let's get airborne."

Sanchez gave a hollow laugh. "Good luck."

Ferris blinked and the words came out in a rush. "The G-
lifters are trashed. It wouldn't fly even if you strapped an
orbital booster to it."

Purcell's face turned red with rage and she went for him,
grabbing Ferris by the throat. "You civvie prick! You said
you could fly it!" Ferris flailed and choked, pulling at the
soldier's grip.

"Let him go!" Zeke snapped. "Purcell, you'll kill him!"

"Damn right I will!" she shouted. "You let us down, you
stupid dink!"

Rogue took Purcell's arm and applied pressure at a nerve
point; she gasped in pain and let the pilot go. "It's not Ferris's fault. We knew the wreck was a long shot."

The woman shook off Rogue's grip and gave him a fierce
look. There were tears of exasperation and anger in her
eyes. "So what are we supposed to do now, blue-boy?
Throw rocks at the Norts until they decide to bomb us into
the mud?"

"Hunters will get us before that happens," Sanchez said
in a low voice.

Zeke turned on the other soldier. "Why don't you shut
your damn mouth? I'm getting sick of hearing nothing but
dead air every time you open it!"

Sanchez shrugged, unconcerned. "Just saying, is all."

"Norts!" The shout broke through the tension. One of the other prisoners, a gaunt figure in a Navy-issue chem-suit stabbed a finger, brandishing a small auto-pistol. "I see a green skin!"

Rogue loped up the ridge and pushed the Souther aside, bringing Gunnar up to bear. "Full sweep," he told the rifle.

"Check," replied Gunnar. "Movement, three o'clock."

The trooper's eyes narrowed as a figure moved around the hulk of a destroyed staff car. It was a G-Soldat all right, but a GI helmet capped the broad, expressionless head. The clone soldier was unarmed, but he sported a familiar, boxy backpack. The gear seemed incongruous on an enemy soldier.

"Helm?" said Gunnar, spotting the biochip slotted in the brow of the helmet.

Rogue drew a bead on the Soldat's eye, he wasn't going to take any chances. "Hold it right there," he called.

The figure glanced up and noticed him for the first time. Rogue saw thin streams of blood at the corners of his mouth and the patch of distended, wet flesh on his flank. The NexGen was trying to hold closed a wide, deep wound. "Hey, Rogue. Knew I'd find ya."

"Bagman," Gunnar grated. "He's hurt bad..."

The Soldat slipped to the ground. "Ah. Here we go again, huh?"

Rogue shouldered his weapon and came to Bagman's side. "Helm, you in there?"

"Yeah." The voice from the helmet was sullen and distant.

"What happened?"

"Heard you calling..." Bagman tapped his head with a finger. "Whatever you did, it worked." He coughed out a mouthful of blood. "Helm... Took a skydive without a grav-chute..."

"I had Norts to break my fall," the synth replied with gallows humour.

"Got to him in time," Bagman gave a lolling nod and removed the helmet. "Here. Don't seem right without you wearin' it."

"Rogue, he's got major internal bleeding. A Nort put a fractal-edge blade through his guts," Helm said flatly.

Bagman pressed something into Rogue's palm with blood-slick fingers. "Your turn now," he gave a faint, pained smile. "My turn, I mean." Bagman touched his head. "What goes around, comes around, huh? Get me outta here."

Rogue looked down at the las-scalpel in his hand and nodded. He thumbed the activation stud and the blade flickered into life.

"I say we ditch the freak and head for the Quartz," said the Souther in the scum-sea war gear. "We get into the Glass Zone, we're home free."

"In your dreams," Ferris frowned. "You want to leave Rogue behind in this hell-hole? You gotta be out of your mind, he's the only fighting chance we got."

"What makes you think you're gonna get a vote, civvie?" said Sanchez. "This is a military unit and you're just a punk-ass independent."

The pilot sneered. "Listen to you! Well, Major General Brigadier whatever the hell you wanna be Sanchez, maybe you haven't noticed, but this little happy band isn't exactly parade ground material!" He pointed an accusing finger at the soldier.

Sanchez stroked his revolver. "Like I said, what makes you think you get a vote?" He tapped the barrel of the gun to his faceplate. "Maybe I just put a round in you and take those nice binox."

"Shut up, all of you!" Zeke barked. "If we want to get out of this alive, we'll stick together and that includes the GI."

"You followin' *his* lead now, Sarge?" Purcell looked away.

Zeke's face soured. "Shut up," he repeated, with less force than before.

The sailor stood up, clutching at his captured Nort assault weapon. "The civvie's right about one thing, there ain't no chain of command in this place. I'm getting outta here and I'm not letting that freak stop me."

"You go right ahead," Purcell's tone was sarcastic.

The Souther turned on her. "What? You gone yellow too? I'm not going back to that Norty zoo, you read me? The GI gets in my way, he's dead! We could take him if we hit him together, he's just one man—"

"You're wrong." Rogue's voice cut through the moment. He stood on the lip of the ridge, just as he had when he'd rescued Zeke and the others from the Soldat snipers. The straps of his backpack framed his chest and in one hand he held his rifle. "I'm not just one GI. I'm all of them."

The sailor's face fell as he met Rogue's wolfish gaze. The Souther looked away, his will to protest vanishing like vapour.

"There's still another hopper out there," Gunnar's synth was clear and direct. "It must have put down somewhere nearby."

"We can find it," added Helm.

"We take out the pilot and the flyer is ours," finished Bagman.

Zeke watched the GI carefully; the clone soldier seemed different now, harder and more focussed. "If we stay low, we could make for allied lines," said the sergeant.

Rogue shook his head. "We're not going to run."

"He's right," said Ferris, flinching as another dart of pain ran through his wound. "This place is laced with sensors. The moment Schrader realises that we've taken the hopper, we'll have a dozen rad-seekers up our tailpipe and *boom*! Titanium rain. We'd never get out of the test range alive."

"Oh, this I gotta hear," Purcell said. "So what's your suggestion then, Trooper?"

"There's gotta be a hundred or more prisoners of war still in Domain Delta, long-range atmocraft too. We go back and get them out and then everybody leaves."

"And what about the ice queen?" Sanchez said. "Schrader isn't going to let you steal her toys just like that."

"I'll handle Schrader. We got unfinished business."

Zeke gave a slow nod. "I'm in."

"Guess I am too," added Ferris.

"You're out of your mind!" said the sailor. "We go back there, we're dead for sure!"

Zeke rounded on the Souther. "Who's yellow now?" he demanded. "You were in the dome longer than us, you know what it's like in there. You think you'll be able to sleep at night knowing you left the rest of those poor buggers behind?"

The sailor went pale as the sergeant's words hit home. "Ah, shit."

Rogue scanned the motley group. "Gather all the weapons and kit you can find in the wreck and divide them up between you. We're taking out Domain Delta once and for all."

Volks approached the central dais in the command centre with trepidation, clasping the digi-pad in one hand. Kolonel-Doktor Schrader was silent and unmoving, her hands placed flat on her control console, her eyes never leaving the projected wall map of the test range. Numbers and symbols marched across the display as the concealed sensor pods buried in the dirt attempted to provide a coherent picture of the area. Volks could only give out probabilities on what was happening inside the battleground.

Schrader remained rigid, locked in place like a statue as Volks came forward. The kapten knew her moods better than any man in the dome, but even he could not predict the caprice of her nature. He was always on edge around her; she was cold toward him one moment, solicitous the next. Volks hated himself for it, but he feared her as much as he desired her.

He had expected Schrader to explode with rage when the disruption signal reappeared but she had said nothing, watching the flickering blips that may or may not have been the whereabouts of her Soldats and their prey. He cleared his throat self-consciously. "Kolonel, hopper one has returned safely, and the battle computer appears to indicate that hopper three has made a landing." She did not speak or even acknowledge his presence. Volks continued. "The observers report that the second flyer seems to have suffered some kind of malfunction. It crashed in sector five, close to the tangler pits."

"I underestimated him," she said quietly. "That was an error on my part."

Volks glanced at the digi-pad where the raw data from the range sensors was scrolling by. "Audio trackers registered explosions congruent to multiple grenade detonations and sporadic weapons fire in several locations." He paused, fearing her reaction. "The... jamming field prevents an accurate reading of the G-Soldat's med-status locators."

"They're dead," she announced. "He killed them. He truly is the finest of his breed. The ultimate survivor." The woman spoke as if she were giving a soliloquy, speaking alone to an empty room.

The Nort blinked in surprise. "Kolonel, that cannot be. Three units, nine newly decanted G-Soldats against one old-model GI... The odds of the Rogue Trooper's survival are practically zero."

Schrader smiled ruefully. "Now it is you that underestimates him." She turned and Volks saw emotion in her eyes. "You were correct, Johann. I should have listened to you. I should have terminated him when I had the chance." She reached out a hand and tenderly stroked his face. "After all I've done to you, you still put my welfare before yours."

Volks's mouth worked but no words came out. He had no frame of reference to deal with this new aspect of the woman, no way to understand the real Lisle Schrader.

Her hand dropped away. "Rogue is coming here, Johann. He's coming to destroy my work."

"I won't allow—"

"I am going to take steps," Schrader spoke over him, pushing past. "I have allowed myself to become distracted. The time has come to take my work to the next level." She left Volks standing there as she made her way to the elevator bank.

"Kolonel!" he called, suddenly unsure of what he should do.

She granted him a brief, real smile. "You've been very loyal, Johann. I'm sorry it has to end this way... But there's no other alternative, you see?"

The lift doors closed on her and Volks felt a sickening sensation in his stomach. For the first time, the officer truly understood that the woman he loved was utterly and completely insane.

"Unit three to Delta, respond." The Nort pilot tapped the communicator inside his chem-suit, in the vain hope that it might improve his signal reception; nothing but jammer-laden static greeted him. "Domain Delta, do you read? This is hopper three requesting status check, over."

He cursed and returned to the radio, fiddling with the frequency selector, searching fruitlessly for a channel that was less garbled than the others. As his orders had stated, the pilot had put down his aircraft at the edge of the target zone and waited for instructions. He was to await the return of the G-Soldat hunters with the body of the Souther Genetik Infantryman, but the orders never specified how long he had to wait. The grav-engines hummed in standby mode, ready at a moment's notice to lift the hopper back into the sky. The pilot felt cramped and uncomfortable, fidgeting in his seat. To be parked here, as a static target on the ground, was against every bit of his training. Perhaps, if it had been any other commanding officer giving his orders, the Nort might have risked showing a little initiative. He wouldn't dare buck the kolonel-doktor's commands, though... Other men in his unit had done so and found themselves flung into the prison, or worse, the labs.

A glimmer of movement brought his attention from the console and he looked up to see a knot of shabby figures coming out of cover toward the hopper. The Nort pilot's hand reflexively darted towards the G-button but then a laser bolt entered his skull through the middle of his forehead and flash-boiled the meat of his brain.

Ferris ducked reflexively as the whine of the las-round came to his ears, despite the fact that the sound of the beam's passage arrived instants after the shot had been fired; had the bolt been meant for him, he would never have heard it coming. "Whoa," he said, covering his twitch.

Zeke gave an appreciative nod. "He's got a dead eye, I'll say that for the trooper. Put that kill shot right through the cockpit plexi and on the bull."

"That's a GI for you," Purcell gibed. "Best money can buy."

Behind them, Rogue stepped out from behind the broken spar of wreckage he had used for a makeshift firing stand and approached. "Your show now, Ferris. Get us in the air."

"Copy that," said the pilot, flipping open the gull-wing door to the cockpit. The Nort dangled at an odd angle, held in his seat by acceleration straps. Gingerly, Ferris began to unlatch the corpse. The dead man's head lolled like a bag of thick fluid; Rogue's shot had popped open the pilot's skull with internal pressure from the liquefied brain matter.

The Southers piled aboard the hopper in a sullen mob, Sanchez automatically looting the craft's interior for anything of use. Purcell positioned herself near a pop-up pintle gun and checked the ammunition. Ferris took the pilot's position and revved the engines. "Good to go!" he shouted over the sound of the thrusters. Back in the saddle again, it was easier to ignore the slow burn from his leg wound.

Rogue was the last to embark, scanning the ground one last time. He turned his back to step into the hopper cabin and in that second a green shape exploded out from under a concealed pit, a camu-cape flickering as it flew away in the downwash.

Ferris stamped on the rudder, yawing the flyer around, but he was too slow. The G-Soldat slammed into the hull of the ship, striking at the GI with a bloody stump, his intact hand clawing a tear in the metal.

"This creep won't stay dead!" Bagman snarled.

The ground fell away from the aircraft as Ferris poured power to the throttles. For one long moment, Rogue teetered on the lip of the cabin door; the Soldat shouldered its way into the cabin, wrestling with the GI. In the cramped interior, it was like a knife fight inside a phone booth.

He was too close to shoot. Rogue spun in place and brought Gunnar down on the Soldat's face, the butt of the rifle breaking the reinforced bones in its jaw. A gun discharged; Sanchez fired wildly, the bullet ricocheting off the hull. The Soldat's stump hit Rogue again, the club of meat ringing his skull like a bell. Dimly, he heard Ferris shout something over the scream of rushing air.

"Hang on!" The hopper's fuselage moaned as the pilot made a vicious turn, standing the flyer on one stubby wing. Rogue saw the opportunity and took it, one hand gripping a restraint harness to hold him steady. He kicked out with both feet and hit the Soldat in the chest. The Nort GI lost his grip and fell away, tumbling over and over. Rogue watched him drop until he hit the ground in a heap of broken angles.

With effort, Rogue hauled himself into a seat. "Take us in," he ordered.

• • •

The man-shapes in the holding cells knew something was wrong; they could tell it from the way that Schrader stalked past them, an unwavering purpose in her eyes. She did not spare them a glance and the scientist passed the biochip chamber and entered the sub-level's main lab. From a concealed flesh-pocket of artificially cultured skin, Schrader removed a needle-like key, protein-chain encoded to her personal DNA profile. The tiny spike fitted into a socket on the lab's central control panel, activating a sequence of remote commands that once given, could not be countermanded.

In a way, it was liberating. Perhaps, after so long down here in the depths of the dome, labouring over microscopes and gene-modules, Schrader had lost sight of what she was truly trying to achieve. It was, after all, only the greatest scientific minds who had the will to take their research beyond the realms of possibility and into rock-crete reality. It was time to redress the balance; time to take the last step.

She glanced at the synthesiser pod where the viral clades were birthing and swarming, hungry for release. "Very soon," she promised them. "First I must discard everything inconsequential."

A prompt on the console offered her a single question. *Commit? Yes/No?*

"Yes," she told it.

In the cages, Schrader's legions of mistakes howled and moaned as the hatches that held them prisoner dropped away. Glass panels retracted into the wall and shuttered doors that had never been opened yawned. Watery light filtered down from the levels above, beckoning them.

Then it began. The ultrasonic pulses drove the mutants out and up from the sub-levels. The half-human test subjects, the Soldat rejects – the things that defied any kind of classification with their malformed bodies and grotesque faces – all of them took their new freedom with wild fervour; but there was something more they wanted, another motive that forced them forward.

They wanted revenge. They wanted it badly. They took it in bloody screaming ruin from everything they came across.

Volks had seen war; he had seen death and brutality, been close enough to taste the stench of it through his oxy-mask. He had been there the night the GIs died in the Quartz Zone, watched his men rip their lander pods from the sky with rockets. He remembered the indigo slick of blood across the glass. Volks had never admitted it to anyone else, but something inside him had broken there in the shimmering wasteland. Even as his army cut their victory from GI flesh, Volks had tasted a fear of something he had never encountered before. Retribution.

Kapten Volks had known that one day it would come. One day, he would pay for standing there, ankle deep in the dead, turning a traitor's betrayal into a massacre that would live in infamy long after Nu Earth was dust.

His fears were there for him on the monitors of the command centre. Every display from the dome's internal security cameras showed the same thing, Nort soldiers in frantic retreat, guns chattering into shifting hulks of blue-green flesh. Creatures with too many fingers on their hands ripped men into shreds; they took up dead men's guns and destroyed anything that moved. Volks could see that the butcher's bill was being paid in full.

She had brought this to bear. It was so clear, now that it was too late for him to prevent it. He had meant no more to Schrader than the microbes that swarmed in her Petri dishes. Volks, and everyone who served her will in Domain Delta, were nothing but tools and now she was disposing of them, using her errors to do the job for her. He slumped against the panel. In all his life, he had never known a sense of defeat so powerful and so sure as what he felt now. Johann Volks owed this failure to himself, his vanity and his obsession for Schrader.

All about him, men were panicking, some of them fleeing their posts, others watching with frozen horror the unfolding mayhem around the complex. Schrader had been careful to pick senior officers with certain character flaws for her staff; they were so much easier to manipulate. The command centre was a hard point, well protected in comparison with the rest of Delta, but it was not impregnable. Tier by tier, corridor by corridor, the tide of death was closing in.

From the perimeter defence station a junior officer called out a warning. "Incoming aircraft!" In the confusion, Volks almost missed the announcement.

"Show me," he ordered.

The operator brought up a camera view of a Nort hopper. The remote monitor zoomed in. Volks saw the numeral "3" on the tail and a dozen cramped figures squeezed into the open-air cabin. The flyer was weaving – no doubt to avoid the aim of the dome's automatic guns – and as it turned Volks got a glimpse of blue. "Freeze that image," he demanded. "Give me a close up."

The picture grew, resolved, and there was the Rogue Trooper, surrounded by grim-faced Souther soldiers.

"The GI!" yelped the operator. "Missile batteries one through six answer ready, Kapten! On your order?"

Volks studied the pixelated face of the clone soldier. He had survived, just as Schrader predicted. "Stand down weapons," he said curtly. "Open a comm channel."

"Sir?" the officer gave him a quizzical look. "Those are Sud soldiers–"

The Kapten's pistol was in his hand and pointed at the operator. Volks noticed it as if it belonged to someone else. "Do as I say."

· · ·

Ferris tapped the threat warning light, confused. It remained inert. "That's freaky. They were goin' for a missile lock and then nothing..."

Purcell spun up the door gun. "Damn Norts are up to something."

"Reckon they got their hands full," said Zeke, peering through Ferris's binox at the dome. "Looks like all hell is breaking loose down there. I see... Well, I don't know what they are, these *things*. They're ripping the Norts apart."

Rogue didn't have to look to know what the veteran meant. "Schrader's pets, all the mutants she bred tampering with GI DNA."

Ferris pressed a hand to his helmet communicator and glanced over his shoulder. "Rogue, you ain't gonna believe this."

The pilot toggled a switch and Volks's voice filled the cabin. "Trooper. Can you hear me?"

"I'm listening."

"I suppose I should not be surprised that you are alive..." There was a lengthy pause. "Lisle... Kolonel-Doktor Schrader has betrayed the party and the people of Nordland, and I... I stood by and let it happen."

Rogue's jaw hardened. "What do you want, Nort? Absolution?"

"Yes," came the reply. "She's going to unleash something horrific on this planet. Everything she touches will become warped and inhuman, like..."

"Like me?"

"Like you," said Volks. "That cannot be allowed to happen." After a moment, the enemy officer spoke again. "I have released the locks on the prison complex. Your comrades are free to escape, if they can. I still have some honour, Trooper. Once, this was a war for ideals and principles. Now it is nothing but a nightmare, a circus for traitors and madmen."

"She has to die, Volks," said Rogue. "You're not going to stop me."

"I won't," said the Nort. "I'm calling for Wildfire, Trooper. You understand?"

"Holy skev..." Zeke muttered.

"You will have little time," Volks continued. "There must be no doubt... There must be an end to it."

Rogue nodded. "Tell your men to stay out of my way." The GI made a throat-cutting motion to Ferris and the pilot severed the link. "Get this crate on the ground, then find something that's fast and big. Get those prisoners out of here."

"What's 'Wildfire'?" asked Purcell.

"Nort code," Bagman answered. "An emergency order for an immediate orbital saturation bombardment."

"Where?" Sanchez demanded.

"Here," said Rogue, as Domain Delta rose up in front of them.

SIXTEEN
BLUE MURDER

Freimann turned the corner and found himself at the business end of a dozen assault rifles. It was a miracle that the geneticist wasn't instantly struck down with a bellyful of las-rounds and for a second he felt like a complete fool, brandishing the prybar he'd salvaged from the maintenance store as if it were some mythical sword.

The Nort troopers looked at him, surprised to find another human being still alive in the carnage of the lower tiers. Some were hooded, others wore their chem-masks rolled back, but even those who covered their faces could not hide their fear. Everyone else in this part of the dome appeared to be dead or... Well, the other people Freimann glimpsed as he ran weren't actually *people* at all. He tried not to think about the blood on the walls and the torn body parts.

"Doktor Freimann?" said one of the soldiers. "Those creatures, what are they?"

"Monsters..." said another man, more to himself than to the rest of them.

The geneticist had to agree. The blue-green things that he had seen tearing men and machinery apart with their clawed limbs were the creations of a mind free from any such distractions as sanity. Even as he had fled from their carnage, Freimann had not been able to avoid the screams of the creature's victims. He gulped air. "They are some kind of genetik aberrations. I don't know where they came from." He lied automatically.

"I do!" said the other trooper, face reddening. "You made them, didn't you?" He grabbed a handful of the scientist's lab coat. "You and that frigid bitch Schrader! They'll kill us all!"

"Get off me!" Freimann swung the prybar in the air and the Nort released him, obeying by drilled reflex more than actual thought. Emboldened by his action, the scientist drew himself up to his full height, pausing to straighten his glasses. "I need to get off this level and you men will escort me."

"There may be other staff on this tier that need to be located—"

"N-No!" Freimann spluttered, suddenly afraid he would be left behind. Fear gnawed at him; if these men knew for sure that he had assisted Schrader in the experiments that created the throwbacks, they would certainly leave him here to die.

The trooper brought up his rifle again. The barrel winked at the scientist as it drew level with him. The other Norts were doing the same thing and the blood drained from Freimann's face.

"Down!" said the soldier, shoving him to the floor.

Freimann hit the ground and saw what the Norts were actually aiming at; a tide of mutant flesh bore down on them, man-shapes boiling along the corridor, some of them running along the walls using clawed feet, a surge of cerulean skin, talons and teeth. He shrunk into a foetal ball and hung on to the prybar.

Gunfire clattered over his head, streaming into the wet shrieks of pain as unnatural throats cried out. Then there were noises like snapping bones, organic tearing, the flash-bang of laser shots, screams and wails and hot splashes of ripe blood.

When silence fell, Freimann dared to look up. His spectacles were dripping with fluid and his view was foggy. There were blurry shapes everywhere, heaps of dark green and blue piled on the pink rags of the Norts. He fumbled, trying and failing to clean his glasses. The men and the mutants had wiped each other out as he had cowered beneath them.

Something moved in the mass of corpses and caught the hem of his lab coat. Freimann screamed and hammered into the bloodied limb with his weapon, smashing apart a skull stained with azure liquid.

It was only when he recognised the texture of human brain matter dripping from the fork of the prybar that the scientist realised he had killed the trooper who had grabbed him. Freimann staggered to his feet. There were noises approaching the intersection, the scratching and scraping of claws on plastiform. He turned from them and ran, panicked breaths roaring through his lungs.

The last series of commands went into the communications array and with that Kapten Volks crossed the point of no return. Of the men that remained with him in the dome's control centre, none of them seemed to be paying attention to anything other than their own little slices of the disaster unfolding inside Domain Delta. A few people jumped as a gunshot rang out from one of the secondary consoles, and a body slumped, the wet rain from a nest of severed arteries falling from the suicide's fresh corpse. Volks paid no heed to the self-inflicted death; perhaps it was a better way to perish than being ripped to bits at the hands of Schrader's stillborn children.

He ran the sequence with mechanical fluidity. An officer of his rank was required to review the pattern of a Wildfire protocol on a regular basis and in his dutiful way Johann Volks had committed the routine to memory in just the same fashion that he had programmed himself to field-strip his handgun in pitch darkness. The command was a last ditch tactic to be employed by officers who knew their positions were about to be overrun by the enemy, but for a facility like Delta it had a secondary function. The Norts knew the power of biological weapons only too well; after all, they were the nation that had unleashed such horrors as black fog, bio-wire and agent magenta on the galaxy. The order, when given by the senior officer at bio-research base, would also serve to forestall any spread of contamination. In a place like Nu Earth, such an edict seemed almost laughable, but the command would bring swift and unstoppable nuclear desolation to anything caught in its sphere of influence.

"Wildfire," Volks told the computer, pressing his ident tag to the scan plate. "Expedite immediate."

The words "*Confirmation?*" displayed on the screen.

Normally, Volks would have required Schrader's authority to proceed. Instead, he fished a second ident tag from a belt pouch and rolled it between his fingers. The oval plastic card was discoloured with blood; Volks had removed it from the body of General Rössa just before the corpse had been burned. At the time, Johann hadn't understood why he felt compelled to do it, but now he understood that on some level, he had known that he would eventually come to this moment. Volks pressed the tag to the scanner and the computer gave a beep of acceptance.

Wildfire command sanctioned. The words marched across the screen. *Estimated time to execution, twenty-seven minutes and forty-three seconds.*

Volks sat and watched the numbers fall ever lower.

Rogue put a double-tap of las-rounds into the head of something that looked like an emerald-coloured cherub and followed it down to the floor from its perch on the ceiling. Thin steam from boiled fluids issued up from the corpse.

"Eh," said Helm, scanning the thing. "That is ug-leee."

The GI moved on without sparing the dead mutant a second glance. Rogue felt no compassion for the enemies that he killed – that was built into him at a genetic level – but he still could not shake the faint sick sensation that had collected at the pit of his gut. Leaving Ferris and the others to secure the landing pad, he'd raced away into the dome proper and without pause, Rogue had killed six of Schrader's "mistakes" so far. All of them were hideous creatures, parodies of his physiology and that of the G-Soldats, but on some marrow-deep level he couldn't elude the feeling that he had something in common with the poor, maddened things. Rogue's emotional palette was stunted by his creators, his responses tuned to the dark end of the spectrum; still, he carried a small beacon of pity for the mutants. He wouldn't let it stop him from killing them, though.

He saw a figure running headlong at him and raised Gunnar's sights to his eye.

The dam of Freimann's panic broke open when he saw the blue-skinned man in front of him. The scientist saw nothing but the promise of death in those blank yellow eyes and he lost all reason. Freimann ran at the blue man, the prybar held high over his head, and he screamed a banshee yell that echoed down the corridor. All the geneticist wanted was to get out of the dome, to escape and run and hide. The fact that the air out there would kill him as soon as he took a breath was far from his thoughts. Freimann was hysterical with terror.

Rogue fired a single shot and blew the prybar out of the Nort scientist's grip. The improvised weapon went spinning away to lodge in a wall and its owner tripped over his own feet in fright.

"Calm down," the GI said, hauling the geneticist to his feet, reading his ident tag, "Freimann."

"Aaaaaaa!" the Nort screamed.

Rogue shrugged and slapped Freimann to silence him. "Better," he said.

"Please don't kill me!" Freimann quaked. "I'm sorry... I'm sorry for what we did to you."

"We?" Rogue repeated darkly. "You worked with Schrader?"

He nodded, head jerking, the words hissing out in a flood of confession. "She told me it was for the good of Nordland, but I never thought she would experiment on people or dig up the dead. Please God, don't let me die here..."

"Well, well, looks like we lucked out. I'm almost glad I didn't shoot you," said Gunnar. "We got ourselves one of Schrader's lab monkeys here."

"How about it, Freimann?" added Helm. "You clean the ice queen's test tubes for her?"

The Nort struggled in Rogue's grip, the insult bringing a little of Freimann's innate pride to the fore. "You insolent synth. I'm a grade six geneticist!"

"Oh, really?" Rogue hoisted the little man off the floor until his feet were dangling. "In that case, you'll know how I can get to Schrader's sub-level."

"Oh, oh no," Freimann shook his head, the fear blooming again. "We were... I was never allowed down there, none of us! It's her private laboratory!"

"There's gotta be a way. If she let those freaks out, I can get in!"

"Answer him," growled Helm.

The scientist blinked. "There are access shafts for the orb-drones... For when the specimens were brought to the other labs for experiments or dissection."

"How do I open them?"

Freimann held out a key card in a shaky hand. "H-here. This will unlock the hatches..."

Rogue tore the card from the chain around the scientist's neck, making him squeal. "Thanks."

"Huh?" said Helm. "I got this good chip, bad chip interrogation stuff down pat."

"Oh?" Bagman sneered. "Which one were you?"

"Synth out," Rogue snapped, releasing the Nort. "We got work to do."

"Wait!" Freimann yelped. "I told you what you wanted! You can't leave me here!"

"Yes we can," said Gunnar, as Rogue walked away.

Freimann sagged against the corridor wall and looked frantically around. He could hear the claws scraping ever closer.

"I take it back," said Helm. "He's the bad chip."

In the black silence over Nu Earth, machines moved with clockwork purpose and patience, shifting themselves from static sleep modes to active battle-ready postures. The various orbital strata above the war-torn planet were clogged with the debris of battle, from the wrecks of murdered starships cut down by photon cannons to the shaggy clouds of fragments left by targeted meteorite bombs.

The life expectancy of an orbital combat drone was three days. Attrition on Nu Earth's space front had pushed both the Norts and the Southers into creating a breed of weapon that was cheap, dirty and disposable; "orbit drone" was a catch-all term for a thousand varieties of unit, each a combination of motive thrusters, a weapons package and a dog-smart artificial intelligence. Some of them carried pulse-fed X-ray lasers, created in the flare of a hydrogen bomb detonation that immolated the firing platform; the ones in very low orbits mounted cluster pods filled with "hard rain" sabots or sleet mines. Drones armed with nuclear warheads were the most prolific, using multi-role ballistic missiles that could be tasked to shoot at space vessels, aircraft or ground targets.

From a Nordland communications satellite on a high elliptical course around Nu Earth, a set of battle orders filtered out to a dozen nuke-armed orbiters and each obediently cleared the lethal payload it carried for launch. Across the night sky, the blunt prows of several multi-megaton weapons turned and dipped to face the same spot on the surface of the blighted world.

■ ■ ■

Rogue expected resistance – a laser-mesh grid maybe, an electrified panel – but there was nothing to stop him as the hatch slid open. He dropped into the shaft. There were no handholds, so the GI spread out spider-style and eased down the channel. None of the dog-chips spoke as he descended; all of them were concentrating on the inputs from their optics, scanning for alarm beams or concealed traps.

He dropped the last few feet and fell into a low crouch. They were in one of the holding cells that faced the sub-level corridor. Rogue tasted mingled animal scents on the air, but no trace of anything alive. The freaks were gone, freed to run out their rampage.

The GI used a limpet charge to blow out the cell window. He moved swiftly, inexorably. Ahead of him lay the biochip chamber and Schrader's private funhouse.

"Anything?" he said quietly.

"Negative," replied Helm. "No organics, nothing on audio. Infrared shows some fading heat traces. She came this way."

"Too damn quiet," Gunnar spoke for all of them.

"I don't like it," added Bagman. "What's she waiting for?"

Rogue frowned. "She wants to look me in the eye." He halted at the hatch to the biochip store; there was no visible locking mechanism and the door was seamless. He surveyed the edges of the frame, looking for weak spots. It would be impossible to blow the hatch open without risking the destruction of the delicate circuits inside.

"Rogue," Schrader's voice issued from a hidden speaker in the ceiling, "let's not waste time with any foolishness, shall we? I have the only key to that chamber." A second door further along the corridor yawned open. "You're welcome to come and take it."

"It's a trap," Gunnar said flatly.

"Sure it is," nodded Rogue. The GI coiled his muscles and threw himself through the hatch as fast as his enhanced reflexes could propel him. He got the briefest impression of a wide laboratory ranged around him before the air went red with laser fire. Rogue ducked and rolled as hot light stabbed at his armoured skin.

"Three o'clock!" spat Helm, and the GI turned his weapon and fired. The rifle spat and shredded a sentry gun protruding from the roof.

Bagman called out "Six o'clock!" and Rogue turned behind a low table, popping up to shoot off a second burst into another automatic turret.

His skin had been seared but not penetrated. The GI swept the room with his rifle and found Schrader watching him from behind a plastisteel shield. The scientist threw him a wan salute with one hand. She was seated at a console, a complex snarl of medical equipment growing out of it to envelop her other arm. Under the harsh lights of the lab, her skin was the colour of snow.

Rogue centred her head between the crosshairs and fired; las-rounds flicked harmlessly off the plex panels. "Bagman," he ordered. "Dispense seal-burster."

Schrader smirked. "Your box of tricks won't help you here, Rogue. I'm afraid the time has come for you to accept the truth. You are obsolete, GI. You and your kind are the old guard."

"Think so?" said Rogue. "I handled your G-Soldats easy enough. If they're the best of your new breed, what you've brewed up down here is nothing special." He gestured at the tanks of fluid, the incubator modules.

She shook her head. "A clone can never really be superior to a natural human, Rogue. You lack the spark... Perhaps you might call it the soul... In the end, you're nothing more than a talking doll, strutting and playing at being alive. True superiority requires the human factor." Schrader's face twitched as the medical machine hissed; it was doing something to her, burrowing things under her skin. "Only by merging both can my vision be complete, you see?"

"Sorry, but I'm not looking for a date," Rogue replied. "Open the chip chamber, Schrader, and I'll think about letting you live."

"And then what?" she asked, an edge of pain in her voice. What little colour remaining in her seemed to be fading away. "Do you have a hundred slots where you could put them, Rogue? Would you gather up all the dead men and carry them back to Milli-Com to be regened, or drag them around Nu Earth while you follow your quest for revenge, just like those in your war gear?"

Anger flared in the GI. "You violated the dead, you ripped apart the bodies of good soldiers for your twisted ideals. You have no right to hoard their–"

"Their what?" she snapped, her voice thickening. "Their *souls*? Is that what you think the biochips are, the spirits of your comrades turned into ones and zeroes? Pathetic!" Schrader got to her feet and tore her arm from the machine. Jets of yellow liquid hissed into the air and pieces of hardware clattered to the floor. Her arm was no longer a slender, milk-pale thing; it bristled with new muscle and the heat of changing flesh. The skin was ice-blue, the indigo hue spreading across the bare parts of Schrader's neck and face even as Rogue watched her.

"What the hell?" he breathed.

Schrader walked awkwardly as bone and skin shifted inside her. She gripped the vial of blue fluid she'd shown to Volks and Rogue and slammed it into an injector. "The human form, while superior, can be improved by the adoption of traits from gene-engineered beings. I have been enhancing myself for quite some time now, grafting GI and Soldat DNA to my own." She weighed the injector in her hand. "I must admit, I have been afraid to take the last step in this process. How foolish." Schrader pressed the device to her neck and pulled the trigger. The contents of the vial vented into her bloodstream and she screamed.

Rogue watched in nauseated fascination as the woman's body writhed and shifted underneath her clothing, the flesh darkening, taking on a pale, sky-blue brilliance. When she looked back at him, her eyes had become blank yellow slits. "Oh, the taste of it!" Schrader gurgled. "Yes, this is how it should be..."

She slapped at a control on the console and the shields retracted. A smile crossed her lips. "Let's play."

The command centre filled with smoke and flame as the hatch finally gave in. Schrader's mutants looted the armoury and found a portable Hellstreak, turning the sun-hot plasma on the barricade. Overspill lapped at the officers who had been too slow to get out of the way, melting the flesh from their bones. A backdraught of sickly sweet roasted meat smell washed over Volks and he suppressed a gag reflex, reaching for his pistol.

Gunfire erupted as the Norts turned their weapons on the inhuman mutants that swarmed through the molten gouge in the barrier. Many died, falling into pools of cooling slag thrown off by the plasma blast, but then more came up and over the bodies of the dead, throwing themselves at the officers in feral fury.

Volks took a breath of searing air and got to his feet. He had nowhere to run to, nothing between him and the mutants but a single clip of ammunition. Blue-skinned death came thundering forward, a chattering, snapping, shrieking flood of murder.

Johann accepted his retribution like a good soldier; while behind him, the countdown display sank ever further.

Schrader exploded towards Rogue in a blur of movement, flashing across the lab in a series of loping jumps, springing from console to table to console. He lit the air with rifle shots, some of them ripping at the trailing edges of her lab coat and setting it aflame, others burning her mutating flesh.

Then she was on him, a banshee howl on her lips, her jaw distending and opening to reveal the buds of new teeth. She raked a clawed talon over his chest and in return he smacked her hard with his rifle butt. Schrader threw punches and he dodged. Her blows were far more powerful than he'd expected, but they were imprecise. The woman had strength to match the best of her NexGen and Rogue had no doubt that his own genetic code was probably part of the nanotech cocktail she had injected into herself, but Schrader was untrained and everything she did was about applying brute force. Still, her small, compact body mass meant she was faster than him and if she could prolong the engagement she might actually be able to win.

They traded strikes and Rogue felt his bones ring with each impact. His mind raced, tactically analysing the fight even as it unfolded. Schrader was mutating right before his eyes, with every passing second she was becoming his equal, getting the measure of her new abilities. He had to get off the defensive and shift the balance of the fight before the woman could use her advantages against him.

Locked together, he couldn't bring Gunnar to bear, but the rifle could still help. He jerked the trigger and sent a yellow-orange flash of las-fire into the ceiling, blowing out a strip of lighting strips. Schrader squealed, the glare from the muzzle dazzling her. She struck out in vicious, blind retaliation and caught the GI across the face with a backhand. Rogue felt his jaw go numb for a moment and the impact threw his helmet from his head. Helm clattered away across the room with a synthetic yelp.

Schrader reeled back, clawing at her face.

"Hurts, doesn't it?" Rogue growled. "GI eyes are extremely sensitive to light and dark and I'm betting your mutant hybrid peepers are just the same!"

"Damn you!" she shouted, sprinting out of his line of fire.

"That's it!" Bagman snapped. "Blind the harpy!"

Rogue nodded. "We gotta work together to nail her." He turned the rifle up toward the ceiling and unloaded the weapon into the lighting strips. The plastic bio-lumes shattered and broke, plunging the lab into darkness.

● ● ●

Schrader's mind and body were caught in a riot of sensations, pleasure and pain washing back and forth as her skin crawled and her bones reformed and changed. She spat like a ferocious wild cat as the lights sparked out; the delicate optical jelly of her eyes burned as the viral clades infested them, rebuilding her retinas to accept new wavelengths of light. She could still hear well enough, though. Schrader caught the whisper of a synth and padded toward it, keeping low. She knew the layout of her inner sanctum by heart and she would use that to trap Rogue and kill him. The thought of murdering the last GI with her bare hands lit a hot flare of excitement within.

"Over here!" she heard Bagman say. "This way, Rogue!"

I have you, she thought, grinning to herself. She could smell the Trooper's scent, the metallic sweat on his heaving muscles.

"Here!" Helm's voice came from the dark, in the other direction, and Schrader froze.

"I see her!" Gunnar snapped, and Schrader caught Rogue's scent again.

Behind me! She twisted and ducked as a combat blade sliced through the air where her chest had been. The GI had dropped his biochipped gear and come for her with a knife. She had to admire the cunning of it, using his own hardware to distract her attention from his approach. Pain erupted inside her, but she forced it away.

Gunnar saw the dull heat-shape of the Nort and locked on to it. "Got her! Firing!" Lasers blasted through the darkness and shots shattered flasks and retorts. Chemicals flash-boiled by the bolts burst into orange flame.

Rogue recoiled as a sheet of fire erupted. "Gunnar, you trigger-happy—"

Schrader hauled a beaker from the inferno and threw it at Rogue, sending a tongue of flame at him. The GI howled and stumbled.

. . .

Rogue beat the fire out and sprinted after Schrader, her shadow thrown into sharp relief by the dancing flames. She vanished through a second hatch and into the biochip chamber. The GI reached the door just as it began to seal shut and forced himself through the gap. The hatch slammed closed and trapped the two of them inside, alone with the silicon ghosts of the dead.

Schrader was in a heap on the floor, panting like an exhausted animal. She had missed the killing blow he had intended with his knife, but she had received a serious wound from the attack. Blood, dark and oily, discoloured the pristine white of her lab coat. Her uniform clung to her in rags where new growths of muscle had burst out of her.

"You're all alone..." she hissed, hauling herself up. "Just you and your pretty blade."

"Enough to end you," said the GI and he nodded at the biochips in the support unit. "And I'm not alone, not here."

Schrader spat out a harsh laugh. "You have no idea how wrong you are." She bared her arm to reveal a wrist communicator unit and raised it to her lips. "Activate electromag pulse."

From all around the room, a series of radiation emitters emerged from hidden panels, crackling with life. Rogue held out a hand, suddenly aware of what the scientist was about to do. "Schrader. NO!"

With a flash of actinic light, a massive surge of electromagnetic energy engulfed the biochip chamber. Naked and unprotected, the delicate protein circuits in the support frame boiled and disintegrated, sending screams of electronic agony into the air. The pulse struck Rogue like an axe blow and he collapsed to his knees, the biochip in the base of his skull burning like a supernova.

Schrader watched, her thin, purple lips pulling back into a cold smile.

SEVENTEEN
IMPACT

"Come on, come on!" Ferris said to the air. "What am I running here, a pleasure cruise?"

The pilot's hands danced across the controls of the Nort transport shuttle and he was rewarded with green lights on all systems. Just like every incident of Ferris's perverse luck, after they'd ditched the short-range hopper Purcell had found a fully fuelled and flight-ready strato-bird on its launch cradle. He suspected that some senior officer on the base had ordered the auto-teks to prep the thing for launch when everything started going wrong, but the poor bastard had never made it through the legions of freaks turning Delta into an abattoir.

The shuttle's cargo bay had a staff car and some skimmers on board, and Ferris wasted no time in releasing them through the drop ramp to make some space. Even as he ran the power-up sequence he could see figures approaching from the prison levels. He'd almost turned the automatic guns on them before Zeke had called out "Friendlies!"

Ferris's hand dropped to the throttle and he toggled the intercom. "Ladies and gentlemen, Freedom Spaceways flight one-oh-one is ready for blast-off!"

"Wait," Purcell's voice crackled, ignoring his flippant comment. "We're still packin' them in."

He glanced at the ship's sensor grid and saw blurry readings emanating from the upper atmosphere that looked suspiciously like missile re-entry tracks. "I hate to be pushy, but how much longer? I see incoming warheads, closing fast."

He heard Zeke yell over the noise of the idling engines. "We go when we're full and not before!"

The floor of the chamber came up to meet him and Rogue sprawled there, his combat knife lost to his nerveless fingers. His head was full of barbed wire, burning razors slashing at the inside of his skull. The GI tried to reach a hand toward the wall of salvaged biochips above him, as if his long-dead brethren might help him. The keening throb of the electromag pulse underscored everything, wailing like a siren made of blades.

The slivers of silicon and protein matrix in the life support web were coming apart, catching fire and sparking. From the speakers of every synth came a death scream, a chorus of absolute agony as the minds of the dead men were overloaded with radiation. What little of their personalities remained intact from the massacre, the tiny broken fragments of self that still inhabited the darkest corners of the dog-chips, were boiled in a sea of radiation. Naked against the punishing onslaught, Rogue's comrades died by horrific, tortured degrees, their consciousness bleeding out.

"Killing... them..." He forced the words out of his mouth. "Stop..."

Schrader cocked her head to watch Rogue writhing on the floor, the thin streams of drool seeping from his mouth, the sapphire blood tricking from his nostrils. "How does it feel to die like this, trooper?" For a moment, she was her old self again, the analytical and calculating scientist. "I took care to ensure that the electromagnetic pulse frequency was exactly tuned to affect biochip circuitry. But you won't perish anywhere near as quickly as your old friends here," Schrader indicated the ruined chips. "Your engram matrix is buried deep inside the cortex, still wired into your primitive grey matter. Your death will be much more painful." She brushed a lock of blonde hair from her eyes and it fell out in a clump, showing a patch of blue-white scalp below; the woman was still mutating and changing. With every moment that passed she was less human and more hybrid. "I've seen your kind a thousand times," she whispered, "on Ararat, Ixion, Horst, Tango Urilla... And all of you eventually learn the same lesson; you are all fodder for the cannon."

Rogue's muscles convulsed as conflicting signals from his brain sent shocks through his torso, his limbs. At so close a range and so large a dosage, the energy pulse induced an epileptic state in the GI. The Southers called such weapons "Haywire" bombs.

Schrader shook her head, blinking away a dart of pain. Even without a sensitive biochip in her brainstem, even with her glorious new flesh, the pulse was still agonising for her to endure. She submitted to the hurt with the knowledge that Rogue's pain would be a thousand times worse; his biochip was a floodgate for the crackling power that would eviscerate his mind.

Rogue crawled forward on his hands and knees. The GI's trembling fingers touched the hilt of his knife where the weapon had fallen and he tried to grasp the blade. Schrader saw what he was doing and kicked the knife away. With a smirk of amusement, she planted another boot in the GI's gut and he crumpled.

Rogue's strength was leaking out of him, dripping onto the plastisteel floor like the droplets of blood raining from his nose, his eyes and his ears. "Nuh... Bagman... Helm... Gunnar..."

"Oh, don't worry. I'll deal with them soon enough." The scientist gave him a look of mock concern. "Don't be upset, Rogue. You always believed you were the last survivor of the Quartz Zone. Now you know for sure." She ran a hand over his twitching torso, as if she were stroking an injured animal. "Soon, you'll be as dead as all the others," Schrader smiled, displaying too many teeth. "The last GI dies at the hand of the next generation. Fitting, yes?"

The strato-shuttle's cargo bay was a mass of bodies, men and women pressing together in desperation. Zeke threw Purcell a worried look. Both of them had rifles at the ready, threatening ragged prisoners who demanded to board the ship and escape from the bloody inferno. There were even some Norts among them, but for the moment no one seemed to care about nationality; everyone in Delta was fleeing the army of Schrader's mutants. They were everywhere – hundreds of them wreaking havoc throughout the dome – but there were other threats as well.

Sanchez grabbed the sergeant's arm. "Can't you hear the sirens out there? That's an air raid warning! Skev the rest of them, we don't go now, we'll never get away!"

"Shut up," Zeke told him. "We got time–"

Gunfire interrupted from the drop ramp, pistol shots cracking the air. From the dome proper the Souther sailor appeared with a handful of men at his heels and charged across the landing pad toward them. "We got company!" he yelled.

Zeke raised his rifle as blue-green things emerged behind the prisoners, howling and hooting. Purcell and Zeke put shots into the mutants, but it seemed liked nothing short of decapitation could stop the stronger ones. As he watched, a prisoner fell and the freaks were on him; ripping and tearing him apart as if he was a rag doll. Within seconds, limbs and internal organs were thrown into the air as if it was macabre confetti for the dead.

"Those things get aboard, we're dead! Tell Ferris to lift off!" Sanchez snapped.

"I'm not leaving anyone behind!" Zeke snarled.

Sanchez turned and fired; his shot struck the Scum Sailor in the chest and he dropped – the prisoners with him faltered and broke apart in shock.

"You cold-blooded son of a bitch!" Purcell screamed.

Sanchez ignored her and slammed the ramp control button. The cargo doors began to slide closed.

"I can't believe you did that..." gasped Zeke.

"What you gonna do about it?" Sanchez was cocksure and angry. "Blue-boy ain't here now to watch your back, *sergeant*." He made the rank an insult. "You're weak, man. You ain't got the guts to make the hard calls."

"Get off." Zeke said in a low voice, grabbing Sanchez's arm.

"What?" Purcell snatched the revolver from his hand before he could react.

"I said, get off!" Zeke shoved Sanchez at the closing ramp and the prisoner lost his footing. He stumbled and slipped, flailing as he dropped down to the ferrocrete landing pad below.

"No!" Sanchez tumbled over the lip of the ramp and disappeared into the melee clustered around the shuttle's landing gear. The mutants crowed as he fell into their grasp.

The hatch slammed shut with a grim finality and Zeke nodded to Purcell. "We're going."

The soldier nodded and tapped the intercom. "Ferris, lift this pig."

"What about Rogue?" said the voice from the cockpit. "Is he on board?"

"Just go," snapped Zeke, as the sound of deformed fists ringing on the hull echoed through the decking. "Wherever the GI is, he's on his own now."

He teetered on the lip of the abyss, clinging to his last moments of life, sparks of pure agony flashing like arc lightning into his mind. His thoughts became fluid, slipping away, fast as mercury, dragging glassy shards of memory from the depths of his psyche. The recollections were chaotic and jumbled.

Trading fire with a sniper in the ruins of Nordstadt...
Serpents and spiders the size of battle tanks...

Rogue had often heard human soldiers talk about death. On Nu Earth, the shadow of it was so constant a companion that no man who fought there could deny his end was only a heartbeat away at any moment. Ordinary men had ways to deal with death. Some of them had beliefs in powers that would pluck them from the void and take their souls to a paradise. Others were afraid that their ghosts would walk the ruins and battlefields forever. To a GI, dwelling on such things was a waste of energy and effort; you're hit, you're dead. That was the end of it.

Ten year-old hands shaking as they hold a loaded rifle for the first time...

Lights of a laser display on the faces of a thousand enraptured Norts...

There was no eternal reward for a Genetic Infantryman, only the promise of permanent servitude in a succession of new bodies, perhaps in another war, on and on until one day there came the shot that left your dog-chip unrecoverable. "Real death", the Genies had called it, as if the other kind wasn't bad enough.

The taste of real air and the chill of the wind over the Oxark Mountains...

Backwash of heat as the sea-shuttle explodes...

Rogue would have no recovery; no one stood by to burrow into his corpse to retrieve his consciousness encoded on plastic. Brain death would occur and the sixty second clock would start to tick, the inexorable fall into nothingness marching closer and closer.

A synthetic scream echoing through an ashen wasteland...

Ghost of a smile on the lips of a blue angel...

A face danced there before him, the image blurred and indistinct. "This is the end, Rogue. Time to go," it told him, the voice it gave distant and muffled. "Die now."

He saw Gunnar, skull streaked with blood, slack with death; Hoffa, choking on poison; Kransky, soulless and empty; Venus, her eyes dancing with promise; Sister

Sledge, blonde tresses framing a face made for deceit; and then a shadow, deep and forbidding, a face that was no face, the mask of the Traitor.

Screaming melting plastic torched skin burning up falling and falling...

Light flashing off the Quartz death reaching up with glass fingers...

"Can't... die... Traitor... must find..." The effort to speak was intense.

A hand caressed his cheek, smearing his blood across the skin. "Poor little GI. Your vengeance will never be satisfied."

"*NO!*" Some last storehouse of will broke open inside Rogue and his hand flicked up like a striking cobra, snaring Schrader's wrist. He crushed bone and tissue and the wrist-comm unit into a mess of plastic and skin.

The Nort screamed in torment, her voice matching the fading whine from the electromag generators as they suddenly cut out.

Rogue shook away the miasma of memory and saw Schrader kneeling over him, struggling to break free of his steely grip. He grabbed her throat with his other hand and squeezed the life from her.

Schrader's fingers were iron rods, ripping and punching into Rogue's flesh. She raked talon-like nails across his arms and chest. "You can't live!" she gurgled, purple blood filling her lungs, spilling from her mouth. "You're nothing! An abortion! A synthetic freak!"

The GI forced himself to his feet, dragging Schrader with him. She shook wildly in his hands, out of control and consumed with her own madness. Rogue pitched Schrader off her feet and threw the woman across the room, into the scorched plastic panel of the biochip support frame. Her body collided with the glass screen in a glittering burst of electric discharge and the screen shattered into wicked shards and shreds of silicon shrapnel.

Beating back the cascade of pain from all over his body, Rogue limped to where the scientist had fallen. Her body

was bent at unnatural angles, her head twisted on a broken neck. Clear daggers of plexisteel protruded from her
chest like jagged icicles and he saw where smashed
pieces of biochip had impaled Schrader's frost-blue skin.
Rogue found his combat knife and balled it in his fist to
deliver the killing blow, but then she spoke.

"Rogue...?" she coughed, her eyes open but not seeing
him. "Father...? I wanted... I wanted you to understand...
I did this for you... I wanted you to love me..."

The GI stood back and let her die.

Heat coruscating from their dark nose cones, the Nort
missiles fell into the embrace of Nu Earth's gravity. The
friction of re-entry glowed cherry red along the leading
edges of the weapons, matching the spears of orange
chemical fire propelling them toward the ground. The
combat computers mounted in the warheads knew of the
presence of their brethren and with blink-fast flashes
from laser communicators, they chattered amongst themselves as they fell. Battle orders were compared in
nanoseconds and a consensus was reached; smart plas-
tics in the steering vanes of the missiles expanded and
contracted, spreading out the pattern of the weapons,
each one of them drifting into an assigned vector.

They passed the abort point and entered their terminal
decent phase. Spent boosters were ejected, exploding
into knots of chaff to disorient enemy anti-missile lasers.
Triggers were armed, the nuclear cores inside the
ground-penetrators and air-burst war shots unlocked.

Then, with the grace of an opening orchid, each of the
missiles shed its outer faring like a fan of discarded
petals. Inside, every weapon revealed a fist of sub-muni-
tions, smaller but no less deadly rockets tipped with
atomic fire. Eight missiles became sixteen, became
thirty-two.

Death rained down on Domain Delta.

· · ·

Ferris pushed the strato-shuttle's throttle bar to zone five full military power and thumbed the afterburner ignition. The Nort ship exploded from the launch cradle and threw itself into the tainted sky on a column of brilliant white flame. The ground was gone, the dusty glass desert a blink in his peripheral vision, there and then vanished.

G-force pressed into him, a fuzzy blanket of weight squeezing the pilot into the acceleration couch. He felt something pressing into his backside – Ferris hadn't had time to get comfortable and a rumple in his flight suit was digging into his skin. The pressure made his thigh go dead and he gritted his teeth to ride out the numbness. Colour leached from his vision as blood retreated from the veins in his eyes, pooling in his lower body. He strained against the multiple-gravity pressure, his arms like lead where they gripped the flight yoke and throttle. Grey sparkles began to gather at the edges of his sight, forming into cowls, tunnelling his vision.

He was dimly aware of a proximity warning from the console; high-speed targets were descending on his flight path.

"Oh shit." The words were slurred and thick in his mouth.

Ferris reacted, forcing the shuttle into a series of rolls and side-slips. There was no way to avoid the incoming missiles.

The sensor grid screamed as the radar returns for the shuttle and the missiles flickered into a merge and suddenly Ferris was slamming the ship around the cloud of nuclear death, cutting a path through the oncoming aerial traffic. Light flashed through the canopy as rocket thrust plumes blazed close to the shuttle's hull, then they were past, and rising still higher into the thinning atmosphere.

A hammer blow echoed through the fuselage and the launch boosters detached themselves. Ferris rode the ship through the turbulence and eased the throttle down from full power; the weight on his chest decreased and suddenly he was aware of the sweat coating his chest.

On the console the sensor grid went wild as a massive radiation spike flared into life.

The missiles knew their targets; some, those with hardened saw-tooth tips, burrowed into the hard-packed earth or through ferrocrete and plastisteel walls before detonating. Others immolated themselves above the ground, turning the air into a soup of gaseous plasma. Domain Delta and everything in it vanished in a perfectly-timed explosion, a string of tactical nuclear warheads casting loose fireballs as hot as the core of a star. Schrader's corpse joined the flesh of her mutant children, the steel and the rock of her secret facility and everything in a twenty kilometre radius became a radioactive wasteland. The Wildfire screamed out across the ruined landscape, churning up the earth that turned into molten slag. Sand, metals and stone were transformed in the flames, the huge energies unleashed in a single instant, fusing the vista into a plain of atomic glass. Delta dissolved into the Quartz Zone, becoming a new part of the warped mirror-landscape, the dead silent and reclaimed.

The hatch to the cockpit hissed open and Zeke hauled himself into the co-pilot's chair. Ferris gave him a nod, working the console. The rim of the nuclear backwash had grazed the ship, tripping a dozen control circuits with sparks of discharge.

Zeke glanced at the aft monitor screen. A bright bruise of searing yellow was growing from the surface of Nu Earth, a clump of mushroom clouds merging into one. The sergeant felt sick and giddy when he realised just how close he had come to being at the heart of that destruction. "What a nightmare..."

The pilot didn't look up. "Reckon I can get us into a low orbit. If you got a preference where you want to wind up, now's the time to say."

"Right," said Zeke. "I'm not sure I wanna go back to the South right away... What about a Freeport?"

Ferris tapped the radar. "We might be able to reach Lost Angels if we're lucky. Used to be a solar power orbital, but now it's a shanty station. Non-aligned."

"Good enough," he paused, studying the monitor. "You think he made it out?"

Ferris gave him a hooded look. "Nothing could have survived those nukes. Not even the Rogue Trooper." He shook his head. "Just when I was starting to like him, too."

Zeke watched the firestorm and said nothing.

In the foothills to the west the echo of Domain Delta's death was muted and hollow, like the grumble of distant thunder. The broken remnants of a highway lay nearby, a relic of the infrastructure of a colonial civilisation that died in the crib. From a distance, the low blockhouse lying next to the road appeared to be nothing more than an abandoned guard post, a pillbox bunker where guns could train on passing traffic; but there were no guns and there had been no traffic on this highway for a decade.

Something moved in the shadows of the bunker. Puffs of rusty dust coiled in the thick, hot air. A heavy iron hatch, sunk into the metal decking to match seamlessly with its surroundings, twitched. Beneath, strength borne from precision gene-engineering forced the hatch open and a blue-skinned figure emerged from the darkness.

"Nothing," said Helm. "No contacts. Rad count's at the top of the line, but we can take it."

"Affirmative." Rogue hauled himself out of the tunnel, brushing a layer of rock dust off his torso.

"Where are we?" Gunnar demanded. "Wouldn't be surprised if Schrader had us pop up in the middle of Nu Nuremburg."

"Nav-compass says we're on the edge of the Black Desert," noted Bagman, "although all the rads in the air are messing up the sat-fix."

"She thought of everything," Helm noted. "Even down to an escape route."

"Pardon me if I don't want to take that ride again," added Gunnar. "Like being strapped to a rocket!"

Rogue emerged from the bunker, blinking. The sky had a peculiar cast to it, a mottled red-orange like the colour of old, dried blood. He slipped a pair of eighty-eight grenades off his webbing strap and clipped them together, dialling a short fuse on the timer. He pulled the arming pins and threw them into the bunker's doorway before sprinting away. The grenades blew with a flat thunderclap of air and the pillbox roof caved in.

"Just in case," Rogue explained. "Don't want anyone using that railshuttle after us."

"Huh," grunted Helm. "It's not like there's anything left back there but fallout, anyhow!"

"Just in case," repeated the GI. "Bagman, dispense digi-map." The backpack manipulator dropped the datapad into Rogue's hand and he studied the display. "We'll head north-west, towards the chem-jungle."

"So here we are again," Gunnar said in a low voice. "Back to square one and our one big lead to the Traitor cooked in her own nuke barbecue. Nice work, Rogue."

"Synth out, Gunnar," he replied. "Schrader had nothing on the Buzzard, I'm sure of it. She would have given him up if she knew where he was... And that's as much a clue as anything."

"How'd you figure?" asked Helm.

"He's not with the Norts anymore. If he was, Schrader would have known it. The Traitor is out there on his own now."

"Like us?" said Bagman.

Rogue watched the fading fire of the nuclear explosion. "Like me."

The GI turned his back on the Quartz Zone and walked away, into the dying night of a ceaseless war.

ABOUT THE AUTHOR

James Swallow has written for the heroes of *2000 AD* in the Black Flame novel *Judge Dredd: Eclipse* and the audio dramas *Judge Dredd: Jihad* and *Judge Dredd: Dredline*. His fiction also includes the *Blood Angels* novels set in the dark future of Warhammer 40,000 and stories for *Inferno!* magazine. Swallow's other books include the *Sundowners* quartet of "steampunk" Westerns (*Ghost Town*, *Underworld*, *Iron Dragon* and *Showdown*), *The Butterfly Effect* and the horror anthology *Silent Night*.

His nonfiction includes *Dark Eye: The Films of David Fincher* and guides to genre television and animation. Swallow's other credits include writing for *Star Trek: Voyager* and scripts for videogames. He lives in London and is currently working on his next book.

CHECK OUT THESE FANTASTIC TITLES AVAILABLE FROM BLACK FLAME!

2000 AD

Judge Dredd #1:
Dredd vs Death
1-84416-061-0
£5.99

Judge Dredd #2:
Bad Moon Rising
1-84416-107-2
£5.99

Judge Dredd #3:
Black Atlantic
1-84416-108-0
£5.99

Judge Dredd #4:
Eclipse
1-84416-122-6
£5.99

Judge Dredd #5:
Kingdom of the Blind
1-84416-133-1
£5.99

Judge Dredd #6:
The Final Cut
1-84416-135-8
£5.99

Strontium Dog #1:
Bad Timing
1-84416-110-2
£5.99

Strontium Dog #2:
Prophet Margin
1-84416-134-X
£5.99

Rogue Trooper #1:
Crucible
1-84416-111-0
£5.99

Durham Red #1:
The Unquiet Grave
1-84416-159-5
£5.99

Nikolai Dante #1:
The Strangelove Gambit
1-84416-139-0
£5.99

NEW LINE CINEMA

Final Destination #1:
Dead Reckoning
1-84416-170-6
£6.99

Final Destination #2:
Destination Zero
1-84416-171-4
£6.99

The Twilight Zone #1:
Memphis/The Pool Guy
1-84416-130-7
£6.99

The Twilight Zone #2:
Upgrade/Sensuous Cindy
1-84416-131-5
£6.99

The Twilight Zone #3:
Sunrise/Into the Light
1-84416-151-X
£6.99

Blade: Trinity
1-84416-106-4
£6.99

Freddy vs Jason
1-84416-059-9
£5.99

The Texas Chainsaw Massacre
1-84416-060-2
£6.99

The Butterfly Effect
1-84416-081-5
£6.99

Cellular
1-84416-104-8
£6.99

Jason X
1-84416-168-4
£6.99

Jason X: The Experiment
1-84416-169-2
£6.99